The Wild Warriners

Four brothers living on the edge of society...
scandalizing the ton at every turn!

Tucked away at their remote estate
in Nottinghamshire are the *ton*'s
most notorious brothers.

The exploits of Jack, Jamie, Joe and Jacob Warriner's
parents—their father's gambling and cheating, their
mother's tragic end—are legendary. But now, for the
first time, the brothers find themselves the talk of the
ton for an entirely different reason...

Because four women are about to change their
lives—and put them firmly in society's spotlight!

Find out what happens in

Jack's story

A Warriner to Protect Her

Already available

Jamie's story

A Warriner to Rescue Her

Available now

And watch for Joe's and Jacob's stories—coming soon!

Author Note

When I wrote the first book in this Wild Warriners series, *A Warriner to Protect Her*, I was pretty certain what sort of direction I wanted the second book to go in. Jamie Warriner is a damaged former soldier with a talent for covert reconnaissance, and I wanted to bring those skills into play for his story. I envisioned some sort of tale involving intrigue—perhaps even espionage. However, as my characters so often do, Jamie took me down a completely different path. The more I got to know him, the more I knew he was actually a deeply sensitive soul underneath all of his monosyllabic gruffness. A man who painted delicate and beautiful flowers was not really ever meant to be so fluent in violence. He didn't need to return to his military ways, he needed saving. It was then that I first began toying with the idea of introducing Jamie to a vicar's daughter.

Around the same time, I was rooting around the attic one day looking for something and came across one of my children's old storybooks, *The Tale of Peter Rabbit* by the wonderful Beatrix Potter. A woman who used her childhood pets as inspiration for her wonderfully vivid and brightly illustrated stories. Before I knew it, my softhearted vicar's daughter had a horse called Orange Blossom and a talent for writing. With his art and her words, surely they were a match made in heaven? If only I could convince Jamie, of course...

VIRGINIA HEATH

---

*A Warriner
to Rescue Her*

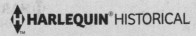

HARLEQUIN® HISTORICAL

ISBN-13: 978-0-373-62938-1

A Warriner to Rescue Her

Copyright © 2017 by Susan Merritt

Printed in U.S.A.

When **Virginia Heath** was a little girl it took her ages to fall asleep, so she made up stories in her head to help pass the time while she was staring at the ceiling. As she got older the stories became more complicated—sometimes taking weeks to get to their happy ending. One day she decided to embrace her insomnia and start writing them down. Virginia lives in Essex with her wonderful husband and two teenagers. It still takes her forever to fall asleep...

Books by Virginia Heath

Harlequin Historical Romance

The Wild Warriners

A Warriner to Protect Her
A Warriner to Rescue Her

Stand-Alone Novels

That Despicable Rogue
Her Enemy at the Altar
The Discerning Gentleman's Guide
Miss Bradshaw's Bought Betrothal

Visit the Author Profile page at Harlequin.com.

For Ellen
For always being there for my children
with either a ready bandage or unconditional love.

Chapter One

⌒⌒⌒⌒⌒⌒⌒⌒⌒

May 1814

The blood-curdling female scream shook him out of his daze instantly. Jamie pulled up his horse and glanced frantically around to see if he could locate the source. All he saw was familiar meadow and trees, and for a moment he thought he might have imagined it. With the warm sun on his face and the leisurely motion of his mount ambling aimlessly beneath him, it was quite feasible he had nodded off. He was exhausted, after all.

Constantly exhausted from his brain's inability to stop whirring when darkness fell, conjuring up memories from his past which haunted him even though he knew both men responsible for the pain were undeniably dead and therefore no longer a threat. Yet the ghost of them lingered in his mind, forcing him to stay vigilant and preventing him from snatching more than a few hours here and there, usually as the sun began to banish the darkness away. Or perhaps it was simply the darkness which frightened him as it had as a child?

After so many months, he was no longer sure. Just irritated with his own inability to move past it.

The second scream, no less curdling or high-pitched, raised all of his hackles, putting him on instant alert. With his soldier's instinct, Jamie raced his horse in the direction of the shriek, which happened to be towards the orchard near the huge wall which surrounded Markham Manor. The orderly trees were arranged in parallel lines with person-width paths of grass in between; aside from the gentle swish of leaves blowing in the summer breeze, silence reigned.

He cast his eyes methodically up and down the rows until he saw something—a dainty skewbald pony casually munching on the tiny, unripe apples that littered the ground around its hooves. As it was wearing both halter and a side-saddle, yet there was no sign of the rider, Jamie carefully lowered himself to the ground and wrapped his own reins loosely about a branch. At the best of times his temperamental black stallion was foul tempered; around other horses he was prone to be a brute. The pretty cream-and-dun pony, with her long fluffy mane and even longer eyelashes, would not stand a chance.

Jamie limped towards the abandoned animal slowly, conscious any sudden movement might spook the strange pony and send it galloping off to who knew where. 'Easy, girl...' At least he assumed it was a girl. If it were a boy the other horses would tease him mercilessly for that effeminate mane.

'Hello!' A slightly panicked woman's voice came from above. 'Is somebody there?'

'Hello?' He hadn't been expecting to address the sky. The sun pierced Jamie's eyes to such an extent he could not see a thing except blinding yellow light. The woman's exact location remained a mystery. Unless she was an angel sent to fetch him and drag him off to heaven, which he sincerely doubted. They had had their chance and failed miserably and if he was bound for anywhere it was probably hell. 'I can't see you!'

'I am in the tree… I wonder if you would be so good as to assist me, sir. I appear to be stuck.'

Surreal words, again unexpected. How did a woman come to be stuck in an apple tree? Jamie did his best to shield the worst of the glare with his hand and squinted through the tangled branches. Two wiggling feet dangled nearly six feet above his head. They were encased in half-boots and were attached to a very shapely pair of female legs, clad in fine silk stockings which were held up with rather saucy pink garters. His eyes widened at the garters. From this perspective they appeared to be completely festooned with flowers. Above them, about an inch or two of creamy thigh was also on display. The rest of the woman was hidden by leaves.

Thankfully, a passing cloud chose that exact moment to block out the worst of the sun, allowing Jamie to get a better look at the rest of the dangling woman. Her slate-coloured skirt, so incongruous in comparison to her choice of vibrant underthings, had inverted and appeared to be wrapped tightly around her upper body. One arm clung to a branch above, the other, and her head, were apparently trapped within the fabric. Her generous bottom was resting on a feeble branch which appeared likely to snap at any moment and, with nothing beneath her except the hard ground, his best assessment of her position was precarious.

'Try to remain still. I'm coming up!'

He supposed it was the gentlemanly thing to do, although Jamie had no idea if he was still actually capable of climbing a tree. Thanks to Napoleon, he could hardly walk, certainly struggled to run and his dancing days were most definitely over. Quickly, he tried to work out the best way to tackle the challenge. The last time he had cause to climb a tree, he had been a scrawny, nimble boy and he recalled it had been a simple procedure by and large. Thanks to his burly Warriner ancestors, and over a decade of growing, he was now an ox of a man. An ox of a man with a useless left leg.

However, that damned leg was not going to define him. If he wanted to climb a tree, he would climb a blasted tree! Putting all of his weight on his right foot, and using the strength of his arms, he managed to hoist himself laboriously upwards. It might have raised him less than a foot off the ground, but he had left the ground. He rearranged his good foot and heaved again. Two foot from the ground! What was that if it was not progress? Slow, laboured, feeble progress. Painful, humiliating, soul-destroying progress.

Oblivious to his grunts of exertion, or the supreme effort it took him to actually climb, the grey faceless bundle above his head decided this was the appropriate time for a conversation.

'I suppose you are wondering how I came to be stuck up this tree in the first place...' At this stage in the proceedings, how she came to be there was neither here nor there. All Jamie could concentrate on was putting one foot painfully above the other. 'It's a funny story really. My pony, Orange Blossom, has a fondness for red apples.' As she spoke, her legs and bottom jiggled, causing the fragile branch to quiver with indignation. 'And rather stupidly, I assumed... *Oooh!*'

The flimsy branch suddenly bent downwards as it split from the main trunk of the tree. Fortunately, she had the good sense to hook her legs around an adjacent branch and managed to halt her descent. Unfortunately, in doing so her dress had now ridden further up her thighs, displaying all of her legs quite thoroughly. As legs went, they were rather nice although now was really not the time he should be admiring them. As he had suspected, those saucy garters were festooned with pink-silk flowers. Her shapely derrière now hung between the two branches and directly over Jamie's head. In her panic, she was wiggling in earnest now in an attempt to free her head from its dull, muslin prison, her visible hand still clinging desperately on to a straining branch above.

Jamie began to inch closer to her struggling form. 'Madam, it is imperative that you remain still!' Because if she fell, it was his cranium which would bear the brunt and the closer he got, the less confident he was he was strong enough to catch her. If her bottom was anything to go by, she was not exactly petite. He pulled himself on to a sound-looking branch and locked one arm around it.

'Take my hand!' Perhaps he could swing her down to the ground? Unless, of course, she wrenched his shoulder out of its socket. Then he would have a crippled arm to go with his ruined leg.

He watched her wrestle within her tangled skirts until her other hand burrowed its way out and her arm made a frantic bid for freedom, but instead of grabbing his outreached hand as he had quite plainly instructed, she used it to attempt to cover her exposed legs with her inverted clothing. Tiny, hard, barely formed apples began to tumble out of the fabric and rained down around him. Two of the lead-lined fruits bounced off his head like miniature cannonballs and made him yelp.

'What in God's name are you doing, woman! Grab my blasted hand now!' For good measure, he prodded her arm to help her locate him.

More wood splintered somewhere close by and the faceless wench squealed again, her bottom lolling further between the branches and coming level with his face. At last, she swung her free arm around and grabbed his hand, but it was a moment too late. Thanks to weak, young wood and gravity, her advancing bottom had begun to gain some momentum and continued to slide on its journey downwards. Acting on impulse rather than gentlemanly manners, Jamie looped his good leg over another branch and tried to halt her descent in the only way now left open to him. Grabbing a handful of a rather pert, round cheek, he unceremoniously braced himself against it to stop her falling.

The headless woman squeaked in outrage and vehemently attempted to remove her posterior from his clenched hand by grasping at anything wildly to haul herself back up again. This frantic new movement proved to be problematic for both the tree and Jamie's tenuous grasp of it. The branch supporting his good leg snapped with a loud crack, sending them both careening helplessly downwards.

He landed flat on his back, with a resounding thud. A split second later the woman landed on top of him. Jamie was hard pressed to decide which event caused him more pain. If he'd had any breath left in his lungs, he probably would have screamed in agony. All that came out instead was a weird hiss, almost as if his entire body was slowly deflating. By some miracle, his eyes still worked. He knew this because he was currently drowning in a sea of hair.

He felt her brace herself on to her hands and lift her head up. Two brown eyes stared, blinking directly into his, far too close to allow him to see anything else. 'Are you all right?'

Hiss.

One hand came to the side of his face and she patted his cheek ineffectually, oblivious to the fact he was munching on a mouthful of her hair. 'Sir? Can you speak to me? Are you injured?'

Jamie flexed his fingers. When no pain shot down his arms, he brought them up to grab her by the shoulders and smartly lifted her upwards. 'Get your blasted hair out of my face this instant.'

She hastily scrambled off him and knelt at his side, peering down in concern. It was then that Jamie finally got his first proper look at her. Big brown eyes, with eyelashes so long they would give her pretty pony a run for its money, a heart-shaped face, obscenely plump lush mouth and a smattering of freckles dusting across the bridge of her nose. The hair which had threatened to choke him was neither red nor blonde. It hovered somewhere in between. But it was thick and heavy and really quite lovely. Even the way the twigs and leaves sprouted out of what was left of her hairstyle was strangely becoming. It was odd that splinters of foliage would suit a woman so.

He managed to lift himself up on to his elbows to

test his neck. He moved it from side to side before stretching out his spine. Nothing broken so far, which frankly, was a miracle after he had been effectively dropped from a great height, then crushed.

'You broke my fall.'

'I am well aware of that.' Jamie gingerly moved his bad leg. The fact it appeared no worse than it had before gave him some confidence. Carefully he raised himself to a sitting position and glared at the woman. She responded by grinning broadly and sticking out her hand. She grabbed his and shook it vigorously.

'My name is Cassandra Reeves. I am the daughter of the Reverend Reeves, the new vicar of this parish. I am delighted to make your acquaintance, sir.'

Well, he definitely wasn't delighted by the way the acquaintance had been made and, because he certainly did not feel like grinning, Jamie frowned instead. Her inappropriate cheerfulness was disconcerting. 'James Warriner.'

'Well, thank you for saving me. I really do appreciate it, Mr Warriner.'

'It's Captain Warriner.' Why he had the urge to make the distinction to her, he could not say, when nobody hereabouts ever called him anything other than either his first name or, sneeringly, '*one of those Warriners*'. Yet to become plain old mister again, when he was still technically an officer in His Majesty's army, was tantamount to accepting defeat. Until he resigned his commission, he would remain Captain Warriner for as long as was humanly possible. He might well have accepted his military career, as well as his life, was well and truly over—his shattered leg was never going to get any better than it was—but the rest of the world did not need to know he was finished. To be barely twenty-seven and rendered useless was a bitter pill to take.

'A military man? That explains it.'

'Explains what?' He was growling because his probing fingers could feel a tender bump forming on his scalp from the impact of one of the apple cannonballs she had fired at him.

'Your abrupt tone.' She screwed her face into a frown and put on her best impression of a man's deeper voice. *'"It is imperative you remain still..." "Grab my blasted hand now!"'*

Jamie stopped rubbing his head and stared disbelievingly at the woman. Was she pulling him up on his manners? Seriously? 'Had you grabbed my hand in the first instance, then perhaps I might have prevented you from falling out of the tree. Your dithering caused us both to fall.'

'My clothing was in disarray.' That, he knew. He had seen those garters and they were hardly the sort of garters he would expect a vicar's daughter to wear. 'It would have been improper to leave it that way.'

'Yet your nod to propriety proved to be remarkably ineffectual, did it not? Not only did it send us both crashing to the ground, it was a completely pointless exercise. Your skirts had been up for some time, Miss Reeves, and I am not blind.'

She blushed then, quite prettily, and those huge brown eyes widened with alarm. 'You might have told me. It was hardly gentlemanly for you to look.'

'Perhaps you would have preferred I closed my eyes and groped around in the branches blindly in the vain hope I might grab you on the off chance?'

'You did grab me, as I recall, and most improperly, too.' Her freckled nose poked into the air as she delivered this set down.

'You are absolutely right. I apologise sincerely for grabbing the only part of your body that I could reach as you careened towards me at dangerous speed. What I should have done was avoided grabbing you in the first place. That would have been the gentlemanly thing to do. It also would have meant that you would have plummeted out of the tree there and then, and thus relinquishing me from the noble task of breaking your fall.'

When he put it like that, Cassie was prepared to concede he had a point. She had practically flattened the man, the poor thing could barely breath a few moments ago. If only he hadn't seen her pudgy thighs. Or manhandled her massive bottom. And if only he wasn't so devilishly handsome then she wouldn't be feeling so self-conscious about her entire, ungainly body below the waist, as well as already feeling ridiculous for getting herself stuck up a tree in the first place. Captain Warriner's eyes were the absolute bluest eyes she had ever seen. Like the clearest summer's sky flecked with speckles of lapis lazuli. With all the dark, slightly over-long black hair and permanently frowning expression, he was exactly what she imaged a pirate to look like. Or a highwayman. Or a mythical knight sat around King Arthur's table. Very few men could carry off chain-mail or a dashing pirate's earring, but she was quite certain Captain Warriner would. She would store his appearance away in her memory for when she needed inspiration for a handsome rogue…

But here she was, weaving him into one of her

stories and the poor man was still sat on the floor. Probably still winded and trying to pretend not to be. Why, he hadn't even raised himself from his seat on the grass.

'I am being unforgivably ungrateful, Captain Warriner. You have been extremely decent in trying to save me and I am truly sorry for squashing you when I landed. If it's any consolation, I did try to avoid you.'

Her fictional, fantasy pirate was still frowning. 'I already know I am going to regret asking this question, Miss Reeves, but how did you come to be stuck in one of my brother's apple trees?'

'I did not realise they belonged to someone, else I never would have taken the liberty.' Stealing was a sin, after all, and she was guilty of enough of them already to add one to the list. It was the Eighth Commandment. Cassie knew all of the Commandments verbatim. Forwards and, because her attention had a tendency to waver, backwards as well.

'Did you fail to notice the twenty-foot wall and giant wooden gates?'

As he was gesturing behind her with his hand Cassie allowed her eyes to turn to take in the towering stone barricade looming against the horizon. Now that he happened to mention it, she had noticed the enormous structure as she had ridden down the unfamiliar lane, but as the gates were wide open, she had assumed it was a public park. Both Hyde Park and St James's had gates, too, although granted nowhere near as imposing, so did the many parks she had frequented in Nottingham, Manchester, Birmingham, Liverpool and Bristol. But she was a very long way from those cities now and she supposed they had no real need for actual parks when lush, green countryside stretched out before you in every direction.

'I did not realise this was private property. I am used to living in big towns, Captain Warriner, where people take the air in big parks. I feel very silly now.'

He waved her explanation away impatiently. 'Anyway—the tree, Miss Reeves?'

She could tell by his expression he thought she was odd. His dark eyebrows were raised in question, but his eyes swirled with irritated bemusement. Cassie knew that look well. It was the way most people had always stared at her. Usually, it only hurt a little bit, because she was quite used to it—but for some reason having this dashing pirate view her in such a manner, when he had barely any time to get to know her, hurt a great deal. Clearly she was now irredeemably odd if an officer in the King's army had spotted it straight away, when Cassie had been trying so very hard not to be quite so odd since she arrived in Retford. To make matters worse, her reasons for being up the tree were, now she considered it, quite daft indeed. Further evidence of her unfamiliarity with country life.

'I was searching for apples for Orange Blossom. The ones on the lower branches were so very small and hard, I thought those higher up might be riper. Because they were closer to the sun…but I realise now, that it is far too early for any of the apples to be ripe. The ones I picked from the top were just as hard as the ones at the bottom.'

'This, I am also aware of. The majority of them fell on my head while you were trying to adjust your clothing.'

Could this day get any worse? She had made a fool

of herself, unwittingly trespassed and stolen unripe apples, then winded the most handsome man she had ever seen after flashing her fat legs at him. 'I am sorry about your head, too,' she said miserably, 'and for climbing the stupid tree in the first place. When the branch beneath my feet gave way, my dress got caught on something and I couldn't move. I shall be eternally grateful you came along. I might still be stuck there otherwise and I promised Papa I would be home by four to listen to Sunday's sermon.' Stuck inside again when she so loved being outdoors.

Captain Warriner merely stared at her, his magnificent eyes inscrutable, though obviously happy to end their acquaintance swiftly. Cassie stood up decisively and brushed the worst of the leaves and twigs out of her hair, chiding herself for her own ineptitude. Why did she always have to be so clumsy and so odd? People were always put off by her exuberance. As one pithy matron had said in the parish before the last one, Cassie was like a cup of tea with three sugars when only one was required. At little too much. Too loud. Too talkative. Far too passionate and prone to cause irritation in every quarter. Why couldn't she simply pretend to be like all of the other young ladies? Why did her silly brain put daft ideas into her head and why did her even sillier head listen to them? Ripe apples and pirates. Two classic examples of her wandering, odd mind.

'I suppose I should get going. Papa will be wondering where I have got to.'

Captain Warriner nodded, seemingly content to remain seated on the grass. 'Yes. Probably best.' He was a man of few words—either that or he didn't suffer fools like her gladly.

'Well, good afternoon then. And thank you again.'
Cringing with awkwardness, Cassie untied Orange
Blossom and began to lead her down the narrow path
out of the dreaded Orchard of Embarrassment. A jet-
black stallion, obviously as unimpressed with her shenanigans as his owner, glared at her in disgust.

You are a very silly human, aren't you?

Don't listen to him, said Orange Blossom loyally,
you meant well, Cassie.

It was cold comfort. Captain Galahad still thought
her odd. For some reason, it was imperative she did
not leave him on such a bad impression.

'I am not normally this silly Captain.' Cassie spun
around only to see him wincing, resting painfully
on one knee, as he tried to stand. 'Oh, my goodness!
You've hurt your leg.' She dropped the reins and dashed
to his side to offer him some assistance. 'Let me help
you up and then I will escort you home.' After causing
his injury it was the very least she could do.

Those lovely blue eyes hardened to ice crystals.
'I'm not a blasted invalid, woman! I can get myself up
off the floor and find my own way home!' To prove
his point, he stood and stubbornly limped towards his
horse.

'Please, Captain Warriner—allow me to assist you.
Your poor leg!'

But he ignored her. He reached his horse quickly
and grabbed the pommel of the saddle to steady himself. Then, with another wince, put all of his weight on
his injured left leg so that he could place his right foot
in the stirrup. He hauled himself upwards using only
the power in his arms. Large muscles bulged under the
fabric of his coat, emphasising his strength and excel-

lent broad shoulders. He arranged himself comfortably before shooting her a scornful glare which could have curdled milk.

'Good afternoon, Miss Reeves. Next time you decide to go out for a ride, kindly remember *this* is private property.' He nudged the foreboding black stallion forward and the pair of them galloped off without a backward glance.

Chapter Two

Jamie dipped his brush in some water and used it to soften the cake of blue paint to create the perfect wash. He preferred to work with watercolours rather than oils. Oil took too long and he was never completely happy with the effect. With watercolour, you could play around with the finish. He loved the translucency it created when he painted skies or water, yet with less moisture you could still create solid lines and definition, and mixed with gouache it could mimic oil paint when he needed texture. It was the perfect combination for recreating scenes from nature, his preferred studies, and definitely the most therapeutic.

He could paint a reasonable portrait if he put his mind to it, but his style was more romantic than practical, far too whimsical for a career soldier and most certainly not something he was ever prepared to discuss. Soldiers were not supposed to enjoy the shape and curve of a petal or the lyrical pictures drawn by clouds—yet he did. He always had. Right from the moment he had first discovered he could draw, somewhere around the age of seven or eight, Jamie had always created fanciful, dream-like depictions of all the beauty he saw around him. His father had always disparagingly claimed he painted like a girl. And as vexing his noxious father was something he had done thoroughly as a point of personal honour, the man's obvious disgust had only encouraged his talent more.

'That looks like the orchard.' His sister-in-law Letty peered over his shoulder, smiling. 'I always think things appear so much more beautiful once I have seen them through your eyes.'

'Hmm.'

It was as far as he was prepared to go in acknowledging her compliment and she knew him too well to push. He watched her move towards her favourite chair and carefully lower herself into it. There was no disguising the evidence of her pregnancy now, and every day it reminded Jamie of what he would never have. Not that he wasn't happy for his elder brother Jack and his wife. He was delighted for them. They both deserved every happiness. A man would have to travel a very long way to find two better people. A part of him was even excited at the prospect of being an uncle— but it was bittersweet. He had always thought he would have a family, although he had never spoken about it aloud because admitting such things was not manly, but he had always hoped he would have a large one. The promise of it had sustained him during his years fighting on foreign battlefields: little, dark-haired versions of himself running riot and driving him to distraction.

But the romantic part of his soul had refused to consider just any woman in those days. He had wanted the whole cake to eat, not just the icing. Fighting for King and country had occupied all of his time and he had stupidly assumed he still had plenty of time left to search for the woman of his dreams; that elusive soulmate who enjoyed nature's beauty as much as he did and who would want to sit with him while he painted because they adored each other. With hindsight, Jamie probably should have married a few years ago, when he was handsome and complete. He doubted any woman would consider the broken man who had returned from the Peninsula. And who could blame them?

Any decent young bride worth her salt would expect her new husband to be similarly brimming with vigour. Two working legs were a prerequisite, as was a sound financial future. Crippled soldiers had few career choices open to them and he could hardly expect a wife to be content to live under the benevolent charity of his brother for ever. He tried not to envy his three brothers. Jack was about to be a father, Joe was finally pursuing his dream of becoming a doctor by studying at medical school and Jacob was having the time of his life at university. Their lives were just starting while his had come to a grinding halt. A wife would definitely not want a man devoid of prospects.

Nor could he ask one to cope with his other *peculiarities*—peculiarities so evident he could hardly keep them a secret from a wife. Finding the right words to explain them to the unfortunate woman, without making himself sound dangerous and ripe for immediate incarceration in Bedlam, was almost impossible. No, indeed, marriage and family were lost to him until he could find a way to fix it all and as he had spent the better part of a year since his return home failing dismally, he did not hold out much hope a solution was around the corner. Mulling the fact was not going to change it. It was the way it was, yet the death of his dream still stung.

Jamie began to sweep the first layer of wash on to his paper, pleased with the hue he had mixed. It was exactly as he remembered the sky yesterday as he had stared mournfully up at it.

'What made you draw it from that perspective?' Letty was still scrutinising the picture and he supposed it was a little unusual to paint exactly what he had seen when he had been flat on his back, minus all of the hair covering his face, of course.

'I thought I would try something different.'

The lie seemed to appease her and she picked up her embroidery, but the truth was Jamie could not stop thinking about those damned pink garters. Or the way the wearer had pitied him when she had seen him struggle. At this stage he had no idea what colour to paint his complete humiliation. Black seemed fitting, but did not quite go with the sky. Maybe he would try to leave it out, in the vain hope he could erase the shameful memory from his mind by creating an alternative memory here on paper.

Their butler crept in stealthily and coughed subtly. Every time Jamie saw him it gave him a start. Six months ago they had not even had a maid—now, thanks to Letty, there was a veritable army running Markham Manor, all transplanted from her opulent mansion in Mayfair.

'You have a caller, my lady.'

A rarity indeed. Nobody called on the Warriners unless they were baying for blood or demanding immediate payment.

'A young lady. A Miss Reeves. She is enquiring as to whether Captain Warriner is at home.'

Jamie could feel the beginnings of nerves in the pit of his stomach, warning of further impending humiliation, but tried to appear impassive.

'Captain Warriner?' Letty was staring at him with barely contained delight. 'How very dashing that sounds.'

'Tell her I am not at home, Chivers.'

'Tell her no such thing! Have her shown in immediately, Chivers. And arrange for some tea.' His sister-in-law tossed aside her already forgotten sewing and sat eagerly forward in her chair. 'Why is a young lady calling for you, Jamie?'

He considered lying, but as the real reason for Miss Reeves's unwelcome visit was doubtless about to be unveiled there seemed little point. 'I tried to rescue her from a tree yesterday.'

'Tried?'

'Yes. And failed. Miserably.'

Further explanation was prevented by the arrival of his embarrassment. Just as it had yesterday, those red-gold curls refused to be tamed by her hairpins. Several very becoming silky tendrils poked out of her sensible bonnet and framed her pretty face. Her lovely chestnut eyes were wary as they darted between him and Letty.

Politeness dictated he should stand in the presence of a lady, but if he stood she would see more damning evidence of his infirmity and his pride was already bruised and battered quite enough. Letty, of course, sprang to her feet in an instant and gushingly greeted their guest.

'Miss Reeves! I am delighted to make your acquaintance. I am Letty Warriner, technically the Countess of Markham, although my husband is reticent about using his title. Do take a seat. I hope you will join us for tea?'

It was all a little over the top, in Jamie's opinion. Yes, a visitor was something of a rarity here, but the way Letty was behaving was a little too effusive. Especially as he was already counting the seconds until Miss Reeves left him in humiliated solitary peace.

'Tea would be lovely,' she said, flicking her eyes towards his briefly as she arranged her bottom on a chair. Jamie could still remember the feel of it in his hands. Firm. Rounded. Womanly. Which of course made him think about the incongruous garters again. 'I came to check on Captain Warriner's recovery. Because of my own lack of judgement, he was injured yesterday.'

Jamie stared straight ahead, but could feel Letty's eyes boring into him. 'Really? Jamie made no mention of an injury. Come to mention it, he also made no mention of the accident which must have led to the injury. All I know is what I have just been told. You were apparently stuck in a tree, Miss Reeves, and my *brother-in-law* tried and failed to get you down.'

She put unnecessary emphasis on the words brother-in-law, clearly making a point to their guest. A point which made Jamie uncomfortable.

He is single, in case you were wondering, Miss Reeves, and desperately in want of a wife. Try to ignore the fact he is lame, futureless and has the potential to kill if the mood takes him.

Miss Reeves blushed like a beetroot, a beetroot with distracting freckles on her dainty button of a nose, and wore a pained expression. 'Captain Warriner climbed the apple tree to save me, but I fidgeted too much and the branch snapped. I am afraid we both fell to the ground. The poor captain absorbed the brunt of the impact.'

An understatement. His ribs had damn near snapped in half.

Letty was grinning like an idiot. 'You fell on top of him? In the *orchard*?' And like a nodcock he just happened to be painting the same blasted orchard and things looked so much more *beautiful* through his stupid eyes.

Miss Reeves nodded. 'I feel awful about it.'

For his own sake, now was the opportune time to intervene, before Letty started to matchmake in earnest. 'As you can see, I am in fine fettle, Miss Reeves. You needn't have troubled yourself by coming all this way to see the evidence for yourself.' His sister-in-law shot him a pointed glance for his rudeness, but Jamie was unrepentant. The last thing he needed was Letty reading more into his choice of painting than he was comfortable with her knowing. Miss Reeves's fine eyes swivelled towards his leg, raised as always on a supportive footstool, and he inwardly cringed.

'But I can see your leg is still injured, Captain Warriner, and that is completely my fault.'

She thought his infirmity was a temporary affliction, and as tempting as it was to go along with the fantasy, his innate sense of futility kicked in. 'This is Napoleon's fault, Miss Reeves. Not yours.'

Now, please go away, woman!

'Napoleon?'

'Indirectly. It was his guns which fired the musket balls.'

'Balls!'

Her voice came out a little high-pitched and he simply nodded. He had no intention of telling her how they had had to dig three of the blighters out of his thigh while he was still conscious and he'd very nearly lost the whole leg, as well as his life, to infection afterwards. She blinked rapidly and Jamie could see her imagination filling in the blanks, those long lashes fluttering like butterflies as she did so.

Very pretty.

Somehow that made it worse. Pretty and pity made him feel less of a man than he usually did. However, under the circumstances, it was probably best to divulge the horrible truth and suffer her pity rather than give Letty false hope that this delightful armful of woman might enter into a romance with a dangerous invalid. 'They left me crippled, Miss Reeves.' And cripples were not attractive. Especially not to freckle-faced fertility goddesses with positively *sinful* hair and saucy garters.

Cassie had no idea how to respond to such a statement. Part of her was sorry he had suffered, another part of her was hugely relieved not to have been the cause of his injury and a bigger part of her kept remembering how very big, solid and manly his body had been sprawled beneath hers. Just thinking about it made her feel all warm and those deliciously *sinful* sapphire eyes were not helping. Once again those exuberant passions she was trying her hardest to suppress jumped to the fore. Fortunately, the arrival of the tea tray meant she did not have to respond and had a perfectly reasonable excuse for removing her bonnet before she began to perspire from her wayward, wicked thoughts.

'Do you take sugar, Miss Reeves?'

'Just one, please, Mrs…er…my lady.'

The pretty blonde woman giggled. 'To be honest, it confuses me, too. Perhaps we should simply dispense with the formalities. Why don't you call me Letty?'

'In that case, please feel free to call me Cassie.' She risked peeking at Captain Galahad, but he made no move to invite her to call him anything familiar. In fact, he looked quite irritated at her continued presence. His gorgeous eyes were distinctly narrowed, which made her babble. 'I am new to the area. My father has recently been appointed the vicar of this parish. We live at the vicarage.' A completely ridiculous clarification only an idiot would make. It would probably be sensible to stop babbling nonsense and wait to be asked a question. Unfortunately, once her nerves got the better of her, Cassie's mouth had a habit of running away with itself. 'I couldn't help noticing you are going to have a baby.' Was it polite to mention such things?

Whether it was or it wasn't, her hostess smiled and Cassie watched in wonder as the young woman's hand automatically went to her protruding stomach lovingly. 'Yes, indeed. But not until the autumn. I appear to have got very fat very quickly.' She handed Cassie her tea. 'Are you engaged to be married, Miss Reeves, or is there an ardent suitor on the cusp of proposing to you in the near future?'

A very sore point.

Cassie's odd personality, off-putting exuberance, unfortunate freckles combined with her father's ferocious temperament had all proved to be highly effective deterrents to the male sex. 'No to both questions, I'm afraid.'

I am doomed to sit on the shelf and gather dust; I only hope it is sturdy enough and wide enough to bear my weight.

'Well, I am sure it won't be long before some lucky gentleman snaps you up—you are uncommonly pretty, Miss Reeves. Isn't that right, Jamie?'

Captain Galahad grunted and appeared very bored. Clearly he disagreed. He was sipping his tea and practically glaring at her over the rim of the ridiculously delicate cup in his large, manly hand. Or perhaps he was glaring at his sister-in-law for asking him such an impertinent question? It was quite difficult to tell.

'Did you enjoy being a soldier, Captain?'

A safer topic might make their exchange less awkward, although this also seemed to annoy him because he frowned.

'It had its moments.'

'You will have to forgive Jamie, Cassie. He is a man of very few words and even fewer smiles. However, beneath that surly, unfriendly exterior he is actually rather sweet. He also paints the most beautiful romantic pictures of the English countryside.' This comment garnered another warning glare. 'Do you have any hobbies, Cassie?'

'I like to write stories. Children's stories.' It was the first time she had admitted that to anyone, but Letty did appear friendlier than the usual person she came into contact with.

'Oh, how lovely! What are they about?'

'As she is a vicar's daughter, Letty, I dare say they are morality tales,' the Captain said disparagingly, clearly disapproving of such things. Sensible men of action like him would disapprove of her whimsical nature and romantic fairy tales.

'Not at all!' There was no way of explaining without sounding odd, but as Captain Galahad was of that opinion already, Cassie confessed all. 'At the moment they are about my pony—Orange Blossom. Or rather how Orange Blossom views our life together. In my stories, she talks. All of the animals talk.'

And she was babbling again.

'I often weave the tales around my own personal experiences. For example, the story I am currently working on is called *Orange Blossom and the Great Apple Debacle*...'

Her voice trailed off when she saw Letty and Captain Warriner exchange a strange look.

'I suppose it all sounds very silly to you, but I have read one or two of my efforts to the children in my father's congregation; they seemed to enjoy them.' Cassie had also sworn the children to secrecy. If her father got a whiff of her vain and pointless hobby, he would forbid her from writing—or worse.

'They sound quite delightful. Maybe you should consider getting them published.'

Cassie already liked Letty Warriner a great deal. 'I doubt my scribblings are good enough for that. But perhaps one day.' After my father is dead and buried—because that was the only way he would allow such self-indulgent frivolity. Unless she ever did manage to escape his clutches just as her mother had done before her. The meagre savings she had secretly accumulated in the last twelve months would barely get her a seat on the post to Norwich and there were woefully no ardent suitors clambering at her door who might whisk her off from her dreadful life. Unless a miracle happened, she was stuck.

Miserably stuck.

Her father had no idea she wrote stories about talking animals. Or about anything at all for that matter and Cassie had no intention of alerting him to the fact. It had certainly never been broached in conversation, not that they ever had conversations. Such an atrocious sin would doubtless require a great deal of solitary repentance, so Cassie had kept it all hidden. Mind you, he also had no idea that she was plotting to run away either. The image of his stern face as he spun manically in his grave at her sinful, open defiance, despite everything he had done to curb her dangerous passions, popped immediately into her thoughts and threatened to make her smile. She hid it by sipping her tea.

Chapter Three

Jamie could see the light of mischief in his sister-in-law's eyes and did not like it one bit. If ever there was time for a speedy exit, it was now, but that meant standing like a creaking old man and then limping laboriously out of the room in front of Miss Reeves. He was torn between the devil and the deep blue sea. Staying opened him up to more mischief—of that he was in no doubt. Letty had a tendency to be tenacious when she set her mind to something and her mind was clearly set. However, leaving and displaying his infirmity was humiliating in the extreme, although why he was so keen to appear less useless in front of the vicar's daughter was as pointless as it was pathetic. She was only being kind, after all.

'I would certainly be interested to read *The Great Apple Debacle*. Will Jamie be in it?'

Pregnant or not, he was going to strangle Letty later, but for now he had to take the bull by the horns and direct this unwelcome conversation or else die of total humiliation. Unfortunately, that meant making conversation. Something he had never been adept at. 'What drew your father to darkest Retford, Miss Reeves?'

'The diocese sent him here. We were in Nottingham for a few months beforehand and they felt his talents might be better used in a rural parish...away from trouble.'

As Jamie had always thought Nottingham was a dire place, filled with poverty and crime, he completely understood. It was certainly no place for a lovely vicar's daughter. 'I dare say your father is relieved.'

'Hardly. My father prefers working in a city, although I cannot say I do. Of all of his parishes, this one is by far the nicest we have ever lived in.' Her face lit up when she smiled and her freckled nose wrinkled in a very charming manner.

'You say that as if you have lived in a few places.'

She nodded, the motion causing one of her burnished curls to bounce close to her neck, which in turn drew his eyes to the satiny-smooth, golden skin visible above the bodice of her plain dress, and, of course, the magnificent way she filled out that bodice. Jamie had always had a great deal of affection for a woman's bosom and Miss Reeves's bosom was undoubtedly one of the finest he had ever had cause to notice.

'Indeed we have. Why, in the last five years alone, we have lived in eleven different towns.' Her face clouded briefly and he realised this gypsy lifestyle was not something she enjoyed. He doubted he would enjoy being moved from pillar to post either. He had had quite enough of that on the campaign trail, although it was not the same. Moving about then had always been temporary and transient as he had always had a very solid place to call home. A place to go back to which remained resolutely constant. If Miss Reeves did not have that consolation, no wonder it made her unhappy. But then she was smiling again so maybe he was mistaken. 'I have lived in Manchester, Newcastle, Sheffield—and obviously London. We have moved there several times although always to different parishes in different corners of the capital. It is so vast; I never had cause to revisit the places we had already lived in. Also we have spent some time in Bristol, Liverpool and Birmingham.'

All industrial, overcrowded places, he noted. 'I think you might find Retford a lot quieter than the places you are used to. Nothing much happens here.'

'That is what I enjoy the most about it. I love all of the trees and nature, so does Orange Blossom, and it goes without saying the air is cleaner. I do so love being outdoors. I have spent hours aimlessly riding around every afternoon since my arrival. Hence I trespassed here yesterday without realising. I am sorry about that, too.'

'Trespassed? Of course you didn't.' Letty was smiling kindly. 'You are very welcome to ride on our estate whenever you want to. In fact, I absolutely insist you do. There are some very lovely spots in the grounds, especially close to the river at this time of year.'

Miss Reeves's eyes locked on his briefly and he saw her trepidation. He supposed he had been rude to her yesterday and, much as it pained him, Jamie felt the need to extend a tiny olive branch. 'The river is a very pleasant place to ride. Even Satan likes it.' Her eyes widened and he realised his choice of name for his horse was perhaps not really suitable in the presence of a vicar's daughter.

'You named your horse Satan?'

'In my defence, he can be truly evil. He has a troublesome temperament and can be hostile around people.'

'Much like his surly owner,' Letty added for good measure. Jamie chose to ignore it.

'Oh! I almost forgot.' Miss Reeves rummaged in her capacious reticule and handed him a package wrapped in string. 'I brought you a small gift. To thank you for attempting to save me and for breaking my fall.' The gesture was strangely touching. When was the last time someone, other than Letty, had extended the hand of friendship to a Warriner? Jamie turned the gift over in his hands before undoing the wrapping. Miss Reeves became flustered and her words tumbled out. 'Please do not get excited. I had no idea what you might want, but as you are a fellow horse lover I brought some carrots.'

She was blushing again. She apparently did that a lot. As promised, three orange spears were nestled in the paper and, despite himself, Jamie felt the corners of his mouth curl up. What an odd, useful and totally charming, gift. 'Satan loves carrots. Thank you.' If he had not been broken and useless, he might have suggested she accompany him to the stables to help him feed them to the bad-tempered beast. But he was, so he didn't. The thought of her politely accepting and slowing her pace while he limped along next to her made him feel queasy. Suddenly, his brief good mood evaporated. He covered the carrots with their paper and placed them on the arm of the chair and withdrew into himself.

* * *

For the next half an hour he remained almost mute.
Miss Reeves and Letty held up the conversation and,
if a response was required, Jamie grunted. To compound his discomfort, the subject of the 'Great Apple
Debacle' was brought up and he was forced to listen
to it regaled for Letty's entertainment. Miss Reeves
had a knack for storytelling. He had to give her that
even though she barely paused for breath. Listening to
her take on the unfortunate events of yesterday, combined with her self-deprecating wit and her insistence
on trying to see the whole sorry affair through the
eyes of her pony, was amusing. By the time she got
to the end, he came out appearing sensible and noble,
while she painted herself as silly and severely lacking
in common sense.

'It definitely would make an entertaining children's
story, Cassie, and if you do eventually consider getting it published, you should ask Jamie to do the illustrations. In fact, the painting he is doing right now is
hugely appropriate, isn't it, Jamie? And from such an
interesting perspective.' The innocence with which
this statement was delivered was astounding and he
gave Letty a tight smile which he hoped conveyed his
intent to murder her as soon as it was politely possible.

'It is just a study of the grounds and I sincerely
doubt Miss Reeves would have any desire to have my
amateur sketches in her book.' Jamie had the overwhelming desire to pick up his stupid, ill-conceived
picture and march out of the room with it. If only he
could still march.

'Nonsense—go and take a look at it, Cassie. Jamie is
merely being modest about his abilities. *Orange Blos-*

som and the Great Apple Debacle would make a wonderful picture book.'

To his horror, the vicar's daughter appeared to find this idea intriguing and clearly something she had never considered before his meddling sister-in-law had planted the seed. 'Pictures *would* be good.' She began to rise from her seat and walked towards him with cheerful interest. His only hope was she would not put two and two together and recognise the orchard. She peered at the painting, bending slightly at the waist to get the best possible view, and wafting some deliciously floral scent directly towards his nostrils. Violets. He had always loved violets.

'Letty is quite right. You are an exceptionally talented painter, Captain Warriner. Even unfinished, I can see this picture is outstanding. And quite charming.' He risked a peek sideways at her and saw her eyebrows draw together as she studied the details more closely. 'Is that the apple orchard?'

'Yes.' The inward cringe threatened to seep out and display itself on his face. Only pride kept his upper lip resolutely stiff.

'Isn't it peculiar the pair of you have both been inspired by yesterday's incident? *The Great Apple Debacle* is already a blossoming story and a half-finished painting.' Jamie sent his sister-in-law a glare which was a stark warning to stop. Typically, she ignored it. 'Have you worked out his perspective yet, Cassie?'

'You are painting it from your position on the ground, aren't you? Just after I flattened you.' Two mortified crimson blotches bloomed on her cheeks.

'It was an interesting view I had not considered before.' Come on, Jamie, old boy, brazen it out. 'From what I remember, the branches and leaves formed an aesthetically pleasing contrast to the sky.' That sounded suitably arty.

'I should probably be going.' She stood briskly upright, still blushing, and Letty heaved herself out of her own chair.

'I hope you will call again soon, Cassie. I should like to get to know you better and I am certain my brother-in-law would, too.' His sister-in-law shot him a pointed look. 'Come along, Jamie, let us walk our guest to the door together.'

Trapped, because Letty knew hell would have to freeze over for him to openly admit he was lame and in pain, he had no option other than to grit his teeth and use the strength in his arms to push himself out of his chair. It was only then he realised he had been stationary for too long and his shattered leg had started to atrophy. It screamed in protest, but Jamie ignored the hot shooting pains jabbing him mercilessly in his hip. Normally, he would wait a few moments for the initial discomfort to subside before he tested his weight on it. Had he not been such a proud man, he might have made use of the hated walking stick gathering dust behind his chair. But if he had to humiliate himself in front of Miss Reeves, he was going to damn well do it without looking completely decrepit and good for nothing. He forced himself to walk despite the agony, knowing full well he was going to regret the decision immediately and pay for his folly later. Hot molten bursts of pain stabbed his left thigh muscle, but Jamie shuffled in his best approximation of a normal man's gait towards the hallway, conscious Miss Reeves was right behind him.

Pitying him.

'Oh, I forgot,' said Letty unsubtly as they approached the front door, 'I need to have a quick word with Cook. If you will excuse me, Cassie—I have thoroughly enjoyed your visit. Please do call again soon and remember I absolutely insist on you riding in our grounds here at Markham Manor. Jamie will see you safely out.'

Yes, he would.

Reluctantly.

Then he would find his brother and demand he keep his troublesome wife in check.

Left alone with Miss Reeves, he limped awkwardly towards the door Chivers was already holding open. Out on the newly gravelled driveway he could see her pretty pony waiting patiently. The incongruous animal suited her. 'Thank you for the carrots,' he said stiffly, 'and for your misplaced concern for my well-being.' Miss Reeves gave him a weak smile and started towards Orange Blossom, turning at the last minute, her expression quite wretched and her words tumbling out in rapid, panicked succession once again.

'I really am sorry about yesterday. Getting stuck up a tree is a ridiculous thing for a grown woman to do—but unfortunately I am prone to act without thinking and often do things which are ridiculous. And I am sorry for not listening to you when you tried to save me, but I was embarrassed because you had seen my unsightly legs. I do not have the words to express how mortified I am to have caused you to fall and then for crushing you. I can be clumsy as well as inordinately stupid and ridiculous. And I am well aware I am ridiculous and more than a little odd. I do try not to be, but as you can see, it happens regardless. I am also aware

that at best you find me irritating. Everybody does—
and quite quickly. I am a cup of tea with three sugars
when one is quite enough. Too loud. Too talkative. I
am trying to be less enthusiastic about everything in
a quest not to irritate everyone I meet, so please don't
panic and think for a moment I would even consider
riding in your grounds again. I realise Letty meant well
in suggesting it and that you were only being polite in
agreeing with her. Nor do I intend to vex you further
by pursuing her idea of you illustrating my silly stories.
I am well aware of the fact you would like to be well
shot of me and the sad thing is I really cannot blame
you. Most of the time I irritate myself. I shall leave you
in peace henceforth, Captain Warriner.'

'I see.' Jamie was not entirely sure what he felt about
all that. There were several things he wanted to say,
and would have if his damn leg still worked, so he
stood awkwardly next to her long-maned pony. 'I suppose I should say good day to you then.' Even though
he didn't want to.

She blinked rapidly.

'Yes. Good day, Captain Warriner.'

She took the reins and then stared mournfully at
the ground. 'Would you be so good as to ask for a riding block, please?'

'No need.' Without thinking he placed his hands on
her waist and lifted her smartly off the ground to deposit her on her side-saddle. Judging from her wide-
eyed look of horror, he had overstepped the bounds of
propriety, but couldn't quite bring himself to care. She
felt good in his hands. Soft. Curvy. Definitely curvy.
'My apologies, Miss Reeves, I realise now that was
unforgivably inappropriate.'

'No...not really. I was taken by surprise that I could actually be lifted. It's never happened before. And I suppose propriety hardly matters when you have already seen my awful legs.'

Some devil inside him began to place her foot in the stirrup because he needed to touch her again, his fingers lingering too long on the silk-clad ankle above her half-boot.

'You have very nice legs.'

What in God's name had possessed him to say that? It sounded like flirting.

'And lovely eyes.'

Good grief! The words he was thinking had just spilled from his mouth when he absolutely *never* actually said what he was thinking to anyone. Her lush mouth fell slightly open and those mooncalf eyes widened. Now he was definitely flirting. Futilely flirting and had no idea what had got into him. To stop his suddenly talkative mouth from humiliating him again he chewed awkwardly on his bottom lip and stared down at his feet.

Please go now. I feel like a total idiot and wish I was dead.

'Thank...you. For the boost...' Miss Reeves blinked uncomfortably as her usually rapid flurry of words trailed off, her freckles disappearing in the rosy glow of her blush. How splendid. Now he had made her hideously uncomfortable with his clumsy, ill-advised, totally mortifying outbursts. 'Good day, Captain Warriner.' Then she smiled shyly and peaked at him through her ridiculously long eyelashes. 'And thank you for the lovely compliments.' She held his gaze for several moments before chivvying her pretty pony on.

Jamie allowed himself to watch her delightful bottom sway down the driveway and decided he felt peculiar.

Unsettled.

Slightly ridiculous.

Almost cheerful.

The good mood persisted even while he loudly castigated his meddling sister-in-law.

Chapter Four

Cassie spent the next morning accompanying her father as he visited some of his new parishioners. Those too old, too ill or too lazy to come to church were always graced with a fortnightly visit. Her father was nothing if not tenacious in his mission to bring the word of God into people's lives, whether they wanted to hear it or not—but at least she was outside. Spending any prolonged periods of time with her father at home was always fractious. She had heard every lecture and every dire final warning for a person to save his soul before Judgement Day and, because she definitely wasn't the world's greatest vicar's daughter, she had long ago stopped listening. Instead, she entertained herself by weaving stories in her head. Not the lofty novels of great writers, Cassie's wayward brain did not work in that way, but wild fairy tales. Feats of derring-do, mythical lands, pirates, princesses, dragons and, lately, talking animals.

If her papa had asked her opinion, which of course he never did, she might have told him his over-zealous, accusatory stance did more to dissuade the reluctant to come to church than encourage them. He was too much fire and brimstone and not enough love or goodwill for his fellow man. The Reverend Reeves was so blinded by his own confrontational fervour he never saw how he raised the hackles of others. Time after time, he had gone too far, upset too many well-respected and reasonable people, resulting in them having to up sticks and move to yet another parish. Usually another parish so far away from his previous one, nobody had heard of him.

Hence they were here in Retford. A tiny rural congregation which was so very different from the city parishes her father preferred, because, as he was prone to point out at least once a day, where there is deprivation and temptation, sin festered. In the fortnight since they had arrived, Cassie already loved the bustling, little market town. Her father, on the other hand, was not so enamoured, but determined to hunt for enough sinners to justify his presence. The wide-eyed farmer and his cheerful wife were probably not the sort of people he was seeking. But it made no difference. Her father was in full flow. As he had only just mentioned Sodom and Gomorrah, it was fairly safe to assume they would be here for at least another half an hour.

Cassie dived into herself. A technique she had mastered around the age of ten and one which effectively blocked out all of the outside world so she could focus on her latest story and allow her characters to speak to her. She had started it last night, whilst listening to Papa rehearse Sunday's sermon, and it was tentatively titled *Orange Blossom and the Great Apple Debacle.* Except, just as it had last night, the flow of the narrative kept being interrupted by thoughts of Captain Galahad, those aquamarine eyes and splendid shoulders.

Apparently, her affection-starved brain was determined to create a completely different sort of story involving him, his mouthwatering strong arms and a willing damsel in distress eager to fall into them so they could ride off into the sunset together. In her mind, the damsel was so thrilled to be going she did not even bother looking back at her hateful father as she headed triumphantly towards her new life. There was no point in pretending the damsel bore a passing resemblance to Miss Cassandra Reeves because she *was* Miss Cassandra Reeves. A bolder, braver version of herself, who batted her eyelashes coquettishly when the dashing Captain complimented her on her legs.

Really, Captain Galahad? Do you think so? Eyelash flutter. *Well, while we are swapping compliments, I think you have a fine pair of shoulders. Perhaps the finest I have ever seen. I do like a man with broad, strong shoulders...*

The word Warriner floated into her ears. The farmer's wife was quite animated with indignation.

'That family are the epitome of sin, Reverend. Debauchers, cheats and *vile* sinners every one of them. There's four of them Warriner boys and all four of them would sooner fleece you than be neighbourly. It's a scandal, I tell you!'

'Those Warriners sound exactly like the sort of people who could do with hearing the benefit of God's word. Perhaps I should visit them tomorrow?'

The zealot gleam was lit in her father's eyes all the way home. Cassie said nothing as she frantically sought a believable excuse as to why he probably shouldn't, then panicked when nothing suitable came to mind that would not result in him punishing her for speaking out of turn. As soon as they entered the vicarage Cassie busied herself with her normal daily chores, hoping he would forget, while her father disappeared in the direction of the church, appearing as preoccupied as he always was. With any luck, he would forget to visit the Warriners, as he so often forgot things that were not top of his list of immediate priorities. Fortunately, his priorities did tend to change like the weather and he had a memory like a flour sifter. Most of the time he forgot he even had a daughter, a very pleasing state of affairs as far as she was concerned as it gave her more freedom than most young ladies of her age. Cassie hauled the heavy kettle on to the stove to boil and got ready to prepare his luncheon.

Despite being well able to afford it, the Reverend Reeves never bothered with servants. Servants suggested he thought himself better than others, which hinted at vanity and vanity was one of the seven deadly sins. Something which was all well and good, but left the entire running of the house up to Cassie. Ungratefully, she supposed, she had come to believe her father kept her as a skivvy to ensure there was never any possibility of her meeting a nice young man and marrying him. She dreaded to think what sort of a rage he would fly into if he suspected she was desperate to leave. It did not help that his sour disposition and hot temper did not lend itself to finding willing employees. Far better to inconvenience his daughter, who slaved for free, and could barely scrape together a few coins for any luxuries whatsoever in the pathetic housekeeping allowance he counted out weekly like the miser he was.

Nevertheless, Cassie enjoyed two blissful hours of her own company, completely devoid of any fiery sermons or pertinent reminders about the need to continually spread the word of God to the seething cesspool of Earth-dwelling sinners. Or any veiled threats about the need for solitary penance to reflect on her wayward tendencies.

'Wool-gathering again, girl?'

His sudden reappearance at the open back door startled her. Without thinking, she touched the pocket of her apron to reassure herself that the key to the door was still there as he resolutely shut it behind him. Something which always created a cold trickle of fear to shimmy down her spine each time he did it. 'Not at all, merely thinking about what I need to do next.' Cassie put down the bread and dutifully pulled out a chair for him at the table. He sat heavily on a chair and began to load his plate with the food Cassie had placed on the kitchen table.

'I have had a most informative conversation with another parishioner.'

'Really?' Already she could feel herself glaze over, but tried to remain focussed, like a dutiful daughter who was not daydreaming about running away would have.

'I made some enquiries into that family we were warned about—the Warriners.'

Cassie felt the icy grip of fear stiffen her muscles, dreading what was coming.

'Yes. Indeed. A thoroughly bad lot. The eldest recently married an heiress, but in Nottingham there is talk he abducted the poor girl and compromised her into marriage.'

Letty certainly did not appear to be the unhappy victim of a kidnapper. Cassie had not met the woman's husband, but she had seen the great affection in his wife's eyes as she had talked about him and unconsciously rubbed the unborn child nestled in her womb like it was the greatest gift she had ever received. 'People do like to embellish gossip, Papa. Perhaps the Warriner family are merely the victims of such nonsense.'

'I fear not, Cassandra. There is too much evidence levied against them for there not to be strong foundations forged on truth. I have heard grave tales, far too terrible to sully your delicate ears, involving avarice, greed, debauchery. Suffice to say I am convinced they are in dire need of the Lord's guidance.'

Oh, dear. 'If they are as bad as you fear, Papa, then perhaps they are best avoided.'

'Nonsense. I have never shied away from the challenge, Cassandra.'

'Of course you haven't, Papa. In a few weeks perhaps you should call upon them, when you are more familiar with your worthier parishioners.'

Her father's response was as loud as it was instantaneous. 'These Warriners are in desperate need of my guidance, Daughter. I will go this very afternoon!'

There would be no stopping him, but there was still a chance Cassie could avoid accompanying him. At least then she would not have to witness the tender new shoots of her friendship with Letty and her only link to the Captain ruthlessly trampled on. Good gracious! A far greater issue suddenly presented itself. As soon as he visited them he would learn she had already done so and blatantly neglected to mention it.

'You came home a little earlier than I expected, Papa, and have rather spoiled my little planned surprise.' Cassie tried desperately to sound nonchalant. Her father hated liars almost as much as he hated thieves, murderers and fornicators, especially when the liar happened to be his own daughter.

He lifted his head and stared at her quizzically. 'I did?'

'Yes! I was about to make your favourite spiced fruitcake. Why don't we postpone our visit to that family until tomorrow?' By which time Cassie might well have thought of something to prevent her father from ever darkening their door.

'You would put cake above the saving of souls?'

'But, Papa—I was so looking forward to making it for you today.' Pleading to his better nature had not worked once in all of her twenty-one years, but still Cassie persisted. Her father smiled his benevolent I-know-better-than-you smile and took her hand, a gesture so uncharacteristic it took Cassie completely by surprise. 'I know what this is about.'

'You do?' Surely he had not been apprised of her unaccompanied visit to the family or, heaven forbid, her sinful behaviour in the apple orchard?

'Yes, and it does you credit. You are a God-fearing girl, Cassandra, and being exposed to the godless frightens you. But fear not. You shall be with me and that heathen family will see what a good example you are of my teachings.'

'But I would rather not do it today. Just this once, Papa, could we…?'

'No! You are a dutiful daughter Cassandra. Being dutiful means doing those things one might find unpalatable without complaining.'

'But...'

'Your mother was headstrong and weak-willed, Cassandra. Do I now see that unfortunate trait rearing its ugly head in you?' He was peering at her closely, looking, no doubt, for evidence to support his suspicion. Again her fingers grazed the heavy key in her pocket. For the moment it was still hers although that could change in a heartbeat. 'You must fight the temptation, girl!' Cassie schooled her features and tried her best to seem compliant, because being compared to her mother always kindled his anger and then her bedchamber door would be locked again.

'No, Father, I merely wanted to make you a cake...' Tears were prickling her eyes as she forced herself to try one last time to escape the ordeal of watching him castigate an innocent family whilst selfishly still avoiding the ordeal of being imprisoned.

'You will do as you are told, Cassandra.' He stared pointedly at the stairs until she capitulated with a terrified nod. 'We will leave within the hour.'

Jamie had spent most of the day riding Satan around the grounds. There was nothing out of the ordinary in that. He rode every single day, for goodness sake, because he enjoyed being out in the sunshine so it was hardly tangible proof he was being pathetic. Nobody apart from him knew he had lingered for the better part of an hour at the edge of the riverbank or that he had rode up and down every row of trees in the orchard until Satan's hooves threatened to carve out a deep trench in the ground. And certainly nobody had any idea he did so in the faint hope he would 'accidentally' bump into the delectable Miss Reeves again.

As if she would have been tempted to visit again after his clumsy, and doubtless unwelcome, attempt at flirting with her. Pretty girls who wore saucy garters and had the sort of figure which would make any man sit up and beg like a dog were not likely to be particularly enamoured of a crippled former soldier who was afraid of the dark. He sincerely doubted she had given him so much as a passing thought since she had ridden away from him. Unfortunately, Jamie could not say the same.

He had done a great deal of thinking about her. Aside from her acute physical attractiveness, and the garters that tormented him, there was something quirky, unusual and refreshingly unique about the vicar's daughter which appealed to him. Maybe because he was prone to being serious and she did, as she said herself, border on the ridiculous—but it was her ridiculousness which was so utterly charming. Jamie had never met anyone who imagined animals talked before, or who climbed trees and got stuck in them or who thought carrots were a gift. Or maybe all of this mooning had come about because Miss Reeves had been the first woman he had touched since his injury...

With a sigh, he limped out of the stable and headed into the house. It was a sorry state of affairs when you misguidedly counted an unfortunate accident as an amorous encounter. He found his brother Jack and Letty in the vaulted Tudor great hall they called the drawing room. His sister-in-law was sewing something which he assumed would clothe the baby one day and, like the besotted dolt he had become, his elder brother was watching her contentedly.

'Don't you have anything better to do than stare at your wife?'

'Not at the moment, no. I find I never tire of it. Don't you have anything better to do than gripe about it?'

Jamie shrugged, reluctant to admit that, no, he never had anything to do any more. His life was aimless because he was now pointless. His easel and paints lay within arm's reach, calling to him, but he resisted picking them up. It would only give Letty another excuse to ask him how his orchard picture was coming along. Instead, he picked up a newspaper and made a great show of reading it.

'Ahem.' The butler appeared on stealthy feet. 'You have visitors my lord. The Reverend Reeves and his daughter would like an audience.'

It was all Jamie could do not to sit bolt upright and neaten his unruly, windswept hair. She was here. Again. Very probably only to see Letty—but that was all right. At least she was here.

And he was pathetic.

'Miss Reeves passed me this note while her father was not looking, my lady, I got the impression she wanted you to read it before I showed them in.'

Chivers handed Letty a letter, which was unsealed and appeared to have been hastily folded. She opened it, scanned it quickly, then scowled. 'Well, I am not altogether sure what to make of this.'

Deliberately, Jamie slowly folded the newspaper in case he seemed too eager to hear what Miss Reeves had to say and schooled his features to appear bored, rather than slightly panicked and yet nauseatingly eager to gaze upon her again.

Letty read the missive out in hushed tones.

Dearest Letty and Captain Warriner,
Please accept my sincerest apologies for the clandestine manner of this note, however, my father would be very angry if he learned that I had visited you unchaperoned or that I had been climbing the trees in your grounds.

I would be eternally in your debt if you pretended this was our first meeting. I know I am asking you to lie for me and appreciate that you are under no obligation to do so and that my request is odd, to say the very least.

I should like to say sorry in advance for what is about to happen. None of this is of my doing.
Cassie

'I suppose we have to honour her request?' Letty folded the note slowly and looked towards first Jack, then Jamie for guidance. They both shrugged in response. It was a peculiar letter to be sure. 'Show them in, Chivers.'

Like the others, Jamie stood. Miss Reeves had already seen him limp so there was no point trying to hide it, and if she had brought her father in tow then the man would expect to see proper manners. Meeting her father suddenly made him feel nervous, as if he were a potential suitor keen to make a good first impression. Where had that ridiculous thought come from? He was not suitor material. He was not anything material any more. Not until he was fixed. If he ever got fixed.

*Stop getting ideas above yourself and just be pleased
she has graced you with her company again. You have
to take whatever crumbs are thrown at you, old boy.*

For some reason, he expected to see a jolly, rotund
man with his daughter's friendly open expression.
The sour-faced, reedy fellow who walked in, ramrod-
straight and unsmiling, was nothing like her. Worse
still, the effervescent Miss Reeves was apparently un-
available for this visit. The pained, slouched woman
who dutifully walked behind her father was a shell of
the vixen he had been thinking about incessantly. Behind her father's back, she screwed up her face and
stared at him mournfully, almost apologetically, then
did the same to Letty. Judging by the stern expression on her father's pinched face, he was not pleased
to be here.

Odd.

Being the ranking man of the house, his brother
stepped forward with his hand outstretched in welcome. The Reverend curled his lip in what appeared
to be disgust and limply returned the handshake as if
Jack's hand was somehow offensive. As a greeting, it
was definitely not particularly friendly and Jamie felt
his hackles rise at the insult.

'We are honoured to meet you, Reverend Reeves.
Miss Reeves.'

Jamie's eyes never left her as his brother spoke and
her expression became more wretched by the second,
yet she refused to meet his gaze and stared dejectedly
at the handkerchief she was worrying in her fingers.

'Allow me to introduce my daughter Cassandra.' She
stepped forward, looking completely dejected. 'Stand
straight, girl! Stop slouching.'

The vicar's voice was clipped and cold and his daughter withered beneath his steely glare. Instantly, for that alone, Jamie decided he hated the man. The sort of man who would openly chastise his daughter in front of apparent strangers was not the sort he was inclined to think charitably towards. The Reverend Reeves was a bully, like his own father had been, and like all bullies needed standing up to. He bit back the urge to give the man a set down on her behalf, fearing it would only make this increasingly awkward situation much worse and might enlighten the imperious vicar of their prior acquaintance. Definitely not what she needed.

To her credit, Letty never faltered. His sister-in-law stepped forward and smiled benevolently. 'My dear Miss Reeves, I am so glad you have come to visit us here at Markham Manor. You and your father are most welcome. May I introduce you both to my husband, the Earl of Markham, and his brother, Captain James Warriner?'

Jamie stepped forward and received his own version of the vicar's limp handshake and bowed politely to the woman who had dominated his thoughts for the last few days.

'It is a pleasure to meet you, Miss Reeves.' She smiled somewhat nervously and blushed bright pink as soon as her eyes guiltily flicked to his.

'How do you do, Captain Warriner. Your lordship.' Then she stepped back behind her father and stared back at her crumpled handkerchief as if her life depended on it.

It was all very peculiar, yet for reasons unexplained they were pretending to be complete strangers. It was obvious she was frightened of her father. Jamie knew how that felt. His own sire had been a nasty piece of work by and large, and one not averse to using his fists when the mood struck him, usually after dark when it was least expected. He had wielded the element of surprise perfectly. And the old Earl had not been particular about his choice of victim. His sons, his wife, servants, complete strangers. Was the reverend also a man like that? The prospect was as unsettling as it was galling. Surely a man of God would abhor the use of violence? But then again, already this man had openly criticised his daughter in front of strangers, so perhaps he was capable of worse and Miss Reeves appeared cowed in the man's presence. It all looked far too familiar for Jamie's liking.

Letty ordered refreshments and invited the vicar and his lying daughter to sit, and did the very best impression of a woman making polite small talk he had ever seen. Throughout the arduous pouring and serving of the tea, the reverend wore a mask of haughty superiority and barely said a word. His daughter said nothing, seemly content to watch her fingers tightly twist her handkerchief into a tangled ball, her lovely brown eyes limpid.

Jamie had just brought his cup to his lips when the good reverend cleared his throat and began to speak in an overly loud voice to no one in particular.

'*"The Lord knoweth how to deliver the Godly out of temptations, and to reserve the unjust unto the day of Judgement to be punished."*' The vicar paused for effect and stared directly at his elder brother. 'A stark warning from the gospels which is pertinent for this family, I believe.'

He watched Jack's dark eyebrows come together in confusion while he tried to come up with a suitable response to what was undoubtedly meant as the most grievous of insults. As usual, his brother resorted to diplomacy, although those who knew him well heard the steel embedded in his words.

'Perhaps the Warriner family of old, sir, but I trust you are not suggesting those of us who stand before you today are the *unjust*?'

Jamie felt his own eyes narrow and would have intervened if he had not seen Miss Reeves stare at him, her sorrowful expression completely wretched. He held his tongue reluctantly.

The vicar was unrepentant and glared back at his brother as bold as brass. 'The whole of Nottinghamshire is rife with stories about the Warriner family. Cheats, liars, debauchers—*fornicators*! But fear not!' One bony finger pointed heavenward. 'It is not too late to save your miserable souls.'

Had the man come here to preach at them? How dare he? Jamie had had quite enough. 'If your intent was to come here and grossly insult my brother and his wife, Reverend, you have succeeded...'

His brother stayed him with a placating hand and a warning glance. 'Reverend Reeves, it is true the Warriners of old were a thoroughly bad lot—and I include my own father in that generalisation—however, I can assure you that his sons have chosen to tread a very different path.'

The bony finger pointed directly at Jack in accusation and wiggled menacingly an inch away from his brother's chest. '"*Enter not into the path of the wicked, and go not in the way of evil men.*"' Almost as an afterthought he added, 'Proverbs,' in case they had the urge to look it up in the Bible to check the validity of his unwarranted sermon.

Miss Reeves, Jamie noticed, had now completely covered her face with her hands and was bent over in the chair, almost as if she were trying to become part of the upholstery. It was obvious she wanted no part in her father's zealous tirade, but felt powerless to stop it. Jack tried to reason with the vicar again. Clearly he had far more patience than Jamie gave him credit for as he'd have sent the man packing smartly. His fingers itched to grab the man by the lapels, toss him on the newly gravelled drive and to hear the satisfying thud as he slammed the door on him. But he and his elder brother were vastly different in character, therefore, Jack still persisted. 'As I have just said, Reverend, my brothers and I have chosen a different path to our ancestors and I can assure you none of us are cheats, liars, debauchers or—'

'"*Behold, the day of the Lord cometh, cruel both with wrath and fierce anger, to lay the land desolate. And he shall destroy the sinners thereof out of it.*"' The vicar's eyes were wide and he was practically quaking with righteous indignation. 'Isaiah!' His finger jabbed Jack's ribs for emphasis and Jamie saw his brother's expression harden although he still did not pull the obnoxious preacher up. 'Repent, Mr Warriner! Before it is too late and your souls are banished to the fiery torment of hell!'

'Oh, this is beyond the pale!' Jamie briskly limped towards the vicar, snatched the teacup out of his hand and clattered it noisily on the table. 'My brother is an earl, Reverend Reeves, not a mister, therefore when you next address him it had damn well better have the words *my lord* at the end of it, else you will have me to answer to. And, whilst we are quoting the Bible, *he who is without sin, let him cast the first stone*!' He grabbed the vicar by the elbow and unceremoniously hauled him towards the door. 'John! Chapter Eight, Verse Seven, I believe. Now, good day to you, Reverend Reeves! Take your unsolicited sermons elsewhere.'

'Do you refuse to hear the word of God, sir?'

'I refuse to listen to a sanctimonious, judgemental, self-righteous diatribe from a man who is little more than a gossipmonger.'

'Gossipmonger!' This, apparently, was the highest of insults as the vicar began to turn alarmingly purple. 'I have it on the highest authority that—'

'Highest authority? Whose?'

The vicar's mouth opened to speak, then closed again, giving Jamie his answer.

'I see. Hearsay? Gossip? History? Surely that is not what the Bible condones, Reverend?' Jamie continued to walk the man to the door where Chivers stood waiting, still holding his elbow firmly.

'Jamie.'

His brother's calm voice penetrated his roiling temper. He understood the implication.

Stand down. We have to be above this.

He glanced at the wide-eyed Miss Reeves and saw the horror in those chocolate-brown depths and realised that his coarse physicality probably frightened her. Freckled-faced vicar's daughters, as a rule, would not be exposed to such aggressive behaviour. Or at least he hoped she wasn't.

Jamie let go of the man's arm and forced his next

words to be cold and final. 'I believe the Gospel of John, Chapter Seven, Verse Twenty-Four, also tells us, "*Judge not according to the appearance, but judge righteous judgement*". Righteous judgement. Based on actual facts rather than salacious rumours. Something, Reverend Reeves, you appear to be incapable of. Show him out, please, Chivers.'

The well-trained butler tried to manoeuvre the out-raged vicar towards the hallway.

'Cassandra. Come along, girl. Let us leave this house of sin!'

Jamie turned to see her stand, those beautiful brown eyes awash with tears. She sailed towards him miserably, wringing a handkerchief in both of her hands, and as she came level she never even looked at him. Whether that was out of embarrassment for her father's behaviour or complete disgust at Jamie's flash of temper he had no idea, but she continued towards the door in the wake of her father. Hunched. Afraid. Subservient. It was a horrible thing to see.

Chapter Five

No matter how much Cassie willed them, the words would not come. She was too distracted to write tonight, not when her cheeks still scalded with shame and her heart was heavy with bitter regret. She had hoped she had finally found a friend in Letty and did not dare put a name to what she had imagined between herself and Captain Galahad. But alas, like all of her brief and transient attachments, her interlude with the Warriner family was dead and buried. Unlike her, she doubted they would be holding a wake to lament its passing.

She closed her journal and carefully hid it under her mattress, sitting down on the bed afterwards and simply staring at nothing. Even by his usual standards, her father had been scathing. He had not even given the poor Earl a chance to defend himself against all of the slander laid at his family's door and that was unforgivable. She had almost said as much to her father as they made the depressing walk back to the village. Almost, because the moment she had asked where he had acquired all of his salacious evidence against the family, he had pinned her with his penetrating stare and shaken his head in outrage.

'Do not dare to side with those heathens over me, Cassandra. Where my information comes from is no concern of yours. *"Honour thy father"*, Cassandra!'

As always, he omitted the end of that particular biblical quote. *'And thy mother.'* Her name was never brought up unless it was to compare Cassie's unfortunate wayward tendencies with the legendary wanton wickedness of her father's absent wife. The wife who scandalously took a lover and then shamelessly ran away with him when Cassie was but a babe. She had no memory of the woman apart from those planted in her head by her father. Memories which should haunt her, but threw up more questions than answers. Answers she would never get, from questions she did not dare ask. However, she envied her mother the escape, understood it and yearned for her own one day. In fact, it really could not come soon enough.

'I was not siding with them, Papa, merely questioning the validity of the charges made against them. They did seem to me to be very pleasant.'

Her father pinned her with another outraged stare, as if she had gone quite mad and needed to be incarcerated in a lunatic asylum. 'Have you learned nothing from my teachings, Cassandra? Appearances can be deceptive!' Then, as he often did, he looked up towards the heavens to seek forgiveness for the silliness of his only daughter. 'Help her, oh, Lord, to develop the fortitude and character you granted to me rather than the weakness cursed upon her by her mother.'

As she supposed it was meant to, this swiftly put a stop to any further impertinent questions. If she pushed too far, he would lock her in her bedchamber again for days on end, forced to pray and endure hour upon hour of his sermons behind the closed door while the inherited badness was exorcised from her soul. It was an ever-present threat; over the years those interminable hours in cloying solitary confinement had made her fear locked doors and crave a constant link to the fresh air of outside. Even in a blizzard, her bedchamber window remained steadfastly open. Just in case. 'Honour they father, Cassandra.'

Cassie watched the satisfaction in his cold eyes as he spied her fear. 'I always do, Papa.' A lie that would probably doom her to an eternity in hell. She obeyed him, sort of, and hated him at the same time. There was no honour in that.

They had walked the rest of the way in complete silence. Despite the utter humiliation, she admired James Warriner's loyalty towards his family. He had stepped in to defend his brother without a moment's hesitation and then he had not thought twice about manhandling her father out of the house. Cassie had never seen her papa so flummoxed before or so effectively silenced.

The Bible quotations he threw back were also to be commended. If her father would listen to her, which of course he never ever did, she was sorely tempted to tell him a man who could correctly quote chapter and verse from the Good Book, without the need to first check the Good Book for reference, was hardly ungodly. Captain Warriner knew chapter and verse and wielded them with the same deathly precision her father did. Yet to better effect.

Then the Captain had practically lifted her father off the floor with those impressive strong arms of his, forc-

ing her papa to do a funny little tiptoe dance as he was
removed swiftly from the Warriners' drawing room.
Cassie would have enjoyed that particular part of the
awful memory had she not been completely mortified
by everything which occurred beforehand. She would
have laughed at the ridiculousness of the spectacle.
Perhaps she would be able to find the wherewithal to
laugh if she ever managed to escape.

It was funny, but in her mind her father had always
been such a towering, terrifying man. A man to brook
no argument. Up against her dashing, serious pirate
he was little more than a weed stood next to a mighty
oak. Solid. Strong. Dependable. And oh-so-handsome
Captain Warriner made her want to swoon. Perhaps,
as her father was wont to point out, she was her mother's daughter after all if she was so easily impressed
and overwhelmed by the sight of a gorgeous man. A
gorgeous man who probably wanted to wring her by
the neck now. So far, she had inconvenienced him,
squashed him, forced him to lie on her behalf and allowed him to be grossly, unforgivably insulted in the
comfort of his own home.

Now, to compound her misery and right the wrong
which he had perceived had been done to him, her father intended to vilify the poor family further from the
pulpit. Cassie had already endured an hour of it over
dinner, scathing, hateful words which blackened the
Warriner name and cast fresh aspersions about their
characters, and that was only the first draft of his sermon. There would be more fire and brimstone by Sunday. No mercy would be shown. Cassie's only hope was
that the family did not attend the service. She had not

noticed them sat in the pews in the fortnight she had been in Retford, although that was hardly a surprise when she rarely paid attention in church at the best of times if her father was preaching the sermon. However, she had a feeling she would have seen Jamie. The sight of his fine shoulders in his Sunday best combined with his dashing good looks would have brought her out of even the deepest of daydreams. And those penetrating, soulful eyes... But there was nothing to be done about it now. Those eyes, quite rightly, would only regard her with wariness in future.

With a sigh, she blew out the candle on her night-stand and swung her legs into bed. She doubted she would sleep, but as *Orange Blossom and the Great Apple Debacle* had come to a shuddering halt in her mind at least she would be comfortable while she stared listlessly up at the ceiling.

As bad ideas went, this one ranked as one of the worst Jamie had ever come up with. It made no difference how well trained he was in covert reconnaissance, lurking in the bushes outside a lady's open window at midnight was not really something any decent gentleman should do under any circumstances. As a Warriner, with the absolute worst of reputations, the repercussions for both himself and poor Miss Reeves did not bear thinking about. Nobody would believe he was there out of necessity because his conscience needed to know that she was safe and well. In fact, he had needed to know so badly he had even braved the darkness to find out, skulking in the bushes for the right opportunity to present itself.

But he had lurked for the better part of an hour already, waiting for her awful father to finally leave his study and head to bed, and now that he was sure the man must be fast asleep, regardless of the impropriety, he simply had to see her. Properly see her, to speak to her, rather than the fleeting glimpses he had seen of her moving about her bedchamber from his hiding place in the foliage.

At least she was still awake. The dim light of her candle did little to illuminate the darkness, but it was some light. There was also a full moon which offered a little more and a reassuring sprinkling of twinkling stars to alleviate the paralysing fear which came from total blackness. In view of the clandestine manner of his visit he had had to leave his lantern hidden down the lane with Satan, which was beyond unnerving. Without thinking, he checked the waistband of his trousers and settled his hand on the solid comfort of the handle of his pistol. Just in case.

In case of what, he would not be able to articulate to anyone. He certainly had no intention of using it on either her father or any locals who might happen to discover him in his current precarious position. Except, the incessant feeling of unease was his constant companion during these dark hours, and he could never let down his guard even though he understood the threat was gone. No matter how many times he gave himself a stern talking to, Jamie knew all too well that bad things occurred at night when he had least expected them, so it made perfect sense to him that he should always face it armed, even though the only danger nowadays came from himself.

The light from her window suddenly died and fear clenched his gut as the darkness choked him. The rational part of his mind reasoned with the irrational and he remembered his mission. Irrational fears had to be ruthlessly ignored until he knew Cassie was safe. Stealthily, Jamie crept out of the bushes and limped towards the vicarage. Her window was tucked to the side, offering him some camouflage. Fortunately, she had also left it open.

'Miss Reeves.' The rustling leaves stole his voice although he dared not speak any louder. Jamie chose the smallest of the stones in his hand and tossed it at the glass, then waited.

Nothing.

The next two stones tapped the window in quick succession. After half a minute of standing poised, Jamie decided there was nothing else for it. A handful of gravel pelted the darkened window as hard as he dared without shattering the glass. Finally, his perseverance was rewarded by the sight of her face peeking through the new crack in the curtains. He waved like an idiot, watching her eyes widen with alarm, and suddenly wished he had given up on his foolhardy plan an hour ago. As if the poor girl would actually want to see a broken, useless former soldier stood below her like Romeo. What the hell had he been thinking?

She flung open the curtains and pushed the window open further. Her head followed. Only then did he realise her hair was unbound. It hung down above him like a silk curtain, momentarily distracting him from the dark or from immediately explaining his presence and making him wish he was Romeo. If there had been a trellis, and if he hadn't been lame, then he would have eagerly clambered up it then. Just to touch her hair.

'Captain Warriner?'

She issued one of those weird whispered shouts which had no volume and appeared completely flabbergasted.

'I apologise for the bizarre way in which I have sought you out, Miss Reeves, but I wanted to talk to you and could think of no other way to do it without raising the ire of your father.' The words were out before he realised how stupid they were. If her father disapproved of her speaking to him in public, properly chaperoned and in broad daylight, his response to seeing his only daughter clandestinely speaking with him in her nightclothes at midnight was hardly going to go down well. The sanctimonious old fool would probably have an apoplexy. He could tell by her expression she thought much the same.

'I was just thinking about you.' A sentence to warm his cockles, dashed by her next. 'And how you man-handled my father out of your drawing room.'

Jamie winced. While he was not sorry he had removed the fellow, he was sorry he had upset her in the process. Very probably frightened her with his sudden aggression. 'Of course, I apologise for my quick temper, Miss Reeves, but you have to understand that—'

'My father was inexcusably rude and deserved nothing less.'

Her head disappeared back inside, leaving the window wide. After an unnaturally long pause she still did not materialise. 'Miss Reeves?' It was very hard to whisper with force so Jamie cupped his hands around his mouth in the hope it might direct the sound better. 'Miss Reeves?'

He heard the tell-tale sound of a bolt being drawn and whipped his head towards it in alarm. And there she was. Stood behind him in her nightgown, a dense shawl wrapped around her shoulders and her lovely hair falling about her face in tousled waves. Bare toes poked from beneath the hem of the garment, reminding him that only the thin linen and one woollen shawl came between her skin and his eyes. Her eyes were downcast and something peculiar happened to his heart, almost as if it had lurched in his chest at the sight of her so upset.

'I cannot tell you how sorry I am about what happened, Captain Warriner.'

He exhaled and continued to scrutinise her. Cassie found herself shifting uncomfortably from foot to foot, then when she could stand it no more she stared down at her feet to watch them dance nervously. When his big, warm hand came to rest gently on her cheek she almost jumped out of her skin.

'Are *you* all right?'

She had been expecting shouting or curt, brittle words of outrage, not concern. Cassie risked peeking up at him and saw the same concern etched on his face. Almost as if he was worried about her.

'Yes. I am quite well, Captain.' Aside from the strange warmth spreading across her skin from where his palm still touched it. His hand dropped to his side and he sighed.

'Your father is an interesting character.'

A very tactful way of phrasing it when, in her opinion, her hateful father did not deserve it. Making a decision she hoped she would not regret, Cassie pulled his arm gently and led them both well out of earshot of the house towards the bushes. Only when she was certain their voices would not carry, did she stop and turn to face him.

'You are being unnecessarily kind. My father is a zealot, Captain Warriner. He is rude, sanctimonious and utterly self-righteous.' And she had never criticised him out loud to another living soul before. Cautiously she glanced up at the sky just in case the Almighty had a mind to smite her for her disloyalty. Then again, if she was about to be consumed by the fires of hell, she might as well continue, because she was so mortified at what her father had done. 'I tried to stop him from coming, but he never listens to me. In actual fact, I am not sure he ever listens to anyone. His overbearingness and forthright opinions are the reason why we move from parish to parish. The bishops try to reason with him, then when they fail to enlighten him to the error of his ways they find a more affable clergyman to replace him.'

As there were no ominous rumbles of thunder or lightning bolts in the star-kissed black sky she dared wonder if the Lord might have similar opinions of the Reverend Reeves. Despite her misgivings, Cassie felt strangely unburdened to have shared what she had kept locked inside her for so long and so relieved that he had come here, of his own volition, to see her that she was decidedly lightheaded. Captain Galahad's dark eyebrows were raised, but other than that his expression was inscrutable in the shadows. Then just one side of his mouth quirked upwards.

'I am sorry if I embarrassed you by throwing him out.'

'You are not angry at me?' Because people usually were. When her father had pushed too far and grievously upset someone, more often than not it was Cassie who they railed against as her father refused to hear them.

'*My* father was a nasty, lying, violent drunk, so you have my sympathy, Miss Reeves. I know how unfair it is to be judged by the sins of a father. Did you think I came here to reprimand you?'

'I asked you and your family to lie for me.'

'After meeting your father, and hearing his condemnation of both my family and you, I can understand why. I doubt he would have been very pleased you had already taken tea with us, what with the Warriners all being cheats, liars, debauchers and *fornicators*!' He imitated her father at the last word by pointing a quaking finger towards the sky, then he smiled and that smile turned her insides to mush. When it slid off his face and his brows pulled together again, Cassie felt bereft. 'I did not like the way he spoke to you. He reminded me too much of my own father. I saw your fear, which in turn has made me wonder if your father is violent towards you, too, Miss Reeves.' There was steel in his tone.

And just like that, he became Captain Galahad again, ready to rescue her or defend her if needed, like a true literary hero would. Cassie was in no doubt he would if she asked him to, something she should not have found thrilling, but did. However, she barely knew him and feared her father's retribution too much to confess the truth.

'My father is not a violent man, Captain Warriner.' At least not in the strictest sense of what violence meant. He preferred to use repentance rather than beat her, although she would prefer a sound thrashing

any day than his cruel choice of punishment. He had
a violent temper. An unpredictable and violent temper which terrified her. Even when not in a temper he
was fearsome. Changeable. He had verbally assaulted
her on at least a daily basis for as long as she could remember. He was cold, distant, frequently spiteful and
disappointed by her. Sometimes, she had genuinely
believed he might lend his unpredictable anger to his
fists, but in each instance he had chosen to lock her
in her bedchamber instead. Manhandling her was not
the same as beating. 'He believes violence is a sin.'

'I am relieved to hear it.' Although he didn't look
entirely convinced he believed her. 'If that changes,
you will tell me.'

It was a command rather than a question. A lovely
command which made her pulse flutter. Nobody had
ever offered to defend her before. Or thrown stones at
her window in the dead of night to see her. And now,
without even considering the gross impropriety of the
situation, she was stood before him in her nightgown,
enveloped by the intimacy of the night and charmed
by the stars. Despite her best efforts not to, a hot blush
bloomed on her face and she stuttered a pathetic response which she had intended to sound glib, but which
came out a trifle desperate instead.

'Th-thank you for your consideration, although I
dare say we shall be summarily moved on to yet another unsuspecting parish shortly so you will be relieved of the obligation.' The reality of the statement
made her voice wobble. Always moving was so unsettling. One day, when she had squirrelled away enough
of the pitiful coins she was able to save from her meagre housekeeping budget, she would find a permanent

home and never go back. It was a dream which sustained her and demoralised her at the same time. At the rate she was going, she might have enough to rent a squalid room somewhere in a decade. Until then, she had to make the best of things, which in turn meant being at the mercy of her father's tempestuous and nomadic lifestyle.

'My offer stands, regardless of your location.'

Cassie wanted to hug him. Feel the contact and the strength in those big arms and perhaps experience what is was to be close to another human being. Just this once—but such nonsense was not acceptable. Not in a nightgown at any rate.

'Again, I thank you for your consideration, but your concern is not necessary. My father is not a violent man, Captain Warriner.' Just a cruel one.

He said nothing, but those blues eyes saw too much, making Cassie suddenly uncomfortable with her need to tell him everything. As a diversion she walked a little way in front of him and stared up at the moon while she waited for either him to speak or to come up with a safe topic of conversation herself. Already she knew he would not be the first to break the silence. Her pirate was a man of few words. 'You know your Bible, Captain.' A topic too close to her father, but the best she could manage in her current state.

'By accident, Miss Reeves, I can assure you. Religion did not form much of my education growing up. We Warriners are all cheats, liars, debauchers and fornicators, remember.'

His expression was serious although his eyes shone with mischief. An unexpected bubble of laughter escaped and lightened Cassie's mood. 'How does one learn the Bible by accident?'

'I spent six months as a guest of Napoleon in his dankest gaol. My only company was an old and mouldering King James Bible.'

'You were a prisoner!' Instantly Cassie felt nauseous. Six months of incarceration did not bear thinking about. The most Cassie had endured was a week, although that week had felt like an eternity, leaving her feeling weak, exhausted and completely dead inside. 'How did you cope?'

She could tell her question had made him uncomfortable because he looked away. 'I did a great deal of thinking and repeatedly read that book from cover to cover.' He came to stand beside her—just a few inches of air separated his arms from hers and the proximity felt intimate. 'I read it backwards once. Just for something to do.'

'I know the ten commandments backwards.'

His mouth curved slowly into a smile which made his eyes twinkle like the starlight. 'Why am I not surprised, Miss Reeves?'

'Perhaps we are kindred spirits?' Why had she said that? Aside from the fact that she really wanted them to be. Silly fool that she was. 'What I meant is we have things in common.'

'Dreadful fathers and a tendency to do things backwards?'

'Yes. I suppose. And we both enjoy creative pursuits. You paint beautiful pictures. I write silly stories. We also both love to ride.' What was she trying to achieve? Did she hope he would want to carry her off into the sunset after a few scant meetings? While she would happily clamber on to the saddle with him, because already she knew him to be kind, brave and honourable as well as being ridiculously handsome and delightfully broad, Cassie forced herself to remember she was an odd, silly and slightly ridiculous specimen of womanhood and one who had caused him nothing but grief. Friendship, perhaps, with a man who probably thought her peculiar, but had still come to see her this evening to offer his protection. She was confusing pity with more. 'Forgive me, Captain Warriner. I babble. I don't mean to, but it happens regardless, and here I am again—babbling when I should plainly shut up.'

'And I remain silent when I should speak. Perhaps we balance each other out.'

Her heart was beating too fast. Words like that gave her too much hope. 'Perhaps...' And for once, no words fell haphazardly out of her mouth. Instead a deep crimson blush began to crawl up her neck and her mind refused to work coherently. 'I should go. My father might wake up.'

'Of course.'

Awkwardness returned between them then, cloaking them in silence. In unison they moved towards the vicarage. Like a gentleman, he walked with her to the back door and stood stiffly as she opened it. 'Thank you, Captain Warriner.' Even though it had been several minutes since his palm had unexpectedly cupped her cheek she still felt it there, almost as if he had branded her with his touch. Marked her as his. Her flesh hummed. 'You have been very kind.'

He nodded and stepped back, looking as uncomfortable as Cassie felt, before wordlessly turning to limp

slowly back up the narrow path. She was about to close
the door before he quietly called out.

'I ride along the river every afternoon. I should
enjoy some company, Miss Reeves, should you feel
inclined to ride there one day.'

Chapter Six

⚜❧

Jamie had made Satan pace the same stretch of riverbank for the better part of an hour before he had forced himself to face facts. She wasn't coming. Not that he had seriously expected she would. He had spouted the invitation to her retreating back because he could not bear the thought of that being their final goodbye and she had merely gazed back at him with wide eyes and a nervous smile before softly closing the door.

Why had he been foolish enough to hope when there were so many reasons why she wouldn't come? Firstly, she hadn't said that she would. Surely that spoke volumes. Secondly, proper young ladies—vicars' daughters—did not meet gentleman unaccompanied and out in the open countryside in case something untoward happened. Unless, of course, they wanted something untoward to happen. Yesterday's clandestine meeting had only come about because he had instigated it and she was too polite to turn him away in light of her father's disgraceful behaviour. Only an idiot would read more into her motives than that. And thirdly, why would a lovely specimen of womanhood like Miss

Reeves waste time in the company of a crippled invalid in the normal order of things? If she was inclined
towards a tryst, then the lucky fellow would be robust
and in possession of two working limbs.

As depressing as it was, you couldn't argue with
logic. Beneath him, Jamie could feel the frustration
of his horse at the inactivity. Satan wanted to gallop
while Jamie was content to wallow in a bit more self-
pity—something which was hardly fair on the horse.
Out of decency, he swung himself off the beast, un-
packed his painting equipment from his bag and began
to remove the halter and saddle. The big black stallion
would appreciate an hour of freedom to fly across the
land. It had been weeks since the petulant animal had
escaped the stable and gone wandering. Satan was determinedly wild at heart, yet Jamie knew full well he
always came back of his own accord when he had had
enough. The horse bolted the moment the last strap was
unbuckled, just in case his owner changed his mind,
leaving Jamie alone with his miserable thoughts. He
limped towards the bank, set up his little easel, then
began the ungainly process of sitting on the ground.

'Hello!'

Any elation he felt at seeing her trotting across the
field towards him was cancelled out by the utter humiliation of knowing she had seen him clumsily manoeuvre his broken body to do something which most
people did without any prior thought or preparation.
Clearly he was doomed to be infirm for ever in the
pretty dark eyes of Miss Reeves. Even worse, without
a horse he couldn't go riding with her as he had suggested, where at least he would give off the illusion of

sprightliness. On a horse, Jamie was his old self. Without one, he might as well be old.

Out of politeness he gave her a cursory wave, wishing now she hadn't come, and busied himself by organising his paints to give off the impression he was occupied. Behind him, he heard a swish of petticoats as she climbed off her own saddle, a saddle which any normal gentleman would have helped her out of. However, getting back up was now out of the question. There was a finite amount of humiliation he could stomach in any one day and he had already surpassed his limit.

'Where is Satan?'

'He wanted to run, so I let him have his legs while I waited for you.' Good grief, now he had admitted he had been awaiting her arrival. Pathetic.

'I can't see him.'

Jamie risked looking up at her and was pleased to note she was too busy scanning the horizon for his temperamental stallion to see his reaction. Lord, she was lovely! Her skin was slightly flushed from her ride, the apples of her cheeks a little pink, lips very pink. In profile, the thickness and length of her lashes was obvious. One slippery burnished curl had escaped her bonnet and shimmered in the sunlight against her neck. The plain, pale grey muslin dress was too drab for her colouring, but from his angle on the ground showed off her splendid figure to perfection; hugging her bosom tightly, then falling in soft folds which caressed her rounded hips. Above those hips he already knew she had a narrower waist. And below were lovely legs. The memory of those garters came flooding back and his cravat instantly became tight and uncomfortable around his neck.

'He will come back when he is ready. I am afraid you and Orange Blossom will have to ride alone.' Something which she would undoubtedly prefer.

Jamie's eyes followed her as she led her own pony down to the water's edge to drink, then briskly marched back up the bank to where he sat. In one fluid movement, she plonked herself down next to him, legs outstretched, and wiggled her feet. 'I am more than content to sit here and while away the time. That is if you can bear my company and my babbling while you paint.'

Of course *he* could bear it. He just did not want to feel so blasted awkward in his own skin. 'I fear you will be bored.' But she was untying the ribbons of her bonnet.

'How could anyone be bored with this stunning view?'

Never were truer words spoken, except his view and hers were completely different. She gazed out to the horizon. Jamie gazed at her. As soon as she lifted the hat from her head, more glowing tendrils fell about her face which his fingers itched to touch and unfurl to fall around her shoulders like it had last night. He had dreamt of that hair when sleep had finally come. That hair. That nightgown. The freckles. Those bare toes poking out to tease him. Oblivious of her impact on him, he watched in fascination as she removed several pins, holding them between her lips, and deftly secured the errant locks back in their proper place, then sat back to rest on her hands before smiling at him.

'I know I should keep my bonnet on because freckles are unbecoming. But they seem to spring up all over the place regardless of whether I wear it or not, so I have decided to embrace them. And I do adore being outside in the open.'

'Hmm.'

He was such a wordsmith! He had had little to charm a woman before his injury. All of the easy charm and talent with the ladies had gone to his youngest brother Jake. Jamie thought the words—he could just never say them.

I adore your freckles, Miss Reeves. I should love to kiss every one of them.

Tree trunks had more talent for flirting than he did. Dead tree trunks covered in fungus and filled with woodlice.

She closed her eyes and tilted her face up to the sun. In doing so, she offered him an unobscured view of her neck and décolleté. There were a few random freckles trailing down her throat, dusting her collarbones and the hint of her breasts visible above the demure neckline of her dress. Jamie swallowed hard, trying not to think of potential freckles on the rest of her breasts and failing spectacularly.

'You can paint while I prattle on, Captain Warriner. You do not even need to pretend to listen. I don't mind. In fact, it would probably be more prudent to ignore me as I tend to talk nonsense most of the time. Most people do.'

Jamie tore his eyes away from her exposed flesh, picked up his brush to start and realised he had forgotten to fill his jar with water. Should he ask her to do it and thereby admit to his infirmity or go to fetch it himself and display it? The latter was too awful to contemplate. He wiggled the jar instead. 'Would you mind?'

'Oh, yes, of course.' She grabbed the jar, stood up and hurried down the bank. 'I suppose getting up and down is difficult with your leg?'

And there it was. He was thinking carnal thoughts about her while she was busy pitying him.

'I am not an invalid, Miss Reeves!'

His voice came out harsh thanks to the anger and shame boiling in his gut. Anger that he was a blasted invalid and they both knew it, and shame that it was, quite rightly, the way she saw him. He watched her wince, but didn't apologise for his outburst. Nor did he look up to take the proffered jar of water when she returned with it up the bank, forcing her to place it next to him on the ground. She sat down heavily while he focussed his efforts on trying to mix a wash and wishing he had not created such a tense atmosphere with his curmudgeonly reaction, when the poor girl had only just arrived and she was only trying to be nice.

'I have a knack for saying the wrong thing, Captain Warriner. I am sorry. Yet again. All I seem to do is have to constantly apologise to you. I am certain you must be already regretting inviting me here.'

Jamie risked a glance sideways and was dismayed to see her bereft, unsure expression. His fault. 'It is I who should apologise for my outburst. You should not be sorry for mentioning the obvious and I need to learn to accept my condition.' Just saying it made him furious. He doubted that would ever stop.

'How did it happen?'

His first reaction was to tell her to mind her own business. He did not talk about it. Ever. The awful memory of that night still haunted him. Except he still felt bad for snapping at her and wanted her to stay a while longer, even if she was only there out of pity or good manners. Unfortunately, the whole truth would likely send her running for the hills.

'I managed to break out of that gaol I told you about last night.'

After he had snapped Capitaine DuFour's neck with his bare hands, stolen his keys and then his horse. He could still hear the definitive crack when the bones had broken. Was still horrified at the surge of elation he had felt when he had killed the man in cold blood.

'The guards shot me as I rode away.'

Three bullets had ripped through his leg, one shattering his thigh bone, a fourth went straight through his body above the same hip, leaving an impressively symmetrical pair of scars on both the front and back of his body. He'd almost bled to death before Satan delivered him to the British lines. Fortunately, he was still conscious and had vociferously forbidden them from amputating the mess. For the next month he had lain useless in the makeshift battlefield hospital, snatching sleep where he could with a pistol under his pillow to prevent them from removing the damn thing while he fought the infection and prayed the splints would achieve a miracle and make him whole again. He still slept with a pistol under his pillow. Just in case. But for altogether different reasons, although he was coming to suspect they were linked. Like DuFour and his father, those surgeons had preferred to sneak up on him while he slept—until he almost shot one of them and they left him well alone.

'The surgeons did the best they could to patch me up, but the damage was extensive. There's nothing to be done about it, I'm afraid.'

She blinked and appeared horrified. 'You poor thing.' He saw the pity and hated it.

'How is your story coming along?'

'I brought it with me, if you would like to hear it.'

Jamie nodded, eager to avoid any further discussion about his useless leg and useless life, and watched her scurry back to her pony and retrieve a small journal from her saddle bag. When she returned and sat back down next to him she was blushing. 'Please bear in mind it is meant for children, so I have used some artistic licence with the actual events…and with the characters.'

'I thought the characters were us.' Although he supposed children would be as unimpressed with a limping, broken soldier as she was.

'They are. After a fashion. But I have changed some things.' She stared down at her hands for a moment before opening the book and he wanted to tell her that she did not need to feel bad for wanting a proper hero for her tale, but kept his own counsel. Saying that would merely alert her to the fact he knew she pitied him and Jamie was not certain he could hide his devastation at that. To cover it, he picked up his brush and palette and began to mix some paint and waited for her to begin, dreading it at the same time. He had rather liked being noble and brave when she had regaled the events to Letty—but now he was to be replaced with a better version of a dashing hero, Jamie was not so keen to hear about him.

'"*Dear Reader, My name is Orange Blossom and I am a pony. My owner is a silly young lady called Miss Dolt, who does silly things—so silly that I simply have to share them with you…*"'

'Wait—you cannot call yourself Miss Dolt. It's insulting.'

'But as I am the one doing the insulting and I am insulting myself, I fail to understand your objection.' Cassie watched his annoyed expression with interest, smiling at him to convey the fact that she was perfectly comfortable with poking fun at herself. She was ridiculous after all.

'Dolt suggests you are stupid.'

'I did get stuck up a tree. What's that if it is not stupid? Besides, it is a book intended for children so I want the character names to conjure an image of the protagonists in their minds. Something which sets the characters apart from one another. Miss Dolt is a friendly name and I want her to be comedic.'

'I still do not like it. There are other friendly names which might conjure an image, too. Nobody wants to read about a stupid heroine. Comedic, yes. Definitely intrepid. Making your heroine appear like an idiot might upset the little girls.'

He might have a point there, although she was surprised a surly soldier would concern himself one way or another about the feelings of little girls. 'What do you suggest, Captain Warriner? Because I can hardly call her Miss Reeves. I would prefer to remain anonymous.' Or risk being locked in her bedchamber for ever.

He scrunched up his face as he pondered, staring at her intently with his head tilted slightly to one side. 'What about Miss Freckles. You did say you wanted to embrace them and if freckles are considered so unfashionable, it might bolster the confidence of all of the little girls who also have them. She can be intrepid but silly sometimes.'

'Miss Freckles does have a good ring to it. And it is such a pretty word even if the freckles themselves leave a great deal to be desired.'

'I happen to like freckles.'

For a moment Cassie was certain he had paid her another unexpected compliment, but instantly he busied himself with applying paint to his paper and she could tell he was more interested in his work. Feeling somewhat disappointed, she idly crossed out the word 'dolt' and replaced it with 'freckles' and added intrepid to the description before reading it out loud again. It worked. Aside from that, it also gave the characters more scope. Now that the heroine was intrepid, she and Orange Blossom could go on all manner of adventures which a completely silly girl would never be able to cope with.

New name decided, Cassie continued to read to him. However, the Captain seemed so absorbed in his work she became certain he was not listening. Which was just as well, because she had reached the part where he saved her from the apple tree.

'*"Captain Galahad charged in on his magnificent jet-black stallion. He was a handsome pirate with sapphire eyes, a single gold earring and a stormy expression..."*'

'Captain Galahad?' His brush stilled and he appeared surprised as he scrutinised her. Cassie tried to brazen it out despite the burning red circles on her cheeks.

'Of course. He is a hero, after all, come to save the intrepid but silly Miss Freckles.'

'Hmm...'

He focussed back on his work with the exact stormy

expression she had pictured when she had written him. Whether he was angry at being likened to a pirate or if he simply thought her as silly as she had written herself, Cassie couldn't say and she was suddenly nervous about reading the next bit. Decisively, she closed her journal. 'I suppose that's quite enough nonsense for one day.'

His brush paused again. 'But I want to hear what happens next.'

'You know what happens next. You climb up the tree to save me and I cause us both to fall out of it, flattening you in the process.'

'But I should still like to hear how you have written it.'

Cassie saw Orange Blossom gazing at her knowingly from the edge of the water. *I bet you wish you weren't quite so gushing about your pirate now, Cassie?*

Yet the Captain was still watching her intently, clearly waiting for the next instalment. In a smaller voice than she'd intended she read the damning passage again.

'"*Captain Galahad charged in on his magnificent jet-black stallion. He was a handsome pirate with sapphire eyes, a single gold earring and a stormy expression. 'She was fetching me apples,' I said, 'and then she got herself stuck.' He saw her dangling feet and knew what had to be done. 'Try to remain still. I'm coming up!' He dismounted briskly and started towards her. The Captain was the bravest of men, who had fought many battles and slayed many dragons...*"'

'He's slayed dragons?'

'Of course. All of the best heroes have slayed dragons. I thought it would make the tale more exciting as well as being a good way to explain how you got your limp.'

His square jaw hung slack for a moment. 'Captain Galahad limps?'

There were frequent moments in life when her silly mind and traitorous mouth got her into trouble. This was one of them. It was now blatantly obvious that she was writing fanciful prose about how much she admired his physique. Unless she could quickly weave some equally fanciful words which would convince him otherwise. 'He was seriously wounded saving the kingdom from a dragon called Napoleon—but he rallied…obviously.'

And now she was making it worse and glowing like a tomato, while he was staring at her in total bemusement. Cassie felt more hideous words bubble up and knew that if she didn't take decisive action then she would babble more of the truth and look even more foolish. She avoided his eyes and began to read quickly, not daring to look back at him until she was certain he was engrossed in his painting again. Not long after that she ran out of words.

'So that's where I am up to.'

He nodded with uninterest and continued to paint, so Cassie sat quietly and stared at the beautiful parkland and wondered if he would even notice if she tiptoed away. Usually, when she wasn't being odd she had a talent for blending into the background. After what seemed like an age he sat back to admire his work, then one corner of his mouth curved up into an almost-smile. From her position, she could barely see the edge of the picture.

'Can I see?'

He shrugged and twisted his small easel around. She couldn't quite believe what she saw. It was a scene from her story. Exactly as she imagined it in her mind's eye. Only funnier. Captain Galahad, complete with rakish pirate earring, was stood at the base of a tree staring upwards with his hands on his hips. Two female feet were sticking out of the leaves and witty caricatures of Orange Blossom and Satan were stood side by side, watching the humans with complete astonishment. The colours were bold and the composition ideal for children to enjoy.

'Oh, my goodness! It's perfect. You have painted it exactly as I imagined it.' It did not take a great deal of imagination to visualise a few lines of her prose written underneath the picture on a page. 'I do believe your sister-in-law is correct. It would make a wonderful picture book. Now that I have seen this I want to see the rest of the story.'

'I suppose I could cobble together one or two more.'

He was frowning. Did that mean he was merely being polite in offering? 'I do not want to inconvenience you, Captain Warriner.'

Inconvenience him? It was not as if he really had anything else to do with his time. Jamie had thoroughly enjoyed creating the whimsical picture. He had also thoroughly enjoyed listening to Cassie read it to him. She did have a talent for comedy and the little children's story definitely captured his interest.

Initially he had been intent on painting the river, but once her voice transported him into her idealised, fairy-tale version of reality, the picture where he was the bravest of men who slayed dragons had practically drawn itself. The finished article amused him immensely and had also inspired him to finish the orchard painting as soon as he got home. Only now he knew that Miss Freckles would be falling towards him in a shower of apples while the two exaggerated horses looked on in alarm.

Miss Reeves's delighted reaction to it had thrilled him too. All at once he had felt useful again. Even if the something responsible was not particularly important in the grand scheme of things, it was important to her and at the very least his pointless talent for drawing had finally served a good purpose.

'I wouldn't have offered if it was an inconvenience, Miss Reeves.'

In his head he had intended to say this with a charming smile. Adding, *And perhaps you would care to meet me here again tomorrow so I can show you my efforts.* However, it came out tinged with belligerence instead.

'Be here tomorrow afternoon.'

Her stunned expression quickly turned to amusement. 'Yes, sir!' Then she saluted him. 'What time should I ready the troops for inspection?'

Jamie felt himself smile. He could hardly blame her for poking fun at him because he deserved it. She was being nothing but friendly and his clumsy, curt remarks probably did make him appear horrendously stiff and humourless. To show her he really wasn't, he flipped out his pocket watch. 'Have them standing to attention at two on the dot, Corporal Reeves.' He was rewarded with a grin that made the gold flecks in her eyes sparkle.

'I was hoping to be a lieutenant at the very least.'

'With hard work and discipline there is always the chance of promotion.'

She leaned closer and nudged him in the arm playfully, giving Jamie a waft of her subtle perfume, then frowned as she caught a glimpse of the time. 'Good gracious! I should be home by now. My father will be wondering where I am!'

She jumped up and scurried down the bank to retrieve her horse, hastily stuffed her journal in the saddle bag and came towards him. 'Would you mind helping me on to my saddle, Captain?'

Of course he didn't mind. It was an excuse to touch her again. Jamie tried to stand as gracefully as possible, which was impossible. When Miss Reeves thrust her hand out to help him he was mortified. Those little gestures of pity reminded him he was broken. 'I can manage!' If only his blasted leg hadn't frozen solid.

'Oh, for goodness sake, Captain Warriner, stop being so stubborn. I have happily asked for your help to get on my pony, so surely I can return the favour?' She saw him set his jaw, offended, and rolled her eyes. 'What did you say to me in the tree?' She mocked his deep voice again. '*"Take my hand!"* Or are you too proud?'

Reluctantly, he did and she hauled him to his feet, then went about the business of organising her pretty pony's reins. Jamie limped towards her and was about to cup his hands to boost her into the seat as she had asked, when the urge to show her he was still a man asserted itself. Damn over-familiarity or impropriety! He might well need assistance getting up, but once he was up he was still as strong as an ox and capable of doing all of those things everyone thought he couldn't.

He slid his hands around her waist deliberately, pulling her gently towards him, then lifted her off the ground. He softly deposited her on her side saddle and then, as he had the first time, he eased her feet into the stirrups. Only this time his fingers lingered longer on her ankles, feeling oddly privileged to know that under her proper vicar's daughter skirts she enjoyed the whisper of silk against her skin. If he slid his hand a few inches upwards, he was certain he would find those incongruous, naughty garters that in all probability only he knew about.

She stared down at him oddly and he knew he had overstepped the mark. 'I really must get home, Captain Warriner.'

Jamie released his hold on her ankle and patted the haunch of her pony. 'Until tomorrow, Miss Reeves.' She blinked twice, then snapped the reins. Quick as a flash, she and her delightful freckles were gone.

'Where have you been, girl?' Her father stood in the kitchen, his face already contorted with anger.

Cassie chided herself for being so careless as to lose track of time. Her father was a man of strict routines. She might not exist to him for most of the day, but the times he remembered her were chiselled indelibly in stone. Four o'clock he expected a hot meal on the table and a pair of ears to listen to him practise his sermon.

She and Orange Blossom had galloped home, slowing only when they turned into the lane which led towards the vicarage. If he had witnessed her riding with abandon he would forbid her from riding and sell her little pony to the slaughter man, exactly as he had threatened. The Reverend Reeves never made idle threats when it came to disciplining his wayward daughter and Orange Blossom had been her only friend in the world for so long her father knew exactly how to hurt her.

For her own good, of course. Always for her own good lest she turn into her mother. Her eyes darted to the clock on the mantel. She was only ten minutes late—yet in less time he had been known to work himself into such a temper he was practically delirious with it. She would have to tread carefully.

'I was talking to some of your new parishioners in the village, Papa. Listening to their ills and offering comfort. Those duties kept me a trifle longer than I wished.' Cassie headed quickly to the fire to see to the bubbling stew she had placed there earlier. It gave her an excuse not to meet his eyes or to allow him to see she was fibbing. Instinctively her eyes flicked quickly to the door. The key was in the lock. A good sign.

'Liar! I saw you as you rode down the lane. You were smiling!'

'The weather is beautiful, Papa, and Retford is such a lovely village I cannot help smiling at all of God's creation.'

'You went to meet a lover, didn't you, Cassandra? A clandestine meeting with a man! Did you disgrace yourself like your mother, girl?'

Instantly, every muscle in Cassie's body tensed while she forced herself to appear normal. She had been having a clandestine meeting with a man, of sorts, so her father's accusation was dangerously close to the mark. Only the illusion of calmness would help alleviate his fears and placate him so she tried to centre herself as she grabbed a cloth, wrapped it around the handle of the pot and carefully carried the steaming vessel to the table. Sometimes, gentle calm worked.

'I saw Mrs Sansam in the village today, Papa. She told me to tell you that she very much *enjoyed* your sermon last Sunday.'

Sticking to the truth, finding things he could easily confirm when he went searching for sign of her sins, was always best. Mrs Sansam, with her bushel of lively children, was always so busy keeping them on a tight leash Cassie reasoned she would have little concept of time. The fact that they had spoken in the early afternoon rather than just now would hardly register if her father questioned the woman tomorrow. Despite his claims of vanity being the most dreadful of sins, her father adored getting praise for his sermons. The tiny compliment was already softening the tension around his jaw.

'Mrs Sansam is a good woman. Godly. She does this parish credit.' People who fell into line were always a credit. Rebellious traits, like imagination or humour, were evidence of ingrained sin caused by ungodly wilfulness, so Cassie hid those parts of her character in his presence, pouring them all into her stories instead.

'I have offered to watch her youngest two children tomorrow, to give her some peace.'

'Peace? Nonsense. Children are a blessing from the Lord, Cassandra.'

Funny, she was *his* child and had never felt like a blessing—more of a curse left to him by her mother when she had made her dash for freedom. As the years had passed, Cassie had developed some empathy for the strange woman she did not remember, yet who kindled her father's daily wrath. To remain shackled to him till death was tantamount to torture. Like her face-less mother, Cassie had the dream of escaping one day. For years she had assumed that would happen when a nice man offered to marry her. However, for that miraculous event to happen she would need to stay in one place for enough time to actually meet a nice man in the first place. Something, thanks to her father, much easier said than done.

Older and wiser, Cassie now realised how dreadful her life might be if she married the wrong man in haste. If she found one with any of the same traits of her overbearing father, then all she would be doing was jumping out of the frying pan and diving into the fire. What she wanted for herself was a pleasant life where she did not have to continually pretend to be something she was not, which meant setting up on her own somewhere. Hence she had begun to squirrel away every spare farthing—aside from those she had spent on a few fripperies she could not resist.

'You are right, as always, Papa.' His mind was moving on, she could tell. The mask of fury was being replaced by the dour expression of a man who believed he was listened to. 'I also thought I would take a small basket to the elderly couple we met last week—you know the ones. The husband is blind. It must be very difficult for his wife to leave him alone to go to the market.'

Cassie tried not to let the palpable relief show as her father sat down at the table. He never sat when he was angry, so the brief, sharp fury she had witnessed upon her arrival must already be dissolving. He believed her.

This time.

Although who knew if she would be so lucky next

time. Although she had never gambled—because gambling was a heinous sin—she had often thought gauging her father's mood would be a great deal like playing hazard. One never knew how the dice would fall and she never knew what might send him into a rage.

'Whilst it is to be commended that you pity those unfortunate souls, Cassandra, and fitting that you should offer them some charity, as I have taught you, try to remember the Lord took that man's sight for a reason. Perhaps he was a sinner and to live for evermore in darkness was his penance.'

Hogwash. But her father put a great deal of stock in the concept of penance.

'Yes, Papa.' She ladled the rich stew into his bowl and then did the same to her own. After her father said grace they ate in silence. The Reverend Reeves believed meal times were for quiet contemplation rather than social discourse. When he'd finished, he sat back to watch Cassie clear away the table. Only then did he retrieve his latest sermon from his study to read to her as she washed the dishes.

As was expected, she listened in silence. Except she wasn't listening. The drone of his voice was easily shut out while she weaved the fanciful stories in her head. And thanks to Captain Warriner's wonderful illustration and desire to create more for her never-to-be-published book of children's stories, she now had a greater incentive to think about her characters than ever before. She couldn't wait until bedtime in order to write the next instalment. In it she would have to find a way to convey Miss Freckles flattening the handsome pirate when they fell out of the tree without alluding to the scandalously splendid pleasure of being in such close, intimate proximity to such a fine figure of a man. Captain Warriner had such strong arms...

'The Warriner family have long been an evil stain in this parish!'

Her head snapped up at the sound of her father's fervent, practised tone.

'The previous Earl was a drunkard and a cheat, swindling many of you out of money and worse. Now his sons are a plague. An infestation of vileness without shame or conscience. Only recently, the new Earl kidnapped his bride and forced her into marriage. Under your noses he kept her prisoner in that den of iniquity—one lone, terrified woman in a house occupied by four vile men. Four soldiers of the Devil himself. Despoilers. Debauchers. *Fornicators!*'

Her stomach clenched as Cassie listened to more of his outrageous vitriol. Grossly unfair words which her father would have honed and rehearsed before he delivered his sermon in a few days. Words which would find their way back to Markham Manor and wound the people within. The good people within. So far she had met only three Warriners and knew they were good people in the same way you could smell a storm in the air. It was a gut feeling. And now, after all the trouble she had already caused him, Cassie would have to apologise to James Warriner once again. She only hoped he meant what he had said to her under the stars last night and that he would not judge her by the sins of her father.

Chapter Seven

Jamie had painted well into the night like a man possessed. Or besotted. Miss Freckles had quite got under his skin. Both the real one and the fictional. Now his saddle bag was stuffed with two more colourful illustrations from the start of the tale, as well as the finished *orchard* painting which was no longer a view of the sky through the trees from the floor. Miss Freckles was hurtling towards the ground, arms and legs waving frantically in the air, big brown eyes wide with alarm and her lovely gingersnap hair in disarray. For good measure, he had added the leaves and twigs to her hairstyle he had found so becoming. He had been tempted to also show a hint of the saucy pink garter, but decided against it on two counts. One, such things were hardly appropriate for the eyes of children and, two, he did not wish to enlighten the vicar's daughter to the fact that he was secretly lusting after her. Jamie sincerely doubted she would be thrilled with the latter.

Horrified more like—yet achingly polite lest she inadvertently insulted a cripple. He would prefer to walk on hot coals before he witnessed that—or limp on hot coals, which was probably more fitting. The most tragic thing about the whole situation was the limp was merely the tip of the iceberg. There was a whole hornets' nest of other issues which he would rather never have to admit to. Ugly scars down his left thigh and above the left hip. The unsightly muscle wastage which came from the infirmity. Those were not things he would want to show a lady.

But even if he did find a woman who could overlook such distasteful physical flaws, because they might not be so obvious if he insisted on making love to the poor thing in the dark, then there was the fact that he was terrified of the dark and therefore prone to react in a manner which shamed and frightened him in equal measure. The fear paralysed him and took away all reason, then he would lash out. Unless he had a pistol in his hand and a light on somewhere close by. Or a big, fat full moon to illuminate the sky. He could cope with it then. Just about. However, even the most forgiving of women would find the prospect of making love to a man with a pistol clutched in one hand, just in case his father or Capitaine DuFour miraculously rose from the dead to come and beat him senseless again, petrifying.

Then there was also the disturbing habit of his trying to attack anyone who tried to wake him up. Granted, he had only done it the once but, as he had almost strangled the life out of his brother Jacob in the process, it had been a memorable event. Significantly memorable enough to mean that nobody ventured into his bedchamber unannounced while he slept and Jamie certainly could not entertain the notion of ever sharing his bed with another. Not when he had hands strong enough to snap a neck in two. It had taken less than a

few minutes to send DuFour to his maker and the sadistic Frenchman had been in possession of a thick and
meaty neck. Very definitely a man's neck. A delicate
female throat would snap like a dry twig in summer
before Jamie had remembered blasted DuFour and his
damned father were already dead.

If he married and miraculously got to enjoy some
conjugal rights, he would have to order the poor woman
swiftly out of the bedchamber as soon as he had done
the deed in case he nodded off. Something he had happily done back in the old days after a vigorous bit of
bed play. Since his return, the only thing his bed was
good for was hiding an astonishing variety of weapons under the mattress. Weapons he had no real cause
to use, but which were necessary to put his whirring
mind at ease. Just in case. Good grief, he was pathetic!

All in all, the chances of him finding a woman who
was prepared to contend with all that, who was also
happy to take on a man who no longer had a career or a
means to earn his own living, or the ability to turn his
hand to something new, were practically non-existent.
Because what professions were there for a hardened,
embittered former soldier, highly trained in the art of
cloak-and-dagger reconnaissance and that one, memorable silent assassination? *The Vicar's Daughter and
the Silent Assassin*—now, there was a title for a book.
Unfortunately, and quite rightly, the sorry pages within
it would send the whimsical Miss Freckles screaming
for the hills.

He spied her in the distance, waiting by the river,
and began to slow Satan's furious pace. She spotted
them and waved. Even from this distance she looked
lovely. Her bonnet had already been discarded, he

noted. The drab-coloured dress only served as a foil to her vibrant hair and delectable figure.

Jamie knew it was delectable. His hands had easily spanned the trim waist twice now, felt the womanly curve of her round bottom, traced the delicate bones of her ankle. He had seen the silky and creamy soft skin above it. He thought about that illicit glimpse of her skin constantly. What he needed to do was stop thinking about her as a woman, because as a woman she was so far out of his reach it was pointless even fantasising about it. But as a painter he could be an acquaintance, a useful acquaintance with skills she could utilise, justifying the powerful need to see her. Which was bizarre as he usually preferred to keep his own counsel and avoid people like the plague.

The preposterousness of his own thoughts made him groan aloud. Useful acquaintance indeed! What on earth was the blasted matter with him? He would do better to remember that she was a vicar's daughter who had been raised to do good deeds for those in need. To her he was probably just another parish invalid she was charitable towards and had to help up from the ground. He needed to put a stop to all of those fanciful, frustrating and fruitless thoughts before they did damage. Lusting after the vicar's daughter was as pointless as it was pathetic.

Cassie heard the approaching hoofbeats and steeled herself for the inevitable before turning around. The sight of him astride his magnificent horse quite took her breath away. The pair of them were well matched. Both dark and brooding. Both a tad menacing and oozing an aura of untamed, unbridled power. Both staring at her as if she were peculiar.

Which, of course, she was.

The Captain pulled his massive horse to a halt and dismounted carefully. Cassie could see the intense concentration this took etched into his brow line and wondered if he was trying to disguise the fact he was in pain. If he was, he certainly wouldn't appreciate her commenting upon it; she had seen the flash of anger when she had offered to help him yesterday, almost as if he was embarrassed to be seen to be weak. Not that she would ever consider him to be weak. The man could lift her off the ground, for goodness sake! Something beyond impressive when there was so very much of her. His big body had absorbed the impact of her falling on top of him from a great height and he had still managed to move afterwards. She might have inadvertently killed a lesser man.

Because she was certain he was self-conscious about his limp, she turned towards Orange Blossom and stroked her mane, and worried about exactly how, and when, she was going to bring up the dreadful topic of her father's impending sermon. Especially after all of the other chaos she had caused him in their eventfully short acquaintance.

You can't tell him yet, her pony cautioned with her eyes, *it will spoil the precious time you have with him. There will be plenty of time to spoil his day afterwards.* And spoil it she would.

'Hello.'

The deep yet soft timbre of his voice made her insides melt like butter.

'Good afternoon, Captain Warriner.' Two piercing

bright blue eyes met hers, disarmed her, and Cassie heard her voice wobble. 'I trust you are well?'

'Yes. I brought these.' All business, he thrust a small pile of paper at her. More of his pictures. Then he turned abruptly back towards his horse to retrieve his painting equipment. Clearly he did not wish to waste time engaging in the sort of inane, odd chatter which Cassie was famous for.

She glanced down at the pictures in her hands and experienced a tight knot of emotion at the beauty of the pieces. Not at all what one would think would emerge from the brush of such a serious and brooding man. The first showed her climbing up the apple tree, a clearly disapproving Orange Blossom staring at her in exasperation. The second depicted the moment she had got stuck. Miss Freckles' arms were poking helplessly from her inverted skirts, the bottom half of her body and her modesty shielded with dense leaves. But it was the third painting which was the most astonishing, partly because Cassie had seen the bulk of the painting before as it was the Captain's unfortunate perspective of the orchard after she had sent him tumbling out of the tree and partly because it was unsettling to see close up his view of her.

In the other pictures, her face had been so small that there were no discerning features. He had made her look pretty, which was flattering, but not drawn in the same intensely personal way that she had been in this picture. Was this truly how he saw her? The falling Miss Freckles had big, brown eyes framed with very becoming, thick lashes. The detail on the irises was phenomenal. He had used several different shades of brown to replicate a real eye, yet amongst all that dark were shimmering flecks of gold. Her O-shaped, startled lips were pink and plump, a lesser, subtler pink emphasised the apples of her cheeks while the dusting of freckles across her nose, hopefully much darker than her actual freckles, gave the face a special charm. The hair was quite splendid. Thick, wavy and a clever mixture of yellow, copper and red tones. Curls and leaves framed her face. The finished woman was quite beautiful. So beautiful Cassie could not take her eyes off her.

'This is wonderful.' Her focus slowly shifted to him and once again he was frowning.

'Hmm.' He stalked towards the softest patch of grass overlooking the river and set up his easel. 'We should make a start on the next instalment to maximise the afternoon.' Cassie watched him limp back towards his horse. 'I shall find somewhere sturdy to tie up Satan first.'

'Poor Satan. Why don't you leave him be and let him wander where he chooses while we work? It seems such a shame to tie him up on such a lovely day.'

'I don't trust him with your pony.'

'If I remember rightly, Orange Blossom and he got on famously last time they were together.' To prove her point, the pony was already ambling towards the stallion. Satan appeared to be quite pleased with this state of affairs and walked towards her while the Captain looked on, frowning. The two horses sniffed each other, then began to chew on the grass simultaneously. Something which appeared to surprise him.

'Well, I suppose we can keep an eye on them.' He did not seem convinced.

'I wrote the next segment last night if you would like to hear it?'

He nodded and lowered himself carefully to sit down on the riverbank. 'It would help to give me ideas for the subsequent illustrations. I believe you left off where Captain Galahad had just begun to climb the tree.'

'I thought it would be amusing to have the two horses introduce each other next and perhaps make this a tale about the start of the friendship between them. The moral being sometimes good things can come out of a dire situation.'

'And there must always be a moral to a fairy tale,' he said dispassionately and Cassie realised he was poking fun at her.

Smiling, she opened her journal. 'I am a vicar's daughter Captain Warriner. There must *always* be a moral.' She quickly located the place and began to read aloud. '"*My name is Orange Blossom—how do you do?*"

"*I am charmed to meet you, Miss Blossom. My name is Stanley...*"'

'What?'

'Satan is hardly a suitable name for children. It might confuse them into thinking your horse is a thoroughly bad lot, when I want him to be friendly.'

'But *Stanley*? Surely there are better names. Satan is a magnificent, haughty and temperamental beast. The name Stanley hardly conveys those traits.' Now he appeared affronted. 'What sort of a name is that?'

'It does have many of the same letters as Satan for a start. And to me it does convey temperamental. My father's shortest tenure as a parish priest was in Stanley near Durham. The temperamental parishioners had him removed in three weeks.' Although, in their defence, her father had insulted the beloved patroness

of the parish because she had a penchant for a dash of
red trim on her gowns. Cassie had been sinfully en-
vious of those gowns and the daring splash of colour.
One day, when she was free, she was going to dress in
all of the colours of the rainbow which were currently
forbidden by her overbearing father. Naming a horse
after that town felt like a tiny act of defiance against
him. Another small insignificant rebellion he would
never know about, like the ostentatious and highly dec-
adent garters she had bought from some travelling gyp-
sies just before she left Norwich and the three pairs of
clocked silk stockings she had found cheap in a market in London almost a year ago. Vain fripperies which
probably made her the worst daughter in the world
bought with some of her precious savings. Yet Cassie
could not find the will to regret either purchase. Those
hidden fripperies made her feel pretty and went some
way to making her miserable life just a little bit more
bearable while she waited for the opportune moment
to make her dash for freedom.

Jamie let her have the name as it seemed to please
her and he was prepared to concede Satan was not really the sort of name to grace the pages of a child's picture book. For an hour he listened contentedly while
she read the latest part of the story while he drew a
caricature of himself, halfway up a tree being pelted
with apples. When her voice trailed off and she lapsed
into silence he risked a sideways peek at her and was
surprised to see her looking troubled.

'What's wrong?' Because he got the distinct impression something was. She inhaled deeply and squared
her shoulders before facing him and in that moment

he was sure she was going to say they could no longer continue to meet like this. He supposed she had already been more than charitable towards him. The severing of their odd little acquaintance was always inevitable.

'I am not sure quite how to tell you.'

'I am a big boy, Miss Reeves. Whatever it is, just say it and be done with it.' He would shrug as if it was of no matter to him, when it was. Her rejection, regardless how inevitable, would still hurt.

'My father has made your family the subject of this Sunday's sermon. I'm so sorry.'

Jamie let out the breath he had not realised he was holding. Relief made him smile. 'Is that all? Why, I am sure the congregation will adore it. They love nothing more than to malign us Warriners.'

'You don't understand, Captain Warriner. I have heard parts of it and he makes foul accusations.'

'Let me guess—we are all liars, cheats and fornicators? Believe me, worse has been levied at us in the past. I am plagued with troublesome ancestors.'

She buried her face in her hands and shook her head. 'I think his sermon goes much further. He is claiming your sister-in-law was kidnapped for her fortune.'

'She was.' Her head shot up and her lush mouth hung slack and Jamie chuckled. He had heard this tall tale repeatedly embellished in the last few months. Why bother with the facts of the event when the fiction offered better scandal? 'My brother found her bound and gagged in the woods. He hid her from her abductors until it was safe for her to return to London and claim her inheritance. During that month they fell hopelessly in love. If you want to know the honest truth, they were each both nearly killed trying to rescue the other one. It was sickeningly romantic, if you are inclined towards that sort of thing.' Which he was. Deep down where nobody else could see it.

Unfortunately, the truth made her appear more wretched. 'I don't know how to stop him. He doesn't listen to me. Aside from the lies he is perpetrating about your brother, he also has written awful things about your father and grandfather.'

'Which will all probably be true. Both men were hideous. We are quite used to being gossiped about.'

'And he has written about you, Captain.'

'He has. Does he paint me a rogue, too?'

'He calls you the Earl's henchman—someone to be feared.'

Feared? At least he was not being referred to as an invalid. 'Capital. I quite like the idea of being considered fearsome. Perhaps it will make your father think twice before he decides to come and lecture my family again.'

'But you will be vilified from the pulpit. Everyone will hear it and judge you.'

'Then perhaps we should all attend church on Sunday. To give your father's sermon some added gravitas. He can malign us to our faces and earn a great deal of respect from his new parishioners to boot. It might even serve to secure his tenure here for a long time. The locals will respect a man who calls out the dreaded wild Warriners. Excitement is thin on the ground here in Retford. The people hereabouts must grab their entertainments where they can. And if it is at our expense, so be it. Please do not let it trouble you.'

Jamie wanted to cup her cheek tenderly with his hand and smooth away the lines of anguish around her mouth with his thumb. Seeing her so distraught gave him a strange ache somewhere in his ribcage.

It's all right, Freckles, don't be sad.

The damning words threatened to blurt out of his mouth. To avoid humiliating himself by acting on the impulse, he set about cleaning his brushes to give his hands something else to do.

'I must say you are taking this well.'

He shrugged. There was no point in getting upset about it. 'The situation was the same long before my birth, so I accept it for what it is. My brothers, Letty and myself all know it is nonsense. I have never really cared what other people think.' Except he suddenly cared what she thought. 'Do you believe all of the gossip, Miss Reeves?'

Her beautiful brown eyes locked with his and held. 'You strike me as a very decent man, Captain Warriner.' That gaze never faltered and he found he could not tear his own eyes away. Around him, all the sounds of nature were amplified. The river water, birds, even the gentle swishing of the grass in the breeze was heightened as he lost himself in those dark depths.

Neigh!

The agitated sound of a horse came from behind and Jamie experienced a rush of irritation. Blasted Satan! Was there ever an animal more spiteful and ill tempered? To pick on that pretty little pony was beyond the pale and to do so when he was having such a splendid moment with Miss Freckles was unforgivable. Except when he turned around, Satan was not intimidating Orange Blossom. The pair of them were rubbing noses and necks quite excitedly.

A little too excitedly.

Judging from her quizzical expression, the innocent vicar's daughter had no idea that all sorts of inappropriate shenanigans were on the cusp of taking place.

'Satan.' Jamie kept his voice low and intimidating while he tried to scramble off the ground before his button-nosed companion received an education. If he could get to the beast before…

Too late.

Satan reared up on his back legs, displaying his ardent intent to the world, while the dun-coloured minx his horse desired batted her eyelashes at him and swished her fluffy tail out of the way. In a split second, his stallion and her pony were doing what nature had engineered them to do and there really was nothing Jamie could do about it. He could hardly try to prise them apart. There was no telling how Satan would react to such an imposition. If he were in his horse's shoes, Jamie doubted he would be very pleased to be thwarted either.

'Oh, my!' Miss Reeves, her eyes like saucers, watched open-mouthed as his horse had its wicked way with hers. Then she turned away abruptly and resolutely stared at the river. 'It feels impolite to watch.'

At a loss as to what else to do, Jamie listlessly stared at the gushing water, too. 'I am dreadfully sorry.'

'Oh, please don't be. Orange Blossom is a shameless flirt. She must take half of the blame for what is occurring.'

More fevered horse noises came from behind them.

'The weather has been quite lovely so far this month, don't you agree, Captain Warriner?'

'Yes, it has. Quite lovely.' Apparently they were now going to make small talk whilst listening to the passionate equine grunts behind them. Jamie sincerely hoped Miss Reeves would not have any questions about what their lusty mounts were up to.

'I cannot remember a time when I have enjoyed the month of May more.'

It was then that the ridiculousness of the situation overwhelmed him and he found his lips twitching. 'I am sure Satan would agree with you.' The bark of laughter escaped then, closely followed by another. Then she began to snigger next to him and before they knew it, they were both clutching their ribs and brushing tears from their eyes, because really what else could they do under the mortifying circumstances? After what seemed like an eternity, peace descended.

'Is it safe to turn around?'

Jamie glanced behind him and saw a smug-looking Satan standing proudly with the flirty Orange Blossom nuzzling his neck affectionately. 'I believe their business is concluded for the day. At least I hope it is.'

'I hope it is, too. I need to get home. But it seems unnecessarily cruel to split them up now, don't you think? They do appear to be very fond of each other.'

Fond of each other! Such a whimsical explanation for what had just occurred, as if the two horses experienced more than the primal urge to mate, and so charmingly just like her to view it that way. 'Then I shall accompany you down to the end of the lane, Miss Reeves, so our lovestruck horses can spend a little more time in each other's company.'

Deciding to abandon his easel until later, Jamie followed her back towards the animals and lifted her swiftly on to her saddle before hauling himself on to Satan. They rode in slightly uncomfortable silence for a few minutes, far too close as apparently their horses could not bear to be too far apart, and Jamie searched his mind for something to talk about which would break the strained tension. In the end, it was Miss Reeves who spoke first.

'Well, at least we have our ending now.'

'We do?' Surely she was not suggesting they finished a children's books with the exuberant joining of two horses!

'Isn't it obvious? The book will have to finish with a wedding now that Satan has compromised Orange Blossom.'

'You want our horses to get married?' What a ridiculously charming and splendidly brilliant idea. Already he could picture Satan in a jaunty beaver hat while his bride would have flowers woven into her mane. He would be best man and Miss Freckles would be the bridesmaid, and they would leave the church under an arch of crossed carrots held in the guests' hands like swords, delicate confetti rose petals fluttering in the air.

'Of course! Orange Blossom has been thoroughly ruined, Captain Warriner. A wedding is only proper. The silly and intrepid Miss Freckles inadvertently instigated their love story when she foolhardily climbed up that tree. It is the perfect happy ending.'

They reached the end of the lane and both dithered, not that Jamie minded. 'My father will be angry if I am late home again. He is a stickler for timekeeping and quite rigid in his schedule. Will I see you tomorrow? Unless you are already quite fed up with all of the trouble I bring to your door, Captain Warriner.'

'I always ride by the river at two. We soldiers are creatures of habit.'

She beamed at him and Jamie felt his heart warm at the sight. 'Then I shall bid you good afternoon, Captain Warriner.'

She nudged her pony forward and Jamie realised he did not want her to go. 'Miss Reeves!' She turned around, pretty eyes questioning, the late afternoon sun picking out the copper fire in the single tendril of hair poking out of her plain bonnet. 'Seeing as our horses are betrothed, perhaps you should call me Jamie. Everyone else does.'

'That would be nice. Until tomorrow... Jamie.' Except when everyone else said his name it did not make his heart stutter. He sat still until he saw her disappear around the curve of the lane, needing to see her for as long as possible. Only when the lane was deserted did he say the words which had almost tripped out of his mouth in her presence. 'Until tomorrow, Freckles. I shall count the hours.'

Cassie could not remember ever spending a pleasanter afternoon in her life. Aside from the shameless behaviour of their two horses, she and Jamie had whiled away the better part of two hours simply talking and working. For once, she had not felt even slightly ridiculous or odd because she was convinced his mind saw exactly what hers did. When she thought up her silly stories, she could see them unfold in her head like a play, hear the conversations and the noises in the scene and be transported away to that place. Jamie's paintings were exactly as she imagined that place to be. Whimsical. Childlike. Utterly charming. It was such

a shame they would not be able to publish them because she was becoming increasingly convinced they
were creating an excellent children's book while they
sat companionably on the riverbank.

She dried the last dish and went to sit dutifully at
the table where her father was scratching away on his
sermon, the quill moving frantically as he scribbled
whatever fevered prose were currently occupying his
thoughts. A quick glance at the paper and she saw the
word Warriner written over and over, and her stomach
sank. He was still on his misguided quest for revenge.
Even though Jamie had told her he was ambivalent,
her father's intentions still bothered her. It did not sit
right to stand by and watch them wronged. He saw
her interest.

'With each new day I learn of new horrors from
that family. I now know the father pushed the mother
to suicide and no doubt his spawn helped, too. She
threw herself into the river rather than spend another
day in hell.'

Poor Jamie. To lose a parent in that way could not
have been easy, especially as he had made it plain his
relationship with his father was fraught. 'What a trag-
edy for the children, to be forced to grow up mother-
less.' Something she could empathise with.

'If only she had had the sense to drown her foul
sons like unwanted puppies at the same time, then the
world would be a better place!'

'Surely you cannot mean that, Papa.' Sometimes,
his cruelty astounded her. 'They were just children.'

'Who have grown up to be replicas of their evil father! A man who was rarely seen in public sober. A
man who shamelessly cheated my parishioners at any

given opportunity. Refused to honour his debts. A man prone to violence! Already we have borne witness to the violence those boys are capable of. Did you not see the way I was assaulted by that man?'

It had hardly been an assault, more an assertion. Jamie had removed her odious father from his presence justifiably, nobly defending his brother. And he had offered to defend her whenever or wherever she needed him. Another nod to his innate sense of honour. How to explain such a thing to her father? Like a coward she decided not to. He would never understand. He took her silence as acquiescence.

'They abducted an innocent woman for her fortune, Cassandra, lured her into their life of sin and now live off her like parasites.'

'I have heard a different version of the tale, Papa, so I am inclined to think all is not as it seems. For every person who claims the Warriners abducted the woman, there is another who says they rescued her from her kidnappers and gave her sanctuary. I am told the Countess married the Earl because she loved him.'

'Who are these liars you put such stock in?' His voice had the calm, icy edge to it which she had learned to fear the most. 'Tell me their names, Cassandra.'

'We are new here, Papa. I do not know their names yet.'

'And now you are protecting these sinners!'

'No, Papa. Please believe me, I do not know their names yet, but they are good people.' Jamie was good, she felt it in her bones and her heart.

Without warning, his arm shot out and he grabbed a hank of her hair in his fist and pulled it hard. 'Liar!'

'I am not lying, Papa. Please believe me!' But Cassie

knew it was already too late. One wrong word and his tenuous hold on his unpredictable temper was lost.

'Your mother was a liar, too!' He was already dragging her to the stairs, his palm now securely anchored in her hair. His strength, combined with her now powerless position, made fighting against him agony. Yet as she fought she also realised her punishment was inevitable. He never backed down when he was like this.

Never.

Cassie forced her feet to move in the direction he wanted in the hope that he would at least acknowledge her lack of rebellion at her impending imprisonment. Such behaviour might lessen her sentence. Panicked tears gathered in her eyes as fear coursed through her body. How she reacted now would determine the length of her penance.

'I am sorry, Papa. I was wrong. I should never have doubted you…'

'Oh, Lord! Help her to see the error of her ways.' They were at the foot of the stairs. The tears were already streaming down her face as the familiar, paralysing terror began to stiffen her limbs and quicken her heartbeat.

'I'm so sorry, Papa.'

'Cleanse her of the wantonness of her mother. Teach her to be meek and to obey your commandments…' Cassie's scalp burned where his fist pulled, his knuckles and fingernails digging painfully into her skull as she climbed each step cowed behind him, powerless to stand straight. 'Teach her to honour and obey her father!' She tried to placate him even though she knew it was futile. It was always futile. He was already lost in the scriptures and talking to the heavens.

"'For the sons of Israel walked forty years in the wilderness, until all the nation who came out of Egypt perished, because they did not listen to the voice of the Lord...'"

When they arrived at her bedchamber, he threw her to the floor as if she were something fetid and rancid he desired to be well rid of, still chanting manically and slammed the heavy door behind her. As the silent sobs racked through her body and she heard the key turn ominously in the lock once again, Cassie curled her arms around her knees and tried to take her mind to a happier place.

A place where horses talked and handsome pirates came to save her.

Chapter Eight

She didn't come. For two days Jamie had sat miserably on the riverbank waiting like a lovesick puppy and for two days he had gone home with his metaphorical tail firmly between his legs. A churning, angry disappointment whirled in his gut as he sat in the drawing room early on Sunday morning.

What a blasted fool he was. He knew better than to build his hopes up when he had known he would ultimately be disappointed. He had confused her interest in his artistic talents as something more, which he knew was unlikely in the extreme and completely impossible given his circumstances, yet he had still convinced himself there might miraculously be something else going on.

The affinity he had thought they had shared, the strange sense of oneness which had overwhelmed him whenever they were together, was clearly one-sided. Why, she hadn't even felt the urge to send word she wasn't coming, almost as if he were of no consequence at all, and that galled. Had she forgotten they had arranged to meet again? Was he so instantly forgettable now that he was no longer a full man?

Wallpaper.

Something one noticed if it was right in front of your face, but forgotten when a more interesting diversion presented itself. He did not want to think about the interesting diversion she had been distracted by. There were plenty of fine young bucks in Retford, any one of them could have tried to turn her pretty freckled head. The surge of jealousy at the prospect came like a bolt out of the blue, rousing his temper at the imagined diverter and his own, physical limitations. He was not the sort of man to turn a young girl's head any longer. It was all so blasted unfair!

But then they had shared a special moment when they last met. He was sure of that. His instincts told him there had been. A perfect moment where their eyes had locked and words were not necessary because it was just them and everything else had become insignificant.

Jamie groaned at his romanticised interpretation of what might have been, for her at least, an awkward moment. The impromptu noise caused his younger brother Joe, home from medical school for a short visit, to regard him curiously.

'Is there a particular reason why you keep sighing and moaning?'

Jamie felt himself frown as he turned back to his painting and tried to concentrate on adding the detail to one of the carrots in the bridal arch he was painting. 'My leg aches.' Symptoms of any sort always distracted Joe.

'Are you using the liniment I mixed for you?'

'Yes.' He wasn't.

'Then why is the bottle still full on your nightstand?'

'Why are you poking around my bedchamber?' Not that Joe, or any of his brothers, would comment on the ready arsenal of weapons placed strategically about the room and tucked under his mattress. They knew he would not discuss those things even though he was heartily ashamed they were still there. 'Stay out of my room.'

'Then take your medicine, you stubborn fool, and I would.'

Jamie grunted and pretended to work, effectively ending the conversation. Or so he thought.

'Letty tells me you've met a young lady. A pretty girl, by all accounts. She says the pair of you have spent a great deal of time together—cosied up by the river.'

'Hardly.' This needed to be nipped in the bud before *he* became the main topic of conversation around the dinner table later. 'She is the daughter of the very reverend we are being forced to see this morning. The one intent on vilifying us from the pulpit with his sermon.' A sermon Jamie was annoyingly looking forward to in the hope he might catch the eye of Cassie and remind her he still existed, and hopefully satisfy himself that there were no young, limp-free bucks on the horizon.

'We, of all people, cannot judge her by her father, Jamie. Letty says the pair of you are working on a children's book together. Based on your eventful first meeting.' One glance at his brother's amused face told him that he and his meddling sister-in-law had been doing a great deal of speculating about the silent assassin and the vicar's daughter.

'No, we are not. I merely did a couple of illustrations for her as a favour.' But Joe was already rising from his seat and walking knowingly towards him, obviously eager to catch him in the middle of another 'favour'. The most whimsical, romantic and damning 'favour' of all of the ones he had created thus far. He quashed the urge to cover his easel with his arms to hide it from his brother's view, but knew he would be sentenced 'guilty as charged' if he did and ribbed mercilessly. Better to brazen it out.

Joe stood at his shoulder and peered at the painting, grinned and then fished in his pocket for his spectacles before bending at the waist to scrutinise it further.

'Are those horses getting married?'

'Miss Reeves has an odd perspective of the world.' One that matched his.

'Is that Satan?'

Jamie gave one curt nod and dipped his brush in the orange paint.

'And the other pony, the pretty one, does that belong to your vicar's daughter?' She was not *his* vicar's daughter. Never would be *his* vicar's daughter.

'Yes. That is Orange Blossom.'

His brother's index finger pointed at the pretty bridesmaid, her coppery hair festooned with pink flowers which exactly matched the ones Jamie had seen on her blasted garter. 'And this must be Miss Reeves. She does look pretty. I can understand what you see in her.'

He ignored that comment to focus on painting the carrot. Miss Freckles was beautiful, not pretty. Heartwrenchingly beautiful, sweet and funny.

'Why are you sporting an earring?'

Jamie did not have to look at Joe to see he was grinning from ear to ear. 'He's not really me. Cassie calls him Captain Galahad. He's a pirate. Apparently.'

'Cassie? Hmm. First-name terms. Very *familiar* first-name terms.'

The anger was swift and irrational. 'Stop it, Joe! Don't try to make something out of that which is plainly not there. Miss Reeves asked me to do some illustrations. That is all. There is nothing else between us.'

'If you say so. But you have been meeting down by the river every day. All alone.'

'No, we haven't! I met her twice. I have not seen her since Thursday. Clearly she has had better things to do than entertain a cripple on her afternoons off.' Jamie instantly regretted the words as soon as they spewed from his mouth. They said too much about how he was truly feeling. He experienced the overwhelming urge to punch his well-meaning brother in the face at the sight of the pity which suddenly suffused his expression.

'I doubt she cares…'

Jamie threw down his brush. 'Don't say it, Joe! Don't offer me platitudes or blasted pity. It is not welcome.' He stood up and limped towards the window, staring out sightlessly on to the garden and tempering his voice lest this awkward exchange continue any longer. 'I'd have thought the carriage would be here by now, seeing as Letty is quite determined to sit in the front pews.'

There was a beat of silence before his brother decided to retreat from the treacherous path the conversation was leading to. 'I will go and check.'

He heard Joe leave the room quietly—only then did he allow his forehead to rest listlessly on the glass. When he saw her this morning he would need to appear unaffected by her rejection and impervious to whatever her awful father said. He would not stare at her, try to catch her eye or give any indication that he had desperately missed her these last few days. As always, his true feelings would remain hidden deep inside where nobody could see them and he would endure the pain silently. If only his brother could mix a liniment for his aching heart.

The Norman church was already half-full by the time the Warriner carriage pulled up in front of it. They made their way slowly towards their rarely used seats at the front, Letty stopping to chat to the one or two people who were beginning to warm to her and ignoring the way a great majority of the congregation felt the urge to whisper speculative asides to one another. Thanks to his years in the army, Jamie had been spared this usual reaction by the locals, therefore it irritated him perhaps more than it did the others. Few people even acknowledged them, which was beyond insulting when Retford had always been their home, yet the infamy of his father and grandfather before him had been so well deserved Jamie understood it even if he did not approve. But his father had been mouldering in the ground for eight years, during which time not a single Warriner had put a foot out of place, so he wished people would simply move on.

Jamie scanned the pews for any sign of Cassie, but she was not there. Neither was her fire-and-brimstone father. No doubt he preferred to make a grand entrance. He struck Jamie as the sort. A grand, ecclesiastical entrance which would signal the start of his retributive sermon. Like his brothers, Jamie staunchly faced the front defiantly in the hope they would see the vicar falter at their unexpected presence.

Out of the corner of his eye he saw a small wooden door open to the side and witnessed the object of his torment emerge. Except Jamie's plan to avoid outright looking at the woman failed instantly. Because something was not right. Her face was pale and drawn. Dark shadows sat under her red-rimmed eyes. There was a tightness about her mouth and jaw he had not seen before and her gaze was downcast. Cassie appeared smaller, slumped and almost broken.

'Well, that explains things,' mumbled Joe to his left, 'Your lady has been too ill to leave the house.'

'Hmm.' Jamie didn't agree, but held his tongue. Whilst it was conceivable she had been ill—people got ill all of the time, after all—mild illness did not usually crush a person's spirit and for some inexplicable reason he knew Cassie's was damaged. There was no light in her eyes. No laughter. No joy. None of the things he associated with her and which drew him to her like a moth to a flame.

Jamie willed her to look across the aisle and meet his eyes, but she did not. In fact, it seemed as if she was completely unaware of the congregation at all, which only served to increase his concern. He could hardly stride over there and ask her what was wrong. Not here, where her father would hear of it, so he searched his mind for a solution. How exactly could he speak to her now when the whole town was there to bear witness?

'Here we go.' Joe nudged him and refocussed Jamie's attention back to the pulpit. The door from the vestry had been dramatically thrust open and the Reverend Reeves strode out in his billowing black cassock.

An overly large wooden cross attached to a leather cord dangled from his neck and he clutched an old, worn bible in one hand like an amulet to ward off evil.

Jamie had the satisfaction of seeing the slightest hesitation in the man's gait as he spied them, although he doubted the rest of the congregation would have noticed it. The reverend placed his free hand flat on the lectern, briefly closed his eyes and inhaled deeply as if he was receiving divine strength from the Lord before speaking. Jamie recognised the reading. It was from Genesis. The tale of the fall of Sodom and Gomorrah was an obvious choice for a man intent on besmirching the Warriner name, yet he found his teeth grinding in annoyance just the same. Around him, the congregation were held spellbound by the vicar's demonic delivery.

The man had a way with words much like his daughter did, Jamie had to give him that, although what he was saying was too much for some. Around him he saw people wince at the odd word while anxious mothers held the hands of their children in case the sermon frightened them. Nothing so dramatic had ever been seen in the tiny market town before.

The cleric paused. His eyes travelled along the row of the front pew, taking in each of the four people present quickly, before returning to burn hot with hatred directly at Jamie. He directed the next words to him, so it stood to reason Jamie stared back unmoved.

'This week I attempted to take the word of God to Markham Manor. It pains me to tell you that it was not welcome. Like the inhabitants of Sodom and Gomorrah, the Warriner family prefer to fester in avarice and sin!'

As he had promised Jack faithfully he would not react with his usual quick temper, Jamie feigned mild amusement instead. Nobody apart from the vicar could see it and, as he had hoped, it riled the man. His eyes bulged manically and an unpleasant foamy clump of spittle gathered in the corners of his mouth—something the congregation did see and it alarmed a few more people. And who could blame them? Foaming at the mouth was not something country vicars should do.

The army had taught him that disgust, fear and dissension were contagious, therefore as weapons they were invaluable. All it took was one person to begin to turn against the Reverend Reeves and others, like sheep, would be encouraged or emboldened to follow. For the vicar's eyes only, he stifled a minute yawn which had spectacular consequences. Arms began to wave, fingers began to point in accusation and the man began to shout quite unnecessarily. From the pews, it all appeared very aggressive. Unfriendly. Distasteful.

This was followed by a long diatribe about his awful father which Jamie was inclined to agree with. The old man had been spectacularly hideous and spiteful. Yet as shocking as it sounded second-hand, the congregation did not truly know the half of it. Not every scar on his body had been caused by Napoleon. He still bore the faint stain of the belt marks across his back which had been generously bestowed courtesy of his father. Painting was for girls. And perhaps Jamie was not quite a man. Therefore, it stood to reason the bad had to be beaten out of him. Something Jamie had endured defiantly for years.

Night after night, once his father had consumed enough brandy to feel up to the task, he would climb up the narrow wooden staircase that led to Jamie's room. His heavy boot would always make the top stair creak. The signal that hell was about to be unleashed for Jamie's own good. When the bedchamber door opened, the belt would be wrapped around his father's fist, in case his disappointing son was left in any doubt of what was to come. Then he would stride to the bed, drag him out by the hair and use that belt or that fist on him until he was satisfied Jamie had learned his lesson.

He had learned a lesson, but not quite the one his odious father had intended. He had learned that the best way to fight back was to refuse to comply. He hid his fear deep inside and never cowered while the violence took place. Each time his father battered him senseless, Jamie would paint something prettier the very next day as an act of rebellion. If his paints were taken away, he used the charcoal embers from the fire to draw, or pieces of chalk dug up from the ground, using art to fortify him and show his father that his spirit could not be crushed no matter how hard his father could hit. Then one day, shortly after his fifteenth birthday, Jamie had fought back. The brandy had numbed his father's reflexes and he had never anticipated that his artistic, girl of a son would ever retaliate, so it came as a shock to find his own belt wrapped tightly around his neck while the artist almost choked the life out of him.

In truth, the animalistic burst of violence had shocked Jamie as well. One minute he had been sound asleep and the next he was choking the life out of his father. How this state of affairs had come to pass he still did not know, except he assumed the man had attacked him in his sleep and in a daze Jamie had allowed the savage which was caged inside him to escape and wreak havoc. Only at the very last minute, when he saw his father's eyes bulge and his face turn purple from lack of air, did he find the ability to step back. But it had taken everything he had to do so and left him oddly unsatisfied not to have finished the deed.

He learned he had tremendous physical power and the ability to separate his mind from the job which needed to be done while that power was unleashed. Both things he had harnessed and used to great effect as a soldier later on, and perhaps that night had been instrumental in his decision to join the army. It gave the terrifying savage inside him an outlet in which to channel the violence. Or perhaps that had simply been to prove a point to himself as well as his father. *I might well paint flowers, but I am a man. And one to be reckoned with.*

His dear papa had never returned in the night again, nor used his fists on Jamie from that day onwards. He gave his disappointing son a wide berth, which suited Jamie just fine. They didn't converse or sit in the same room and his father never again so much as referred to him, let alone tried to disparage him. And Jamie had openly continued to paint. Still continued to paint. So his father had never won. Neither would the Reverend Reeves. Jamie stared back at him dispassionately, doing his very best impression of a man bored senseless and totally unmoved by the hate spewing from the vile reverend's foaming mouth.

All at once, he felt a warmth spread up the back of his neck and sensed she was watching him.

Cassie had not expected Jamie to be sat in the church. Not really. And after three nights of incarcer-

ation she had been too traumatised to give anything
much thought other than her palpable relief at being
free again to pay much attention to the congregation.
Her father had only released her a few minutes beforehand with the terse instruction to 'get ready, girl!', so
she had hurried to take her seat in the church in case
he changed his mind and locked her in again.

The aftermath of each new punishment always left
her drained and befuddled, a state which got worse
each time and took days to shake off, to such an extent that the effort of putting one foot in front of the
other was almost too much. But as soon as her father
had begun his litany of the Warriner family's many
flaws she suddenly had the overwhelming sense that
he was there. For reasons Cassie did not understand,
his presence soothed her. It did not matter that he was
glaring at her father with barely disguised disgust or
that he would, in all likelihood, never want to speak
to her again after the sermon. He was there. That was
all that mattered.

As if he sensed her watching him, he turned slightly
and his intelligent bright blue eyes sought hers. It was a
look which spoke volumes. She could see his concern
for her clearly, saw the question about her whereabouts
and knew instinctively he wanted to speak to her. She
also watched his gaze flick back towards her father
furtively, in case her father noticed the meaningful,
silent exchange between them and she was grateful for
that, too. Jamie understood there would be repercussions if her father got wind of any sort of relationship
between them, even though he could have no earthly
idea of exactly what those repercussions entailed, but

she felt enormous relief knowing he would never approach her here.

Cassie offered him a tremulous smile to show him everything was all right, when it really wasn't, and then directed her focus back to her father. Like the dutiful daughter he wanted her to be, hoping this was not a temporary freedom and that he would leave her unpunished for another few weeks. Her eyes wandered to an enormous statue of the crucifixion behind her father and, to blot out the sound of the terrible words filling the church, she prayed that she would miraculously find enough money to run away from her tormentor, rent a little room somewhere and never fear the sight of a lock again.

As soon as the sermon finished the church was silent. It was obvious nobody could quite believe her father had said such dreadful things about the family while they sat there in front of him. In many of the faces she saw outright sympathy for them—and felt some relief that her father might perhaps have made things inadvertently better for Jamie and his family. The way the Warriners all sat proudly without saying a word actually made the tension worse. Everyone was waiting to see how the family would react. Her father included. Cassie knew him too well not to notice he was nervous, too.

The Earl of Markham stood and solicitously helped his pregnant wife to stand. She beamed at him and threaded her arm lovingly through his before they both walked the short distance to the altar.

'Thank you for the sermon, Reverend. It was most… enlightening.'

This caused a flurry of incredulous and slightly impressed whispers from behind and her father to snarl. Ignoring it all, he then led his wife proudly towards the door, the pair of them chatting pleasantly to each other as if nothing untoward had just transpired. Behind them, Jamie followed, walking next to a man who was the spitting image of him. One of his brothers, no doubt, although which she had no idea. As the rest of the congregation stood and began to gather themselves ready to leave, visibly deflated to have been denied a grander spectacle, Cassie watched Jamie whisper something to his brother and slip stealthily out of the church. Clearly he had had quite enough and had no intention of hanging about, not that she blamed him. Not after so much of her father's hateful words had been directed solely at him. The devil's own henchman. Who painted talking horses who were going to get married.

Miserably, Cassie made her way out into the churchyard to talk to her father's parishioners. Papa was quite particular about her properly fulfilling her duties and while she was still forced to live under his roof she had no choice but to live by his rules. Normally, she quite enjoyed talking to the parishioners. It was a tiny piece of human contact in a week filled with coldness. But today she was in no mood to care. She would be stuck here and, judging by the eager faces of some of them, nobody was in a great hurry to get home today. Not when the entertainments might not yet be concluded.

Outside, she could see no sign of Jamie. Several people immediately crowded around her and began to speak with incredulity that her father had been so bold. A few congratulated her on his performance, to which Cassie could not pretend enthusiasm. Never in her entire life had she been so ashamed of being Edgar

Reeves's daughter than she was today. He had gone too far and he had lied. For a man who claimed lying was the most grievous of sins, they had spilled from his lips like a fountain, all because Jamie had had the good sense to throw him out. Cassie had seen how he had directed his poison towards Jamie and at times she had almost allowed her complete abhorrence to show on her face. If she were braver, she would have stood up and demanded her father should stop, except she could not face another minute staring at the same four walls. Walls which crept closer and closer with each passing minute, which suffocated her with their proximity and terrified her by with their impenetrable sturdiness.

'Good morning, Miss Reeves.' The other brother had sidled up next to her and was smiling kindly. 'My name is Joseph Warriner.'

Cassie glanced towards her father and saw him engrossed in an impassioned conversation with quite a crowd, oblivious of her existence. 'I am pleased to meet you, Mr Warriner.' And then in a tiny voice she felt compelled to add an apology. 'I am so sorry for all of the things my father said.'

He brushed it away with a smile and a casual flick of his hand. 'We have heard worse, Miss Reeves, I can assure you. But that is neither here nor there. I have been sent on a mission by Jamie. He has told me to tell you that he has finished the pictures and that they require your approval. He said you know where to find him.'

At the same moment her father looked up to locate her, Joseph Warriner had already swiftly moved on and, to all intents and purposes to the eyes of the world, they might never have spoken at all.

Chapter Nine

It was another two days before Cassie was able to go out alone without fear of retribution. She might not be under lock and key but that did not mean her father was ready to give her all of her freedom back. There was all manner of laborious tasks which he suddenly needed doing, which would also help to purge her soul of badness, and he insisted she accompany him on visits to every parishioner who had not heard his epic denunciation of the Warriners in church, which meant she was forced to hear it regurgitated again and again. Fortunately, fate, or rather the Bishop of Nottingham, intervened and her father was summoned urgently to the diocese.

Cassie left it an hour before saddling Orange Blossom and riding into town. As soon as she could confirm that, yes, the post had left and, yes, the Reverend Reeves had been on it, did she hurriedly turn her pony towards the Markham estate.

She saw Jamie the moment she passed through the giant open gates. He was sat astride Satan, winding his way up and down the rows of trees in the orchard,

looking every bit as ferocious and wild as his mid-
night-black horse.

'Cassie! Are you all right?'

He manoeuvred his horse alongside hers smartly,
searching her features for any sign that she was not.

'I couldn't get away sooner. My father needed me
at home.' But those eyes of his saw too much and she
could tell he remained unconvinced. For a moment she
was tempted to tell him the truth about exactly why
she had been absent for almost a week, then instantly
decided against it when she remembered how he had
manhandled her father out of his home and how intensely he had offered his help if ever she needed it.
If Jamie took her father to task on her behalf, no matter how tempting the fantasy of it was, she would ultimately be forbidden from ever seeing him again and
would probably spend the better part of a month imprisoned in her bedchamber. Maybe longer. Her father
would definitely move to another parish, as he had in
the past when questions were asked about her welfare
by well-meaning parishioners, and then she would lose
Jamie and this lovely place in one fell swoop. It was
not worth the risk. Far better to keep her punishments
private until she could escape them for good. 'And I
have been ill. A bad summer cold.'

'I see.'

Cassie knew he did and she was certain he saw
everything, which made her nervous. 'I am eager to
see what you have painted. I have finished the story.'
Scribbling away into the small hours in the two days
since she had been free because picking up a pen, even
moving from a spot, was too terrifying with the door
locked. The only way she could survive it was to climb

into herself and live in the imaginary world in her head. 'Perhaps we should ride down to the river so I can read it to you?' Without waiting for his agreement, Cassie set Orange Blossom into a gallop, partly to escape his disconcerting gaze and partly to exorcise the demons of her incarceration. It was good to be out in the open again. Walls, doors and especially locks always put her on edge. There was nothing between her and river except half a mile of meadow, fat, woolly sheep and an infinite cloudless sky.

Bizarrely, she was smiling by the time they reached the bank, something which surprised her so soon after her ordeal. Racing Jamie and Satan had been a pointless exercise because they had easily passed her as she had known they would. Jamie's horse was all muscle and power, much like his owner, so he practically flew. Her pony did her best, but they ended up trailing in the wake of the lightning-quick black stallion and his impressive, able rider. Seeing Jamie race across the fields, his big body crouched low over his horse with effortless grace, was quite something. If she needed further proof she was her mother's daughter, even though she knew she shouldn't, Cassie's eyes feasted on the sight of his rear, his broad shoulders and the flash of bare skin visible between the collar of his shirt and the soft, black hair curling gently at the nape of his neck. Not that she had ever been particularly competitive, but losing this race had turned out to be such a pleasure it felt like winning.

'What kept you?'

He had already dismounted and was stood nonchalantly, leaning against his panting mount, examining his fingernails as if he had been stood there for hours.

Smug, male satisfaction at his victory was written all over his handsome face. All of that thick, dark hair was delightfully windswept, making him appear boyish and young and far less burdened than she had ever seen him. Playfully, she ignored the jibe and spoke to her pony instead. 'We had to let them win, didn't we, darling, otherwise the boys would have sulked all afternoon.'

'You didn't let me win. I won fair and square and we both know it.'

'A gentleman would have let Orange Blossom win.'

'That is not in my nature, I'm afraid. I grew up with three very competitive brothers and I like to win.'

'Did you win often?'

'All the time.' When Cassie turned he had moved to stand beside her, waiting to help her down from her saddle. Instantly, her pulse jumped at the prospect of feeling his hands on her waist again and the power in those strong, capable arms as he lowered her to the ground. No sooner had she let go of the reins, than she enjoyed the sensation of those warm palms searing through the fabric of her gown just under her ribs. Because she needed to touch him, too, Cassie placed her hands on his shoulders, ostensibly to steady herself although she did not need steadying. They were as firm and as hard as she had imagined. Jamie was a solid, impressive specimen of raw, powerful maleness.

Who smelled divine.

As he helped her down, Cassie had wanted to bury her nose in the exposed skin of his neck and simply inhale him. Errant, wanton thoughts like that would only serve to get her into more trouble, so she quickly stepped out of his reach as soon as her feet touched the grass to rummage in her saddle bag.

'I brought us some cake and some lemonade.' She pushed them into his hands and tried to ignore the odd expression she saw flit across his face. Confusion? Bemusement? Discomfort? A picnic, even like the tiny one she had prepared, was something courting couples did. Under the watchful supervision of a chaperon. Immediately, she recognised it as what it was and realised she was being far too forward and slightly pathetic. Worldly-wise and eligible men like James Warriner would hardly find anything appealing in a frecklefaced, odd sort of a vicar's daughter who largely lived inside her own head. He was here on sufferance or out of a sense of duty, because he was kind beneath all the surliness and she was being overpowering again.

To avoid making him uncomfortable she would need to clarify. 'I did not have time to have luncheon,' she lied, avoiding his eyes. 'And it seemed rude to pack food for only myself to eat. I hope you don't mind.'

Embarrassed and horrified at her own lack of forethought, Cassie pulled out the pork pie, wrapped cheese, rosy-red apples, fresh bread and butter she had also lovingly packed—because the way to a man's heart was through his stomach and because she was a fool who had wanted to do something nice for him without fully thinking through how it might be perceived. In truth, Cassie had so been looking forward to spending time with Jamie again, the notion of a cosy picnic had seemed perfect. She really should have considered the obvious message it sent.

Jamie remained silent while he helped her arrange it on the stupid embroidered tablecloth she had also

brought with her, then watched warily as she handed
him a delicate china plate festooned in brightly painted
flowers. Her secret plates, procured one day on impulse and hidden in her bedchamber. This was their
inaugural outing, yet another thing which marked this
encounter as special.

'You really did think of everything, didn't you? It
might have been quicker if you had simply eaten lunch
rather than prepare all of this.'

The blush which had been threatening to bloom for
a good five minutes suddenly exploded like a crimson
firework on her face and neck. She tried to cover it by
sawing off a slice of bread. 'Yes, I suppose so. However, in my defence, it is such a lovely day I wanted
to enjoy the sunshine.' If she kept her bonnet on he
might not notice. Her hot, irritating bonnet. Which if
she kept it on much longer would have to remain on for
the duration as her hair would become plastered to her
heated head. But if she kept it on, then her face would
glow in that unsightly, deep pink way and, horror of
horrors, perspiration would trickle down her cheeks.
There was nothing for it, the bonnet had to come off.

Hastily, her fingers went to the ribbons at her neck
and wrestled with them. Nerves made her clumsy and
she knotted them hopelessly.

'Here. Let me help.' Which, of course, was the very
last thing she needed, but because she had worked herself up into a state she had no choice. Cassie lifted
up her chin and tried to stare up at the solitary wispy
cloud, the empty sky, a random fly buzzing in the air,
anything to avoid looking at him. So close she could
see the shadow of stubble on his chin. Could count
every eyelash. Sniff him like a dog in season.

'I have altered the story so that Orange Blossom and Stanley fall hopelessly in love whilst you try to save the intrepid and silly Miss Freckles from the apple tree.' Oops. It was meant to be a fairy tale—most definitely not about him, although it was. 'I mean Captain Galahad saves Miss Freckles, but then as you are Captain Galahad…what I mean is Captain Galahad is largely based on you. Not that you are a pirate, of course. I mean I know you were in the army and not on a pirate ship. I suppose those two careers are vastly different.' Her voice was getting higher pitched with panic and the disconcerting sensation of feeling his fingers accidentally brushing the sensitive skin at her throat as he worked the knots in her ribbons.

He was touching her skin.

Good gracious, it felt good!

'Did you enjoy being a soldier? What made you join the army in the first place? Because you are an artist, so one would assume you would have become an artist rather than a soldier? Did your father insist you join the military? I know second sons have a tendency to either take a commission or join the clergy. Although I can't really see you as a vicar. Even though you do know your Bible. Would you have liked to be a vicar, do you think?'

'Which of those multiple questions would you like me to answer first?' Those glorious blue eyes locked on hers for a moment and he was almost smiling, which was devastating, until Cassie realised he was smiling because he probably thought she was an idiot. A babbling, blushing, ridiculous idiot.

'I know you think I am silly, Captain Warriner, I am well aware of the fact I tend to babble.'

'I thought we had agreed that you would call me Jamie.' The stubborn ribbons finally came free and his hands finally left her skin. 'And I sympathise with the babbling. When I am nervous I tend to grunt, which makes me appear rude when I do not mean to be.'

'You get nervous?'

'Have you heard me grunt?'

Yes, she had. Quite a bit. And he was smiling again as he broke off a sizeable chunk of pork pie, then popped it into his mouth. After a moment he stopped chewing and appeared stunned. 'This is delicious! Surely it did not come from the local bakery? If it did, they have certainly improved their standards since the last time I went in there.'

'I made it.' His obvious admiration for her efforts made her feel proud. 'We don't have any servants at the vicarage so I do all the cooking.'

As well as the cleaning, washing, listening to endless sermons, visiting parishioners. Being a dutiful daughter. Wishing she was somewhere, anywhere, else and having to resort to making imaginary worlds to pass the endless hours of drudgery.

'Until Letty married my brother, neither did we. When I came home from the war I became the cook for a short while. I can't say I was very good at it. I can roast a chicken and boil a carrot. At best, my food was edible. My brothers were hugely grateful when I was relieved of the duty.'

Would it be considered rude to ask why Markham Manor did not have servants? Surely the Earl was not a skinflint like her father? Cassie nibbled on her food and tried to think of a polite way of asking. After half a minute he burst out laughing. It was a wholly masculine sound which she felt inwardly all the way down to her tingling toes. 'I quite admire your restraint, Cassie. I can see you are burning up with curiosity and ruthlessly suppressing the question. Shall I put you out of your misery?'

She nodded sheepishly, supremely aware of other tingles in the most outrageous places, and watched him lean back slightly as he made himself comfortable, turning his face to soak up the sun and stretching his bad leg out. The sudden urge to scramble on his lap made her breath hitch.

'We were broke, Cassie. Poor as church mice and everyone hereabouts knew it. Nobody would extend credit to the Warriner family because we were a bad risk. I am not sure my father ever paid a debt in his life, but he certainly racked up a great many of them. All of them had to be settled after his death, which took more years than one would imagine. We couldn't even afford labourers to tend the fields. Jack, Joe and Jacob worked them from dawn till dusk and I sent back my wages to supplement them while I was away. When I came back I became the cook and housekeeper all rolled into one. Obviously, I could not draw a salary when I couldn't fight for His Majesty, so the purse strings were even tighter. They were grim days indeed.'

'But they are over now? Your fortunes have been restored?' Cassie swept her eyes over the well-tended fields. Markham Manor appeared to be thriving.

'I forget you are new to this area and therefore do not know all of the scandalous gossip. It is technically Letty's fortune. She was an heiress. A very wealthy heiress. And one everyone believes had to marry my brother because he had either kidnapped her or compromised her.'

'How unfair. It is obvious they are in love.' The emotion had positively shone out of both of their eyes when they had proudly left the church after her father had grievously slandered them. His cruel words had not mattered because they had each other, a state which made Cassie long for her own happily ever after. However, mentioning love in any shape or form made her self-conscious in front of this man. To keep sane whilst locked in her bedroom, Captain James Warriner had featured in a great many happily-ever-afters. In all of them he had rescued her, declared his secret, undying love for her, then ridden off with her into the sunset.

'In love—like Orange Blossom and Stanley? Tell me the ending of the story, Cassie. I should like to hear how two horses fall hopelessly in love beneath an apple tree.'

So she did. Reading her story from the very beginning to the end. He smiled in all the right places and occasionally chuckled. The deep, throaty rumble continued to do odd things to her insides and made her breathing a tad erratic, forcing her to inhale slowly and purposefully to avoid appearing vexed.

'"...*and Stanley nuzzled my mane as we walked off into the sunset, ready for our next adventure with the heroic Captain Galahad and the intrepid but silly Miss Freckles...*" The End.'

'I would have thought Stanley would have kissed his bride, seeing as that is the tradition.'

Jamie would have kissed his bride. Quite thoroughly and at the first available opportunity. Then he would have taken her somewhere quiet and kissed each and every one of her freckles.

'You cannot have kissing in a children's book. It's not proper. Besides, horses can't kiss—they nuzzle, which I always think would be a nicer way to show affection than kissing at any rate.' Her button of a nose wrinkled in disgust, which amused him greatly. But then she was a vicar's daughter after all, so all talk of passion in any form was something she was obviously unfamiliar with. Unless it was between horses, of course.

'Clearly you have never been kissed.' And he would give his back teeth to be the first one to kiss her.

'This may well shock you, Jamie, but, yes, I have.' She giggled conspiratorially while a knife wedged through his heart at her surprise admission. 'It was wholly uninspiring and quite messy. I fail to see what all of the fuss is about.'

'Then the gentleman who kissed you clearly didn't do it properly.' Thank goodness! The relief was palpable. The idea of his Freckles feeling passion in another man's arms was abhorrent.

She snorted prettily and swatted his arm, something she did quite a lot and which he enjoyed immensely. Usually. 'Gentle*men,* Jamie. There has been more than one. Although in truth, they couldn't really be classed as gentlemen. Scoundrels would be more appropriate a term, with the benefit of hindsight, of course, although I must confess I suspected as much at the time. Which is odd, because from the books I have read, the kiss of a scoundrel is supposed to be the best sort—yet I found them quite dull, really.'

More than one! And by her own admission the hideously unworthy men who had dared to steal those kisses were scoundrels to boot! The dagger of jealousy had him furious instantly. 'You allowed scoundrels to kiss you? Willingly?' If any of them had dishonoured her he would hunt them down and take pleasure in tearing them limb from limb. 'Did the wretches do more than kiss you?'

This she found immensely funny. 'Of course not. I *am* a vicar's daughter. But I confess I was curious to know what the process entailed, so when the opportunities presented themselves I allowed a few kisses.' She shrugged as if it was of no matter, when it most definitely did matter. It mattered to him. 'I suspect I am one of those women who does not melt into a puddle at the merest touch of a man. Odd, really, when I had always thought I would be prone to swooning...'

'Then all I can say is not one of those scoundrels knew the first thing about kissing!' Jamie sounded belligerent and didn't care. He still could not quite believe his ears. Of all the conversations to have with a vicar's daughter...

'Of course they *knew* about kissing.' She spoke to him slowly, as if he were a silly child who needed the simplest of concepts explained to him. 'All scoundrels know what they are doing when it comes to romancing a woman. Seduction *is* their stock in trade.'

Romancing a woman! Flowery words, heated, stolen glances. Trysts! *Seduction!* Jamie's world turned red, then white as anger turned to incandescent, irrational, unquenchable rage. How dared they? If anybody should have been the one to induct her into the art of kissing, it should have been him. Unlike those charming scoundrels he appreciated her. Respected her. He definitely wanted her. Infinitely more than any of those faceless seducers could ever imagine. But then, if he were to hazard a guess, none of those vermin were broken and lame and scared stiff if their candle blew out in the night. He'd bet his horse on the fact that they were very nimble on their despicable, conniving feet and thoroughly embraced the promise brought by the dark. Not a single ugly scar would mar their good-for-nothing bodies, so it stood to reason her lovely freckled head would be turned at the splendid blasted sight of them!

And she had kissed them.

Them!

Knowing full well they were scoundrels from the outset, because she had wanted to be kissed. Not him, of course. He was vastly inferior to those two-legged charmers in her gold-flecked eyes, more was the pity. His kiss would not be dull or messy. It would be spectacular and she *would* swoon. Jamie would make damn sure she swooned.

Before he could think better of it, he hauled her against him and pressed his mouth to hers. She gave a tiny squeak of surprise, while he shamelessly poured all of those boiling, jealous feelings into a kiss that positively burned. Jamie didn't care.

It needed to burn.

He had to sear his mark on her and banish the memory those faceless, unworthy scoundrels from her lips. Brand her as his, enlighten her to how spectacular a kiss could be if done correctly, by someone who was just as much of a man as those charming rogues who made seducing beautiful women their stock in trade. Despite his crippled leg, damaged mind and ruined prospects, he was still very much a man… Except somewhere along the way he got lost in it all.

He forgot that this was a kiss borne out of fury and frustration at what might have been, if he had not gone off to war and come back a shadow of his former self, and rejoiced when it turned into something important. Passionate, affectionate and filled with the promise of more.

The white-hot rage which had consumed his mind only a few scant moments ago evaporated like the early morning mist, replaced instead by something indescribable, almost like an exquisite rainbow bursting behind his eyes. But one unlike any he had ever witnessed before. One which assaulted all of his senses, not only his sight. She smelled of violets and cut grass and sunshine. Tasted of ripe strawberries on a hot summer's day. Felt perfect in his arms. Warm, soft, womanly. Desire ripped through him and Jamie welcomed it, feeling vibrantly alive and whole again for the first time in over a year. A proper man again and one who was quite capable of pleasuring a woman.

This woman.

He desperately wanted her bare skin against his, from the tip of her button nose to the ends of her pretty pink toes, to slowly unwrap her like a treasured gift and worship her with his eyes, mouth and fingertips. He wanted to peel her out of her proper vicar's-daughter dress and lay her bare to the sunshine and find out once and for all if there were other freckles on her body. Secret freckles that only he would know about. Freckles he would brand with his kisses, too, before he made her his in every way possible. Here on this riverbank, in broad daylight, before he took her home with him for ever.

His greedy palms smoothed down to her hips and then back up again to cup her face before they plunged into her silken hair. Of their own accord, his fingers found the pins that held it and plucked them out, filling his hands with the tumbling mass as he began to ease her slowly backwards on to the grass. And throughout it all, all he could hear was the rapid beating of his own heart as it rested deliriously against hers, as if it was meant to be there.

Always.

Which frankly scared the hell out of him.

And probably out of her, too.

Jamie abruptly ended the kiss and sat up, his chest rising and falling rapidly and his breeches considerably tighter than they had been a few moments ago. He had no right to be kissing her possessively. Or in anger. Or kissing her at all for that matter, despite the sight of her lying rumpled on the ground and looking positively ripe for the picking. Cassie had certainly made no flirtatious overtures or given any hint that such impertinence was welcomed. Theirs was a platonic relationship based on their mutual desire to complete her storybook. Why, she hadn't felt the urge to visit him in almost a week, even after he had passed on a message through Joe at the church days ago telling her explicitly that he would be here. Waiting. Where he had waited, like the besotted fool he was, for three interminable days. Therefore, it stood to reason that the turbulent feelings choking him were one-sided. One-sided and doomed to be unreciprocated.

Yet as fruitless as it all was, the last thing he wanted

was to frighten her away. Meeting Cassie by the riverbank, talking to her, painting while she read to him or wrote were already the brightest, shiniest, most important parts of his day. To think he might have ruined what they had with one, irresponsible, irrevocable moment of jealousy terrified him more than the yearning in his heart as he gazed at her. Her clothing was in disarray, her lips swollen from his onslaught and her eyes screwed tightly shut, blocking out the hideous, maimed sight of him while he had foisted himself upon her like an animal, oblivious to everything except the overwhelming need to take her.

Poor Cassie. His inappropriate, unwelcome personal desires were his alone to contend with and they shamed him. He had to fix it. Perhaps make it seem as if it had not meant the world to him. Lie if need be.

At first, Cassie was unaware the kiss had ended. Her eyes remained closed, her mouth eager and every nerve ending in her body positively vibrating with need. It had been a wonderful, impromptu surprise and a revelation. Who knew both of the scoundrels she had fleetingly kissed before Jamie had done it completely wrong? Or that, as she had always suspected, she was prone to swooning after all?

His mouth had been all urgency and passion, his strong arms had held her tightly, not that she had had any desire to escape. Far from it. From the outset she had instinctively burrowed against him, shamelessly flattening her suddenly aching breasts against the firm wall of his chest and replicating the movements of his lips against hers. His teeth. His tongue. When he had pushed her backwards, she had surrendered gratefully, running her palms brazenly over his shoulders and moaning her appreciation loudly into his mouth…

Which probably accounted for why there was at least a foot of fresh air between them now and he was blinking down at her in horror. Like her wanton mother before her, Cassie had gone too far and disgusted him with her enthusiastic and newly awakened passion. Hadn't her father warned her almost daily that a good man would never condone a woman who would lustily give of herself for her own satisfaction?

Well, now she had tangible proof. Jamie was mortified at her scandalous behaviour. Passion had no place in an honourable life or a marriage. The act of marital congress was for the creation of children and any unseemly, sinful urges of the flesh should be mercilessly ignored or she would end up like her mother. Shamed. Shunned. Her soul destined for eternal damnation. Five minutes in the arms of Captain Galahad and she would happily have burned in hell and not given a damn.

'I believe I have proved my point. Your scoundrels knew nothing about romancing a woman.'

The coldness of his words were a slap in the face. He had done this to prove a point? Not because he had wanted to. Not because she tempted him or appealed to him in any way, but because he had wanted to teach her that her scoundrels were not quite as skilled at the art of seduction as she had been led to believe. And that he was better.

He held out his hand and hoisted her up, refusing to meet her eyes, then turned away from her. That blatant rejection stung and she felt her cheeks burn with shame. Like a needy fool she had allowed him to take all of the liberties she had denied those other would-be seducers and would have allowed him to take so many more had her pawing, mauling hungry passion not repulsed him.

Or perhaps he was not repulsed, merely uninterested and unaffected by it? She was hardly the sort of woman who sparked besotted admiration in the male sex. She was an odd, freckled vicar's daughter. Three sugars when one was enough. By his own admission he was vastly competitive. There might be a chance the kiss was simply a way to gain one-upmanship over those men from her past, just as he done with his own brothers growing up.

Would he stoop so low?

It went against everything Cassie thought she knew about him.

Whilst such a convoluted explanation appeared unlikely, already Cassie could see the heated moment was forgotten as far as he was concerned. Jamie was blithely munching on an apple and rummaging in his saddle bag. When he produced some sketches and handed them to her as if nothing had transpired between them at all, she seriously considered the notion he had done it to win. While it hurt, it did give her the opportunity to appear as unaffected and worldly-wise as he apparently was. A kiss was nothing to him. Simply a physical act which could be mastered with practice. Something he was instinctively good at, like riding or painting. Something he could use to prove a point.

'I should like your thoughts on the wedding picture.'

She did her level best to act as composed as him, something which was inordinately difficult on account of all of the riotous loose hair tangled about her face. Evidence of his petty victory. Cassie tucked as much of

it as she could behind her ears and pretended to study
the picture rather than weep pathetically and drown in
the ocean of tears which were forming behind her eyes.

As always, the painting was perfect. His attention
to the tiniest of details was impressive and endearing. Stanley was staring at Orange Blossom with pride
and adoration, looking smart in a beaver hat set at
a jaunty angle, her pretty pony had wildflowers and
leaves woven into her long mane, while scarlet rose petals thrown by the wedding guests floated about their
heads as they wandered beneath a formal, whimsical
arch of crossed carrots.

Behind them stood Miss Freckles and Captain
Galahad. Miss Freckles was clutching a posy which
matched the bride's headdress and was beaming at the
happy couple. But it was the Captain who caught her
eye and made her heart bleed. Because in this painting
he was not watching the bride and groom. His piercing
bright blue eyes were slanted towards Miss Freckles
with an expression which almost matched the black
stallion's. Bemused adoration.

The tableau mocked her and she wanted to rip it into
tiny shreds that matched the cheerful painted confetti
and throw the whole lot in his arrogant, smug point-
proving face.

'It's lovely.' *And I am dying inside.* 'And we are
done.'

'Yes. *Orange Blossom and the Great Apple Debacle*
is finally finished.'

As endings went, this one was quite tragic and he
was missing the point entirely. 'I am going home, Captain Warriner. I shan't bother you again.'

He paused, his half-eaten apple hovering inches

from his lips, and frowned. 'If it is the kiss you are worried about, you needn't. I merely wanted to show you that those scoundrels you put such stock in were not worthy. I meant nothing more than that.'

Cassie found herself scrambling to her feet and striding towards her pony, hurt, irritated and insulted by her brooding companion's blatant ambivalence, when he had just kissed her until she was insensible and that kiss had been so profound.

To her.

To him it meant nothing. He had just said so.

Yet he had asserted his dominance and power over her. Whilst the way he had gone about it was wholly different from the way her father exercised his dominance, he had used those kisses to put her firmly in her place. Something which made her angrier the more Cassie thought about it. What was it with men that they had to be in charge? And why did they have to break a woman's spirit to do it? To think she had been considering a happily ever after with a man who would stoop so low to prove a point. Ha! She still had her original escape plan to revert back to. One where she created her own happy ending. Devoid of domineering men who hurt her feelings and made her feel insignificant! She might have to tolerate her father until she could escape, because he was her father, more's the pity and she had nowhere else to go. But she certainly did not have to tolerate Jamie.

When he made to stand up to assist her on to her pony as he usually did, looking confused by her obvious overreaction, she wanted to slap him. The prospect of his hands on her body again so soon after it had betrayed her so wantonly was out of the question. 'Do not trouble yourself getting up. I do not require your superior help in this matter as well. I could get on my own pony before you came along and I dare say I shall manage well enough going forward. You see, there is a tree stump over there.' To prove the point, Cassie marched Orange Blossom swiftly towards it while he struggled to get himself off the ground and deftly used it to put her own bottom into her own saddle much quicker than she had ever sat on her saddle before. 'Good day, Captain Warriner. Thank you again for lending me your painting talents. And I am glad I could facilitate another petty win for you and feel I must congratulate you in your exemplary seduction skills. Kindly keep them to yourself in the future.'

Chapter Ten

❦

Well, he had made a spectacular hash out of that. Even Satan was staring at him incredulously.

Could you have been more boorish or offensive, you stupid human? You ravished the poor girl, failed to apologise for groping her and made it sound as if you were teaching her a lesson for having the audacity to be delightful enough to inspire men to kiss her. What a thoroughly charming creature you are!

To add insult to injury, Jamie could now apparently hear his horse speak! Or maybe it was his own disgusted voice in his head? Either way, he couldn't argue with the sentiment.

What had started as the perfectly pleasant afternoon he had longed for had deteriorated rapidly into one of the worst days of his life, thanks entirely to his legendary quick temper and a rampant case of jealous lust. The only day he could remember which had turned out to be worse was the one in which he had been shot four times and almost died from the injuries—although as he watched her lovely bottom disappear in the distance, that cute freckled nose defiantly poking up in the air in outrage at being treated so abominably, he would have swapped the shame he currently felt for those destructive, life-changing bullets in a heartbeat.

If there had been a convenient brick wall close by, he would cheerfully smash his stupid head against it. Maybe he would go and find one, do it anyway and be damned. He doubted it would hurt more than his heart did. Who knew it was possible to grievously insult a woman in so many different ways in such a short space of time.

Jamie began to snatch up his things in utter disgust at his own ham-fisted behaviour. Seeing the remnants of the lovely picnic she had prepared still strewn across the grass only served to further sour his mood. The poor girl had departed in such a hurry she had left it all behind. Even her leather-bound journal, the one in which she wrote her precious stories, sat discarded on the tablecloth. He picked it up and began to flick through it. The moment he saw the name Captain Galahad, a fresh wave of shame washed over him, his fingers tracing the flamboyant, sloping handwriting lovingly. Her words. Words which summed her up perfectly. Cheerful, funny, vivid. Generous of spirit. Thoughtful. And he had behaved with such thoughtlessness he wouldn't blame her if she never ever wanted to see him again.

He rode home listlessly and was grateful when he collided with nobody when he arrived. The drawing room was empty and silent, so for ages he sat miserably and stared out of the window. It went without saying he owed her the most enormous, grovelling apology it was possible to give, no matter how humbling or mortifying it was likely to be. He needed to explain why he had kissed her in the first place—or a watered-down version of why he had kissed her. One which kept his growing affection for her a closely guarded secret—and then allow her to decide if she still wanted to cut him out of her life afterwards.

What was he thinking? For her to cut him out of her life he had to be in it in the first place, which he was entirely sure he was not. For almost a week she hadn't given him a passing thought bar today, preferring to fill her afternoons with other, more enticing activities, than sit and talk to him. A humbling realisation indeed. Jamie rubbed his hands over his face and caught the lingering scent of her perfume. His fingertips smelled faintly of her, from where he had plunged them into her hair and greedily run them all over her body. When he closed his eyes he could conjure her at that exact moment. Tumbled on the ground, hair fanned out around her head, the gold-and-copper strands standing out in stark contrast to the rich green grass, her lush mouth swollen from his kiss. So lovely just thinking about it made his heart quicken. There seemed no point in stifling the urge to paint her, because when she sent him packing later, he would at least have that perfect image to remember her by.

With her father away overnight, Cassie was not in any hurry to go to bed. Not when she could sit and write at the kitchen table by the light of a proper lantern without fear of discovery or retribution. In her haste to leave Jamie she had left her journal behind, so she was forced to used loose pages of foolscap until she could find some manner of retrieving it while deftly avoiding him. Besides, she did not need her journal to write. Loose pages would suffice and she still had every intention of filling them. Opportunities to write at a table were few and far between, and too splendid an opportunity to waste. Hours and hours free to indulge in her passion for writing. Just her, her writing equipment and the whimsical stories in her head.

Utter, utter bliss.

Unfortunately, no matter how much she willed them, no words came out of her pen because all she could think about was *him*. The glorious feel of his lips on hers and the bitter sting of his reaction afterwards. Both events befuddled her mind in equal measure and effectively chased away the fantasy world she loved to write about.

Why was she wasting so much thought on him anyway? He was not the first person to reject her and she very much doubted he would be the last. And anyway this relationship, like all the others she'd had in the past, would be transient. They would move away from Retford sooner rather than later, or her luck would turn and she would be able to claim her independence, therefore it was probably for the best she did not allow herself to become too attached to him. Although she already was. At least this way she would have time to get over him before she left rather than mourn his loss afterwards. It was also better that she was positively fuming at the audacity of the man.

Proved my point!

Of all the outrageous reasons to kiss her. Well, he had certainly proved it and now she had to prove her own point and that was James Warriner could go to hell. She wouldn't care. She wouldn't! All Cassie had to do was what she always did. Pick herself up, dust off her dented pride and pretend it did not matter, even if it did.

Tea was undoubtedly the answer. A nice, hot cup of tea in which she would shamelessly dunk a vast number of the sugar biscuits she had baked a few hours ago to take her mind off *him* then as well. *He* had spent far too much time occupying her thoughts. Enough was enough. Cassie decisively grabbed the empty kettle from the hearth and went to fill it from the jug, only to find the jug empty. With a huff, she strode out of the back door to go to the well and fetch more.

A dark head suddenly popped out of a bush to her side and she screamed. The instinct for survival kicked in and she instantly threw the metal jug at the intruder as she darted back towards the house and heard the decisive clunk as it hit him smack in the face.

'Ow!'

She knew that voice.

'Jamie?'

'That was a blasted good shot, woman. Do you play cricket?' He was whispering and rubbing his temple as he emerged limping from the leaves. 'Because you have a very strong arm and excellent aim.'

Cassie's heart was beating so fast she put her hand to her chest to try and calm it down. 'What in God's name do you think you are about, James Warriner? You gave me the fright of my life. What are you doing in the shrubbery?'

'I came to return your journal. You left it by the riverbank.' He began to pat down his pockets and then groaned. 'And apparently I have left it back at the house. Sorry. I shall fetch it back to you tomorrow.'

He touched his fingers to his eyebrow and she saw

a stain of something dark there. Blood. Instantly she felt guilty for throwing the heavy jug at his head, but really…he had rather brought it upon himself.

'I think your forehead is bleeding.'

'It's only a little graze and I dare say I deserve it. My behaviour this afternoon was… What I mean to say is… Well, frankly, I'm not entirely sure quite what came over me earlier, but I am heartily ashamed of myself, if it's any consolation, and I came here to offer you a grovelling apology for being an overbearing brute. I wish the whole sorry episode should never have happened.' Sorry episode? Cassie's teeth began to grind afresh. 'And I think it would be best if we pretended it had never happened. Let's go back to being friends again. I've been stood in this damn bush for close on an hour waiting for your father to go to bed so that I could throw myself on your mercy and beg for your forgiveness.' He was still whispering even though there was no need.

'My father was summoned to Nottingham. The Bishop is not very happy with him. I don't expect him back this evening.' Why was she telling him that when she was justifiably still furious at his scandalous behaviour? 'Not that it matters. I am not speaking to you. You kissed me to prove a point!'

'Not my finest hour, I will grant you. I also behaved like a total cad afterwards.' He bent down and picked up the jug, then handed it to her. 'You can throw it at me again if you want. I promise I won't duck.'

He looked charmingly boyish and contrite. Too charmingly boyish and convincingly contrite that part of her resolve to continue to be furious at him began to waver. The thin trickle of blood next to his eyebrow chiselled away a bit more.

'Perhaps you should step in so I can take a look at your cut before you go.' Her tone was brittle because she was nowhere near ready to accept his apology. The only excuse for kissing a woman senseless was desperately wanting to kiss the woman in the first place. Especially when the kisses were as lethal as his were. Throwing them around willy-nilly to prove a point was irresponsible and calling them a 'sorry episode' was just plain insulting. If he hadn't been wounded by her hand, she would have given him his marching orders smartly. But he was injured and, although she could not muster up any guilt to have been the cause of it, it was her Christian duty to help him.

He followed her meekly into the kitchen and stood awkwardly by the door while she fetched some witch hazel and gauze. Cassie laid the things on the table and motioned snippily for him to sit. She watched his eyes dart about the sparse kitchen, taking in the plain walls whose only decoration were the large, rough-hewn crosses which had been nailed on all four sides. It was such a miserable, depressing kitchen, but matched the rest of the miserable depressing house. 'My father disapproves of unnecessary fripperies. When you move as often as we do, you learn to keep material possessions to a minimum.' And now she was making excuses when she shouldn't care what he thought. Except she knew he loved colours and…well, there weren't any. 'We can't all live in a grand house, Captain Warriner.'

'I notice I am back to being Captain Warriner again.'

'I think it's for the best.' He didn't flinch when she began to clean the wound, but those deep blue eyes stared into hers mournfully, somehow making the simple matter-of-fact act something intimate.

'Would you like me to beg?'

The idea had its merits. 'No, of course not.'

'But you are not ready to forgive me either.'

Cassie stepped away and began to clear away the witch hazel. 'I accept your apology, Captain Warriner, and wish for you to leave immedia—'

There was a great deal of scraping as he pushed the chair back and began to lower himself to his knees on the floor. She saw him wince with pain although he tried to cover it.

'What on earth are you doing?'

'I am about to beg. I believe to do it justice, one should be on their knees. If your father has a hair shirt lying about somewhere, I shall happily put that on, too. Or I could flail myself with birch twigs.' He shuffled towards her on his knees, which had to have hurt him a great deal although he bore it stoically, a sad puppy-dog expression in his handsome face that did not quite hide the discomfort he was feeling. 'Or you could flail me with birch twigs. Or that jug.'

'Please stand up. I have caused you enough injury for one night.' Cassie held out her hand and helped to hoist him up, regretting it instantly when he stood too close and towered over her, forcing her to tilt her face to look into his. And he was still holding her hand. It was so disconcerting, she snatched it away and she took a step backwards to put some well-needed distance between them. Distance he closed instantly.

'Please forgive me for being such an insufferable buffoon earlier. There is no excuse for my crass, boorish behaviour and I will do anything to hear you say you forgive me.'

'Anything?' A smile began to tug at the corners of her mouth as she found herself being charmed by him regardless. Her father had never apologised to her once in his life. Cassie rearranged her features into a frown and promised herself she would remain impervious. 'I believe I shall need tangible examples before I commit to forgiveness, Captain.'

'I could brush your pony down every day for a month. That would take for ever. She does have a ridiculously long mane.'

'Only a month? No, thank you. I like to brush her myself and Orange Blossom likes to look pretty.'

But she would be guaranteed to see him for another month. Weak, pathetic, needy fool.

Cassie folded her arms in a show of strength. She would not be charmed by him. Not now. Not ever.

'I have asked you to leave, Captain Warriner, yet you are still here. Please go.'

'I could take you shopping and buy you whatever you wanted, then carry all the packages afterwards. I hate shopping. Every minute will seem like an eternity.' She wanted to giggle, but took another step back instead, but it escaped loudly from her silly mouth when he stepped towards her again, an arrogant and mischievous gleam in his eyes. Her pulse began to flutter and tiny butterflies appeared in her tummy. The interaction between them now felt like a game and one she was apparently happy to lose.

Fortunately, she could hear Orange Blossom's voice from the stables. *Don't stand for it, Cassie! He kissed you to prove a point, remember?*

'Tempting, but, no. My father disapproves of unnecessary fripperies. Besides, forgiveness should never be bought.' She backed up and found her bottom pressed against the wall. There was nowhere else to go and despite her disappointment in his behaviour she really didn't want to. This felt like flirting, not that she had ever really flirted before to have anything to hold in comparison, but there was something quite wonderful about having this surly man pleading in such a wholly delightful manner.

'What if I promised to illustrate every one of your stories for ever?' He was watching her intently. Ready words failed her. Would he really do that? And if he did, wouldn't it be marvellous!

'I suppose...'

'Wait!' His playful expression was replaced by a frown. 'Listen.'

It was the unmistakable sound of a carriage. And it appeared it was heading towards the vicarage. The pleasant butterflies turned into tentacles of panic which wrapped themselves around her gut and windpipe.

'It's my father! He cannot find you here, Jamie!'

Chapter Eleven

Necessity meant he had to react quickly. The sudden movement, combined with his ill-advised drop to his knees, made his leg muscles tighten and almost give way. Jamie pushed through the pain with gritted teeth to move stealthily towards the window. The Reverend Reeves was indeed currently alighting a shoddy-looking carriage, and one which had very effectively blocked Jamie's escape route. Poor Cassie looked rightly terrified.

'Is it him?'

Jamie nodded and scanned the lower floor for an exit or a suitable hiding place. The lack of furniture rendered the latter redundant.

'Oh, my goodness! Oh, my goodness!' Her panicked face was white, her dark eyes round with fear. 'You cannot be here! You cannot be here!' She had started to yank at his sleeve.

'If I leave now he will see me! Which way is your bedchamber?'

'You cannot go there!'

'Would you rather he found me here. With you? Alone?'

That seemed to bring her up short. 'Turn left on the landing! Hurry!' An instruction which was completely unnecessary when Jamie had just heard her father bid the driver goodnight. He was no more than two stairs up when she called him back. 'Here—take these and hide them.' She thrust the paper, pen and ink bottle into his arms. 'He cannot know I write.'

There was no time to ask her why. Questions would have to wait—unless her father discovered him and shot him, in which case the point was moot. Ignoring the screaming pain in his leg caused by climbing at a speed it was no longer capable of, Jamie miraculously managed to dart into the moonlit bedchamber at the same moment the vicar came through the door.

Carefully, he tiptoed towards the wardrobe and silently placed her writing materials inside, hiding them under some clothing in line with her odd instruction. Her father did not know she wrote stories when those stories were her essence, just like his painting was his? How did one keep a secret like that? At some point he would have to ask her.

Jamie lowered his backside slowly on to her bed and gently removed both of his boots, as he had so many times before when he was somewhere where he shouldn't be. Although on all of those occasions he had been spying on the enemy, not creeping around in the bedchamber of a vicar's daughter. He placed his boots quietly on the floor by the bed and fleetingly considered how lovely it would be to do this every night before he climbed under the covers. With her.

Cuddle up contentedly with her in his arms. Kiss her freckles goodnight.

Probably strangle her as she slept innocently beside him because the blind terror of the darkness had rendered him insensible and unleashed the coiled violence which lurked inside him. A very effective way of shattering a romantic fantasy!

It dawned on him then that if her father discovered him bootless in her bedchamber he would assume something untoward would have occurred, until he realised there would be no pretty way of dressing this up and explaining his presence if he was discovered. The absence of his boots would hardly make a difference. Her father had the lowest opinions of the Warriner family so it stood to reason he would think the worst. Debauchery. *Fornication!*

If only.

But poor Cassie would be ruined by his foolish actions and then probably forced into marrying him. Bizarrely, the idea of being caught so thoroughly in the parson's trap with Cassie did not make him the least bit nervous. Thinking about the abject disappointment such an arrangement would have on her did. Already he cared too much about her to see her life ruined like that, or worse, putting her in the path of danger caused by his hands.

He really should not have risked coming here again. At night. Something so clandestine was bound to cause trouble—but he had been pulled here by his own guilty conscience, eager to make amends and put their blossoming friendship back on to an even keel and bluff his way out of stealing that kiss. He certainly should never have taken her up on her offer to come in so she could tend to his wound. That had been madness. Although he had been lured in by the hope she might accept his apology and because he had desperately wanted to spend some more time with her. Alone. Potentially, he had made the mess worse than he had this morning, something he doubted he would ever forgive himself for. Especially if he *had* ruined her.

On stockinged feet, he crept back to the door and opened it a crack to listen. If Cassie was in trouble, they would face the music together. There was no way he would remain hidden like a coward to leave her to bear the brunt of her father's anger. If he took one look at his daughter's guilty, panicked face and put two and two together then they were done for. But there was no noise coming from the austere little kitchen at all. Which was an even greater worry.

Jamie crouched low and eased his head and shoulders out of the door to spy over the landing. The Reverend Reeves was stood all alone in the centre of the kitchen, his eyes scanning a letter of some sort. Cassie was nowhere to be seen. A painful minute ticked by and she burst through the back door clutching the exact same jug she had tossed at his head with such precision only a few minutes earlier.

'Here we are, Papa! More water. Now I can make you tea. Did you have a good trip? Was the bishop well? Would you like some supper? I could cut you some ham or cheese. Which would you prefer?'

She was babbling, a sure sign of her nerves, and he willed her to breathe for both their sakes.

'Shut up, girl! What is the matter with you? The last thing I want to hear after a long journey is your nonsense. You are such a silly girl, Cassandra—I keep hoping that you will outgrow those irritating traits you inherited from your mother, but, alas, with each year you grow more and more like her. She never knew when to shut up either. Make the tea and do it quietly.'

Jamie had not warmed to her father when he had first met him, even before the man had opened his mouth and insulted his family. However, hearing the way he spoke to Cassie at home made his blood boil. He watched her face fall and her shoulders slump, as they had the last time he had witnessed her with her father, before she meekly did exactly as the foul man had asked.

While the kettle boiled, she sawed off slices of meat, bread and cheese despondently and piled them on a plate, her eyes darting furtively back towards her father to see if he had any suspicions that something was amiss, but the man was too engrossed in his correspondence to care. When she placed the food in front of him, the dour vicar never even acknowledged it, not with a slight gesture or with any words of thanks, but he clasped his hands together and loudly thanked the Lord for what he was about to receive.

Clearly his only daughter, the one who cooked and cleaned and slaved for him, was invisible. Something which Jamie should have been grateful for, seeing as there now appeared less of a chance the Reverend Reeves would notice Cassie's guilty behaviour, but which made him sad for her sake regardless. It was no wonder she had made so many flippant remarks about how irritating she was, or how he could ignore her while she 'prattled on', or that she was odd and ridiculous. Her father had drilled those beliefs into her with his callous disregard and cruel words. He understood first-hand how demoralising that could be.

Jamie was forced to watch her sit dutifully opposite him while he ate, then clear away the plate while her father immersed himself in his Bible. Then she sat with him again and was completely ignored for another twenty minutes before the old man rose and announced his decision to go to bed. After watching them for so long, Jamie was not surprised when Cassie was left with the task of blowing out all of the lamps and closing the windows. His daughter was little more than a servant to him, except he doubted she received the same benefits a real maid would enjoy. Like wages.

As the vicar climbed the stairs, Jamie slunk back into the bedchamber and softly pushed the door to. It was then he noticed the darkness. The moonlight had disappeared, lost behind a dense wall of clouds, and he felt the stirrings of the blind panic which only solid darkness could create.

His heart was racing already. Cold beads of sweat erupted on his forehead and trickled down his neck. His palms were hot and moist.

Not here!

He could not lose control here. Not while Cassie's security depended on his silence. Better to focus all of his energy into his current predicament, the one which could have dire consequences, rather than give in to the irrational fear which was already clawing at his belly mercilessly. Instinctively, he touched the trusty pistol tucked into his belt and fought for calm. All he could do was wait it out until the pious reverend was snoring, then leave the same way he came in. Until Cassie came into the room, there would be no candlelight and until the clouds floated past he wouldn't see the moon, so Jamie needed to take his mind off the dark.

Something which was nearly impossible when his

heart was racing so fast he could barely breathe. He had to slow it or suffer one of the paralysing attacks of nerves which rendered him hysterical.

He had to breathe.

He clawed at his cravat and carelessly tossed it to the floor, loosening his collar. Already his behaviour was nonsensical. Just once he needed to bring it under control. For Cassie.

Months of rotting in that foreign gaol had taught him to focus on something pleasant when the panic engulfed him. Something not linked to his fear, something his mind could hold on to when he lost control of his own emotions and his own mind. It had been a technique born out of necessity then and one he had not used in months because he had a ready supply of candles at home and had therefore not needed it. But under the circumstances, it was worth a try. The reverend was none the wiser as to his presence here. Jamie would be damned if he would allow his own irrational hysteria to alert the man to it.

He lay down on the mattress and began to slowly inhale a lungful of cleansing air. It smelled of Cassie. Violets. Cut grass. Sunshine. Slowly he blew it out again and closed his eyes to the darkness, trying to picture her as he had painted her this afternoon. Tumbled on the ground, her glorious hair fanned out about her head. Lips swollen from his kiss. The sun was shining. It warmed his back as he lowered himself on top of her. He inhaled again and the tight bands of panic began to loosen around his ribs. He was kissing her, his beautiful Freckles, and she was kissing him back and there was a rainbow. A glorious, vibrant rainbow...

* * *

Cassie felt quite peculiar for all manner of reasons, the biggest being the fact there was a man in her bedchamber. As scandalous, outrageous and terrifying as that was, underneath all of those frightened emotions was a quiver of excitement. Because the man in her bedchamber was Jamie. They would be alone there together for a little while before he could slip out quietly into the night. They would have no option but to sit together on the only surface available to sit on—her bed. Something she should not find so thrilling, but she did. More proof she was a thoroughly bad daughter, not that she needed any.

Once all of the lights were extinguished, Cassie took the stairs slowly with a single candle in her hand and her strained nerves bouncing all over the place. She pushed open her bedchamber door and immediately saw him stretched out on her bed, filling the narrow mattress with his big body. A pertinent reminder he was all male. Gloriously male and scarcely a few feet away from her father across the hall. He rolled on to his side and appeared immensely relieved to see her. When he smiled her mouth dried. The collar of his shirt was open, displaying a tantalising V of skin she had not seen before, and his dark hair was rumpled from her pillow. A pillow she would have to sleep on when he was gone. Cassie doubted she would ever wash that particular pillowcase again.

He waited until she closed the door before whispering, 'Is he asleep?'

Cassie shook her head. 'He usually reads for an hour or so.'

'Then I suppose you are stuck with me for an hour.'

Her lips tingled. 'I suppose so.' She was stood awkwardly in the middle of the floor, clutching the candlestick for all it was worth, wondering what it would be like to stretch out next to him on that mattress. Like a lover. He mistook her posture as wariness and shuffled to sit.

'Fear not, Cassie. Your virtue is safe with me.' More was the pity. As she was undoubtedly her mother's daughter she might easily be convinced to part with it where he was concerned. He patted the mattress next to him. 'You might as well sit.'

She did. Reluctantly. Instantly feeling the heat emanating from his body just a few inches away from hers. Even though all disappointingly proper, it was an oddly intimate position to be in. Several painful minutes ticked by in necessary silence, reminding her of how potentially dire their current situation was. Too close for comfort, they listened to the sounds of her father readying himself for bed, neither of them daring to so much as breathe loudly in case it alerted him to Jamie's presence.

If he was found here, then she genuinely feared her father's reaction. Aside from the fact he now loathed the Warriner family unjustly, he had a particular axe to grind with Jamie and venomously hated him above all of the others. It also did not bear thinking about the way he would respond to finding a man in her room. It would confirm all of his worst fears and suspicions. Her mother was a disgrace in his eyes and Cassie was already almost one although she had never done anything to deserve the comparison. Briefly kissing two scoundrels in two separate churchyards hardly counted. Having experienced a proper kiss with Jamie, she now realised how innocently chaste the previous two had actually been.

Her only foray into proper wanton abandon had been with the man currently sat next to her. If she were being honest with herself, even here, with her father across the hallway, if Jamie decided he had made a mistake earlier and really needed to kiss her again she would happily fall into his arms and let him.

The silence next door had stretched for almost five minutes, suggesting her ill-tempered father was finally ensconced in his bed, when Jamie shifted his position to lean a little nearer.

'I feel I owe you another grovelling apology for putting you in this predicament, Cassie. I can see now my coming here was a dreadful idea.' He was speaking close to her ear, something which apparently had the power to scramble her wits and make her forget that her father was so close and that she was potentially in the worst trouble of her life.

'So long as my father remains ignorant of your presence, it doesn't matter. Fortunately, as I am sure you heard, he rarely notices me.'

'I preferred it when my own father was oblivious of my existence. Things were always easier when he left me alone. Does your father's lack of interest bother you?'

If only he knew. 'It used to bother me a great deal. Now I find it gives me certain freedoms which would otherwise be denied me. Like riding every afternoon for hours on end unchaperoned.' This conversation was dangerous because she desperately wanted to confide in him about the awful times her father did notice her.

Jamie seemed to understand her situation, almost as if he empathised. He was very open about his own father's many shortcomings, even sharing the fact the man was violent towards his sons. Cassie knew if anyone would know what she was going through, it would be Jamie. 'My father can…'

They both stilled at the sound of footsteps across the hall. Her father was rummaging for something in a drawer. His shoeless feet padded back towards his bed, the bedframe creaked slightly as he obviously lowered himself into it. Jamie crept towards the door, opened it a crack and then shook his head as he closed it again.

'The light is still on.' In two, stealthy strides he was back at the bed and once again sat directly next to her. 'I am afraid you are stuck with me a little bit longer.'

For several seconds they were both so quiet the only thing she could hear was the soft sound of his breathing. Sitting here like this, so close to him and yet not close enough, was unsettling and exciting. Cassie needed to do something to take her mind off such thoughts and, since her own confession had been cut off, she was not entirely sure she should be that open about her situation just yet, just in case Jamie tried to come to her aid and inadvertently made her situation worse—something which would be very difficult indeed when she only had a pitiful stash of farthings in her wardrobe and nowhere near enough to be in a position to leave. 'Tell me about your father, Jamie.'

'He was a nasty piece of work and a tyrant to all four of us boys, but he used to single me out especially. Painting, in his opinion, was something only girls did. Especially the sort of painting I do. My father was keen for me to grow into a proper man. I think he genuinely thought if he beat me hard enough then he could make it go away.'

'Then I can only assume he failed in his endeavour, seeing that you still paint. And quite beautifully.'

'It turns out I have a stubborn streak,' he said with an undisguised touch of irony which made her smile. 'My painting became my one act of open defiance. I remember reading somewhere the only way to deal with a bully is to stand up to them. I was not big enough to fight fire with fire, so my pictures were a way of telling him he could not control me. The angrier it made him, the more I drew. A small, petty victory over the man I hated most in the world.'

Like Cassie's pretty secret plates or her pretty pink garters. All of her writing. 'Do you still paint out of defiance?'

He paused for a moment, those dark brows drawn together while he thought about it, giving Cassie the opportunity to gaze at his profile in the candlelight unhindered. His skin golden. Those spectacular eyes as blue as the deepest ocean. After a moment his mouth slowly curved upwards. 'No. Now I do it because I need to. We both know my efforts at conversation often leave a lot to be desired, but I can talk with my paints and say things I would never dare to say out loud.'

'Like what?' He was staring down at his hands where they rested on his knees, suddenly awkward in his skin and all the more endearing because of it. Not so tough and brash underneath it all perhaps?

He groaned and shook his head, smiling sheepishly. 'It doesn't matter.'

'It matters to me and it matters to you. Tell me.'

'If this conversation ever leaves this bedchamber,

Cassie, I might have to hunt you down and wring your pretty neck.'

Pretty? In whatever context the compliment warmed her. 'Go on, Captain Warriner—you cannot leave it unsaid now as I will hound you until you confess all. What can you say with paint you would never dare say out loud?' She nudged his arm playfully and wondered if he was blushing. In the dim light it was difficult to tell, but as he was hiding his eyes behind his floppy hair and his shoulders had dropped, she was certain he was embarrassed. Eventually, he scraped his hands over his face before slanting her a look of surrender.

'To me, the world is a beautiful place. Trees, flowers, animals, even clouds fascinate me. I love the patterns and shapes. Appreciate the colours and proportions. All things which horrified my father, who might have been more accepting if I had painted grand battle scenes or epic pictorial commemorations of classical literature, like the great masters. But I would prefer to paint a marigold than a masterpiece.

'Or a pair of talking horses getting married under an arch of carrots.'

'So much more interesting than a battle scene for sure.'

'Did you really mean it when you said you would illustrate all of my stories?'

She heard him exhale. 'I did.' No doubt he regretted the offer now. 'If you will forgive me for my appalling behaviour this afternoon and my monumental folly in coming here tonight, I will illustrate all of your flights of fancy gratefully.'

'You would do all that solely for my forgiveness?'

'Not entirely. I have a selfish reason to want to do

it.' Cassie's pulse began to race at the words, hoping he was about to make a declaration of some sort, because in these last few minutes he had opened up to her in a way he never had before. Shared confidences. Sat so close to her they were practically touching when he could have moved to the opposite end of the bed quite easily. Quite properly. Yet right now, they were cosy.

Close.

At his instigation. And it felt so right. If he felt it too...

'The thing is...'

He regarded her shyly and her heart leapt.

'I find I actually enjoy painting your whimsical stories. I think I might have a knack for illustrations.'

Cassie deflated as her silly, fleeting hope was crushed, not that she would allow him to see it. Of course he was not as overwhelmed by their intimate predicament as she was. He had only kissed her to prove a point, after all, and she had forgiven him for it. Sort of. 'You do have a knack for illustrations. I am sure all manner of people would pay handsomely for your skills.' She risked peeking at him and could see her words had pleased him even though his had disappointed her.

'I doubt there is much money to be had from drawing caricatures.'

'I believe Hogarth and Gillray would disagree with you. They made a fortune from their talent for caricature and satire. You have a good eye for the amusing and funny details, Jamie. Like Hogarth. A wedding arch of carrots is very funny.'

'But I only thought of the carrots because you had painted such a vivid picture in my mind with your witty words. Maybe our combined talents could earn us both a living? Your stories and my illustrations do make a pretty good picture book, if I do say so myself.'

Cassie sighed and shook her head. 'Alas, I can never publish them. I daren't. My father would never allow it. He disapproves of common entertainments and works of fiction in general. If you are going to make a career out of drawing, it cannot be with me.' Although it would be a splendid way to earn her own independence.

'You write in secret.' It wasn't a question. He had probably worked out as much when she had begged him to hide her equipment.

'I do. It is a guilty pleasure I allow myself, but not one I could ever seriously pursue, as much as I might want to. At least not while I live under my father's roof.' Was that too blatant a hint that she was open to him rescuing her? Probably. It made no difference. Jamie failed to pick up on it, or if he had, he was letting her down gently.

'Many writers publish anonymously or use a pseudonym to disguise their real identity. Perhaps you should acquire a *nom de plume. Orange Blossom and the Great Apple Debacle* by the intrepid Miss Freckles.'

She could not help smiling at the thought. 'Illustrated by Captain James Warriner.'

'It would never sell with the name Warriner attached to it. We are far too untrustworthy a family.' He was smiling, too, and somewhere during their exchange he had leaned a little sideways so their shoulders were lightly touching again. It was playing havoc with her pulse.

'Then you also need a—what did you call it? A *nom de plume*?'

'It's French. Literally translated it means a pen name. But as I don't work with a pen but with a brush, mine would be a *nom de pinceau*. A brush name.'

'You speak French?'

Of course he did. Fluently. Had he not he never would have been able to blend in so well in the French lines or gather the essential intelligence and reconnaissance he had been sent in alone to retrieve. A whole hornets' nest of things he really did not want to talk about. 'Only a little.'

'I suppose you had to, fighting Napoleon and all. Do you miss being a soldier?'

'No.' The word came out without Jamie having to consider it, yet as he said it he realised it was true. He missed being able to walk properly, that went without saying. He missed not earning a salary. He sometimes missed the respect which came from being *Captain* Warriner, decorated soldier and all-round reliable fellow in the King's Army. But he did not miss the dangerous and unpredictable existence of being in a war. The knowledge came as a revelation. For as long as he could remember, being an officer had defined him, then not being able to be that soldier had cruelly defined him. Now, here on her bed, talking in whispers with a beautiful freckled woman who was slowly driving him out of his mind with longing, he was not entirely sure what he was any more. An artist? Cassie had certainly given him something to ponder. The idea of earning a living from his art excited him more than anything had in a very long time because one did not need good legs to draw and he loved doing it.

That idea and Cassie, of course. As he sat beside her in her bedchamber, the single candle picking out the copper in her hair and the gold speckles in her eyes, his mind was wandering away from the problem of her father in the next room and on to other more carnal thoughts. One man. One woman. Hundreds of glorious freckles.

And one bed.

Beds were for sleeping in and for making love in, and right at this minute he was desperate to do the latter. Painfully desperate and becoming more so with each passing second. The enforced intimacy created by having to whisper and huddle together in order to hear the other was not exactly helping. He shivered every time her lips dallied near his ears. Several times he had been sorely tempted to just close the short distance between them, kiss her and be damned. He had even rationalised how he could worry about all of the ramifications and obstacles later. Once the deed was done.

If she was open to the idea, of course.

He was resourceful and wily after all, Napoleon's bullets had not robbed him of those skills, so perhaps he could find a way to figure it all out.

She licked her lips, drawing Jamie's hungry eyes to them and reminding him of the way they had tasted only a few hours before. The lingering memory of her soft mouth pressed against his was not helping to cool his ardour. His was a scant few inches away. He could close the distance in a heartbeat. Without thinking Jamie found himself drawing closer, then stopped short. He had promised her that her virtue was safe with him after his ungentlemanly behaviour earlier. If he stole another kiss, she might never trust him enough to forgive him again. Yet the air between them positively crackled with promise and she hadn't backed away.

Did that mean she might be open to the idea, too? 'Cassie, do you think…'

What?

Do you want to spend your life leg-shackled to a cripple who might attack you in the night because he has mistaken you for the sadistic Capitaine DuFour? But it will be all right, my darling Freckles, because you will have your own bedchamber, preferably one a good half a mile away from mine because I cannot be trusted. I also sleep with an arsenal, don't you know. And I just might, if I am in the full grip of my irrational and ferocious panic, take that pretty neck of yours in my bare hands and snap it as I did le Capitaine's. Like I almost did to my brother's. It took the other two to pull me off him then, as I was so insensible I was like a wild animal. A rabid dog. A monster.

No.

He wouldn't do that. Even though she was staring right back at him and he could have sworn he saw matching need mirrored in her eyes. 'Do I think what?' Her voice was breathy. Or was he imagining it?

Seductive.

God help him. Or perhaps he was mapping his own desires on to her and seeing things which were just not there.

'Do you think your father might be asleep yet?'

She sat a little straighter and he saw the confusion in her face. 'He might be. Do you want me to check?'

Jamie nodded and grabbed his discarded boots from the floor. The sooner he could escape her intoxicating presence the better. For both of their sakes. She scurried to the door and poked her head out, then motioned the coast was clear. Boots in hand, he started down the stairs, trying to ignore the ominous darkness which awaited him. It would be all right. Satan was hidden a short way down the lane, tethered to some branches and stood next to his lantern. Even if it was no longer alight, Jamie had oil and flints in his saddle bag and could soon remedy the situation. And the moon was probably out again, or at least he hoped it was, and he had his pistol tucked into his belt.

He was halfway down the staircase when the vicar woke up. 'Cassandra? What are you doing, girl?'

Jamie froze and waited anxiously. 'I left a light on downstairs, Papa. I am going to put it out.'

'You are such a stupid girl! Can I not trust you with even one simple task? You'll burn the house down one day.'

'Sorry, Papa. I shall try harder in future.'

Noisily, and for effect, she clomped down, too, giving Jamie a chance to get to the back door and open it without too much fear of being heard. She hovered close by, her fingers nervously wringing the edge of her skirt as her eyes kept darting back towards the top of the landing in case her father followed.

The worst part was, Jamie did not want to leave her. He did not want to be denied her company or leave her at the mercy of her dreadful father. He had the overwhelming urge to ask her to come with him. Then what? It was a silly, futile hope. 'Will you be all right?'

'Yes. Believe it or not, to me he appears in good humour. When he is angry he is a lot less affable.' Although she had intended those words as a joke, they set alarm bells ringing in Jamie's mind.

'Will I see you tomorrow?'

'If you want to.'

'Of course I want to. We have another storybook to create, don't we?' Lord, how he wanted to kiss her goodnight.

'Then I shall see you tomorrow, Jamie. In our usual place.'

Our usual place. How splendid that sounded. 'Goodnight, Cassie.'

For the next fortnight they met every day for two blissful hours, Cassie writing a new adventure for Orange Blossom while Jamie translated her words into whimsical pictures which delighted them both. Sometimes they rode idly along the riverbank, sometimes they shared stories over the home-baked delicacies she brought them, and sometimes they sat in surprisingly comfortable silence, gazing up at the clouds and the ethereal patterns they made in the sky. It was almost sheer perfection. Almost, because the spectre of that one, passionate kiss hung over them. Unspoken about and yet so prominent in her mind at least. When the Reverend Reeves was once again summoned to the diocese in Norwich, Cassie suggested they spend the whole day together to work. By midday, they had done precious little actual work as they had ridden over the entire length and breadth of the Markham estate talking. Jamie had an idea about dragons which she knew would make a good story.

It was Jamie who suggested they deposit their mounts at his brother's stable for a well-earned rub down and some oats, so they set up his easel and her pens on their favourite spot by the river beforehand, intending to stroll back horseless after they had eaten some lunch with Letty. The beautiful Countess of Markham was thrilled to see her and made no mention of her father's outrageous sermon. Even when Cassie tried to apologise, it was cheerfully waved away. 'Who cares about such nonsense? Jamie tells me the pair of you are actually going to try to get your storybook published. How exciting!'

'We might. One day.' They hadn't seriously talked about it since the night in her bedchamber.

'Cassie is concerned about putting her name to it as her father would disapprove.' Jamie made a disgusted face at the mention of her father before taking another bite of his food.

'And Jamie is convinced attaching the name Warriner to anything is doomed to see it fail. I need a *nom de plume* and Jamie needs a *nom de pinceau*—which is apparently French for paintbrush.'

'Whatever names you choose,' Letty replied knowledgably, 'they must be memorable in order to stand out on the cover. No Smiths or Jones for surnames. And no Johns or Janes for the Christian names either. You need something with a bit of dash—it is a great shame you will not use your own name, Cassie, because Cassandra is the perfect name for an author.' She dipped her spoon in her pudding and licked it thoughtfully before grinning. 'Why don't you amalgamate both your names? Seeing that you are now a partnership.'

'I'm not sure I follow.'

Letty ignored the stern look Jamie shot her and continued to speak to Cassie as if he did not exist. 'What I mean is, as you are both keen to maintain your anonymity by using pseudonyms, why not create just the one. Cassandra James—the talented new author and illustrator of humorous storybooks for children. People in London will fall over themselves to buy them. The pen name will be a delightful nod to your real selves. A marriage of sorts.'

Despite the obvious attempt at matchmaking which had Jamie scowling across the table, Letty's idea did have merit. *Cassandra James*. It was a lovely name and she enjoyed the sound of the syllables. *Cassandra James*. It was almost musical. However, it was not just the *nom de plume* which excited her. The idea that they could publish a book, and one that people would actually pay for, opened up a world of possibilities. A way to fund her future independence in a quicker way than squirrelling away the odd coin from the frugal housekeeping money. Such a possibility seduced her. 'I rather like it, Jamie. But it is up to you. Do you feel uncomfortable with the idea of being published as a woman?' Because if he didn't, Cassie now knew she needed to find a way in which he would be happy to have the book published. It was her ticket to freedom.

He shrugged as he wiped his hands on his napkin. 'My vile father always said I painted like a girl—pretending to be one for the eyes of the world will have him spinning in his grave. I rather like *that* idea.'

'Right, then. It's settled. *Orange Blossom and the Great Apple Debacle* by Cassandra James it is!' Letty tossed her own napkin on the table. 'I happen to know a publisher in London. My father invested heavily in his fledgling business years ago so he owes my family a favour. Even if it is not the sort of thing he publishes, he will be able to point it in the direction of someone who does. Give me your story and paintings and I shall send them to him this very afternoon. By the time I have finished, books by the talented Cassandra James will be famous.'

Her excitement was infectious and Cassie suddenly wanted to go along with the idea before she had time to think about it and decline. How marvellous would it be to see her story as an actual book, and one perhaps which hundreds of children might enjoy? Aside from the potential money it might make, it would also be another guilty little act of defiance against her overbearing father, yet another reason to do it. 'Do you have my journal, Jamie?' He still hadn't brought it back to her and she was hoping he hadn't mislaid it.

'Yes.'

'Splendid. Chivers!' Letty was already ringing the bell. The butler appeared through the door as if he had been stood outside poised for such a request. 'Chivers, I will need to send an express to London this very afternoon. Can you get someone to fetch Mr James's charming horsey paintings, which are piled by his chair in the drawing room, please?'

'Have you been rummaging through my things again, Letty? I've told you a hundred times, do not touch my painting equipment.' Jamie looked pointedly at Cassie as if he were greatly put upon. 'There is no privacy in this house. Something which has got worse since my brother married this witch.'

'I did not see Miss Reeves's journal there, Jamie. Where, pray tell, is that?'

The Countess was grinning again and Cassie swore she heard Jamie actually grind his teeth. 'Oh, I think you know, dear Sister-in-law. Let us not play *this* game again.'

'Honestly, I do not know.' Although it was obviously she did. 'Come along, Jamie, Chivers hasn't got all day. Tell him where to find Miss Reeves's small, *brown* leather-bound journal.'

The butler's eyes were darting between the pair of them like a spectator in a tennis match. Letty was grinning and Jamie was scowling. A good ten seconds of impasse ticked by until Jamie grunted what sounded like. 'Nightstand.'

Poor Chivers appeared confused. 'I did not catch that, Mr James.'

'Yes, do speak up, Brother dearest.'

'It's on my blasted nightstand, Chivers!' He stood up, looking charmingly annoyed. 'Come along, Cassie. We have *work* to do.' Then he limped away as smartly as his injured leg would allow.

Cassie thanked Letty for lunch and hurried after him down the hallway. Instead of exiting towards the back door in the kitchen, Jamie veered down another passageway. 'Where are we going?'

'I need to fetch some more paint. I am running out of blue.' He opened an ancient-looking door and disappeared down a narrow staircase. With nothing better to do, Cassie followed his retreating back and was surprised to find herself in a rabbit warren of a cellar. There were literally doors everywhere. He grabbed a burning lantern before he opened one. Inside was an artist's store cupboard which even Michelangelo would envy. Hundreds of tubes of paint, brushes and jars were cluttering the shelves. As he began to rummage for the exact shade he wanted, he quickly turned towards Cassie. 'I could probably do with more paper as well. Would you mind grabbing some from the cupboard next door? It's piled to the left as you walk in. Be careful. It's a bit of a mess.'

Cassie did as he asked, pushing open the heavy oak door expecting another cupboard—except it was hardly a cupboard. More a cavernous room. Piles of paper and easels of varying sizes were stacked haphazardly against one wall. Everywhere else was evidence of Jamie's art. Beautiful pictures were piled on or against every available surface. It was like Aladdin's Cave.

Cassie couldn't help herself. To have such an unexpected opportunity to see his work, to witness first-hand the things he could paint but never say, was a tantalising insight into a man she was becoming inordinately fond of despite her better judgement. Shamelessly she began to flick through them, amazed by the level of intricate detail he could create using just a brush and his own extraordinary talent.

He really did see beauty in everything and his choice of composition was staggeringly romantic. Vivid sunsets, delicate butterflies, intricate cloud formations. Birds, deer, trees and plants. All of the prettiest things nature had to offer, except people, and all painted with the gentle, loving care of a man who could not say it, but felt it all so deeply. She could see as much clearly with every detailed, considered and romantic brushstroke. It was obvious he truly loved creating such beauty.

Another part of the feeble dam she had constructed around her heart washed away on a wave of affection so strong, it staggered her. Leaving Captain Galahad behind when she inevitably left Retford was going to be the hardest thing Cassie had ever had to do. He was the only true friend she had ever had—yet there was no point in trying to pretend otherwise, he was so much more than a friend. At least, she wanted him to be more than a friend and occasionally she thought he might feel the same way as well.

There were those oddly charged moments when she caught him staring at her, for instance, when he would quickly look away, but not before she had seen his blue eyes swirling with some undecipherable emotion. The way his hands lingered on her waist or ankle when he helped her on to her pony. The way he glared at his sister-in-law every time she hinted there was something between them, which she did at every available opportunity and each time Jamie became flustered, grunting one-word responses. By his own admission, a sure sign he was nervous. And then there was the way he painted Miss Freckles. The tiny caricature was so pretty, with her wild hair and big brown eyes, Cassie wondered if that was how he saw her. The real her.

It was obvious that the fictitious Captain Galahad was hopelessly in love with the intrepid but silly heroine they had created. It positively shone out of his painted turquoise eyes as he gazed across the paper at the woman who appeared oblivious to his feelings. Miss Freckles, she noticed, never gazed at him with the same adoration. Her eyes were always turned towards Orange Blossom or Stanley or whatever scrape she had currently dragged him into, almost as if he was insignificant. Perhaps that was how he felt. He was so sensitive about his limp after all and had felt the urge to prove himself better than those scoundrels enough to kiss her that one time…

That thought brought her up short. Was Jamie's art imitating life? Was there a chance he had deep feelings for her, too? Things he could never say with words—only paint? And perhaps his kiss—because it had been a very heartfelt and passionate kiss, regardless of his claim to the contrary—was tangible proof? Maybe he had concocted the whole story about proving a point to cover up the real truth? Unless she was being ridiculously fanciful again. If she were really as intrepid as Miss Freckles, or even the shameless flirt Orange Blossom, she would be bold.

She might be bold enough to instigate another kiss to find out if he was truly immune to her charms as a man proving a point would be. She could sneak into the cupboard next door, slide her arms around his waist and whisper something seductive close to his ear.

I was wondering, Jamie, if you would allow me to conduct a little experiment...

Which, of course, she wouldn't. Cassie was ultimately a coward despite being her mother's daughter. The trouble was, the more time she spent with Jamie, the less guilty she felt about her fanciful daydreams involving him, her and the magnificent sunset they rose off towards together. She supposed she should try harder to stop thinking such wanton thoughts, seeing that they would only confirm her father's worst fears for her rotten soul and get her into a mountain of trouble, but the simple truth was where Jamie was concerned she couldn't find the motivation to care.

A vibrant study of a flower caught her attention and she pulled it up level with her eyes to get a better look. In the centre of the fat pink rose was a bumble bee, the wings appearing almost translucent and, if she was not mistaken, every fuzzy hair on its striped back individually defined using the finest of brush strokes.

No doubt exquisite, but the pale glow from the lantern outside was too weak to see them properly. Cassie took a step backwards to try to catch some of the light on the picture, her hip grazing against something hard in the process. Whatever it was, it moved. She heard it slide to the floor on a whisper. Then the door violently slammed shut behind her and her heart literally stopped beating in her chest.

Chapter Twelve

〜〜⤴⤵〜〜

Jamie found the blue he needed, then remembered he should also stock up on some black paint as well, as he was going through it at a rate of knots getting Satan the deep, opaque colour that did his temperamental horse justice. He stuffed everything he needed into his pocket and left the little storeroom.

'Cassie, did you find the paper?'

The passageway was empty and silent, and he assumed she must have headed back upstairs without him. He could hardly blame her; he did climb stairs pathetically slowly. More like a feeble old man than one supposedly in his prime—but his damaged thigh muscle found that particular movement the most challenging of all, so he supposed stairs would always be his nemesis. The flash of temper which always accompanied any reminder of his infirmity was tinged with self-pity. Obviously Cassie, despite her inordinate patience with his blasted physical limitations, occasionally felt constrained by him. Hence she had skipped up the stairs smartly rather than wait for him to hobble along with her.

The fresh dose of self-pity mixed with the awkward self-consciousness which his brother's meddling wife had sowed with her thinly veiled hints about his relationship with Cassie. When you put those two states together, he found his previous buoyant mood significantly deflated. He had been so looking forward to spending a whole day with her, rather than the few stolen hours she managed in the afternoons. Riding, chatting, laughing. He was always happier with her by his side, even if he was just a friend. He had managed to convince himself that was better than not having her in his life at all. But as usual the truth crept in when he found himself looking at her longingly and wondering *what if*?

Jamie returned the lantern to its hook and scowled. In all honesty, maintaining the charade of being happy with their state of affairs was proving more and more difficult with every passing day, not helped by unsubtle hints from his family suggesting it was quite apparent he wanted more. Today, over lunch, had been positively cringeworthy. Letty's well-meant and playful words had wounded.

Partnership! Marriage of sorts! As if he could seriously contemplate a marriage of any sort in the state he was in. The final humiliation had been having to admit to keeping Cassie's journal on his nightstand like a lovesick milksop, another glaring clue to his intense feelings towards her. Although only he knew he had taken to sleeping with it tucked beneath his palm, a little part of his freckle-faced temptress to help ward off the demons of the darkness which still lived inside his own broken head. At least he hoped only he knew.

What was worse was that he really only had him-

self to blame. He knew damn well his relationship with
Cassie could only be platonic—yet he still hoped and
yearned for a miracle. Hoped that one day he would
miraculously wake up fully healed and nimble, the
hated limp gone and his irrational nocturnal behaviour gone with it. But miracles had proved to be decidedly thin on the ground as far as he was concerned.
Annoyed, Jamie stomped loudly on the first step and
then stopped abruptly when he heard a strange noise.
It sounded like sniffing—or perhaps sniffling.

Definitely sniffling.

Quiet, almost imperceptible sobs which he might
never have heard if his military training and years of
covert missions had not made him acutely aware of the
slightest sound out of place.

'Cassie?' He started back the way he had just come,
wondering if she might have got herself lost in the
cavernous and winding cellar. It was highly plausible.
Jamie and his brothers had played hide and seek down
here for hours when they were children. 'Cassie, are
you still down here?'

He heard another snuffle and realised it came from
the paper store. If she was in there, why didn't she answer him? 'Cassie!' The shout went unanswered.

Unless she couldn't answer him. Perhaps something
had fallen on her or she had tripped? There were all
manner of easels and canvases in that room, things
which he had been meaning to properly tidy up since
he returned home from the Peninsula and could never
quite find the incentive to. Thinking of Cassie hurt sent
a chill through him as he grabbed the lantern again.

'I'm coming, Cassie!' He tried the handle repeatedly
before acknowledging it was futile. The blasted door

wouldn't move, which meant something was wedged behind it. Very probably an easel because he had carelessly stacked them next to the door for his own selfish convenience. If one of the bigger ones had knocked her on the head, she could well be out cold.

Or worse.

Jamie put his shoulder against the ancient oak and put his full weight behind it, enough to open the door a crack to see inside. She was on the floor and, by the looks of things, hunched up in a ball because she was in agony. If she had broken a bone because of his slapdash organisational skills, he would never forgive himself.

'Stay still, Cassie, I'm coming to get you!' He began to push at the door again repeatedly, slowly shifting whatever piece of his equipment which was blocking it. 'Where are you hurt?' No response, but he could now see her shoulders quivering in the dim light cast by the lantern he had placed on the floor. She was sitting. Curled into a ball, her arms tightly wrapped around her knees, face buried in her skirts. Clearly something dreadful had happened.

'Cassie! Where are you hurt?'

The door was open enough for Jamie to squeeze through. He rushed towards her and crouched down to touch her shoulder, his heart racing and fighting for calm. If he had hurt her, even inadvertently... 'Cassie?'

She looked up then, an expression of complete terror etched on to her lovely face, eyes wide. Even without the aid of the lantern Jamie could see she was as white as a ghost.

'Jamie?' Her fingers came up to claw at his lapels where she clung on for dear life. 'Oh, thank God!'

He ran his hand gently over her face, her shoulders,

arms, then along her legs to ascertain the extent of her injuries. 'Where are you hurt?'

'Not h-hurt.'

He might have been relieved at this statement, but her breath was sawing in and out rapidly, and for a moment he thought she might pass out, but then she shuffled closer and collapsed against him, wrapping her arms about his neck and hugging him desperately while she dissolved into hysterical sobs, practically panting with the exertion, which alarmed him. Because in a rush, he suddenly understood what ailed her. Jamie knew only too well what a blind panic looked like and how all-consuming one could be, and for whatever reason, the quivering woman in his arms was in the grip of one.

'You need to breathe, Freckles.' He smoothed his hand over her hair and forced his tone to be matter of fact, forced his own ribcage to rise and fall slowly as he inhaled and exhaled for her. 'Breathe with me... in...slowly.'

He felt her struggle to emulate him with some difficulty, but at least she was listening. She could hear his voice over her terror.

'And out...slower. That's right, darling, and again...'

With no clue as to what was wrong and with Cassie in no fit state to tell him, all he could do was gather her close so she could feel the motions of his chest and rock her in his arms, telling her over and over again that everything was all right, because he was here and he would sooner die than let anything bad happen to her.

Cassie began to focus on the rhythmic beating of his heart, the gentle rise and fall of his chest and the feel of his hands idly sliding up and down her back. Focussing on Jamie, on being held by Jamie, helped to banish the paralysing terror which controlled her. He was so strong. So dependable. Strangely she knew with him she would always be safe. Instinctively, she buried her face in his neck and tried to focus on each breath. His own was so measured it served to slow hers. This in turn began to calm her frenzied pulse and painfully loud heartbeat.

'It's all right, Freckles,' he soothed and instantly it was. 'I have you, my darling. Nothing can hurt you now.'

Such beautiful endearments, the sort a man might whisper to his sweetheart.

Or croon to a hysterical woman in order to calm her down.

As her wits returned, Cassie began to wonder how she would explain her bizarre behaviour to a man who held his own emotions so very firmly in check. A man who had fought Napoleon, stoically fought pain every single day since and one who had endured six whole months of incarceration rather than the few minutes she had been accidentally shut in a storeroom.

Accidentally being the case, as she knew full well she was in Markham Manor and not the vicarage, her father miles away in Norwich. However, when that door had slammed she lost all sense of place and reason and did what she always did when the key turned ominously in the lock. The brave man holding her probably thought she had gone quite mad, which for a moment she had, but it was a madness which was transient and only possessed her when she could not get out. She doubted Jamie would understand such nonsense. Not when she barely understood it herself.

He sensed she was more in control and spoke quietly into her hair. 'Are you all right, Cassie?'

As tempting as it was to lie in order to save face, she couldn't bring herself to do it. Not to him. 'The door slammed shut.'

'An easel fell down and jarred the door. Did it hit you as it fell?'

'No. I am well.' A glaring, blatant lie. Her heart was beating a rapid tattoo in her chest, her lungs burned from the after-effects of her frantic, desperate breathing.

'You are not well—you are shaking.' Something she probably would not stop doing for at least half an hour and which effectively called her out on her lie. How to explain without truly explaining and appearing more ridiculous than ever?

'I have a fear of locked doors, of being trapped inside places. I know it's irrational, but when it happens I freeze. The panic seems to strangle me and I can't... I c-can't—' Bitter tears of shame began to fall, choking off her confession.

'Breathe.'

Cassie nodded, surprised he could finish her sentence. 'It's silly.'

'Fear is not silly, Cassie. It is real and visceral, regardless of whether the cause is imagined or not. Did you have a bad experience as a child? Were you locked in somewhere and couldn't find a way out?'

It was yes to both answers, although she could never tell him the whole truth. For as long as Cassie could remember her father had shut her in a room when he thought she had been bad. When she was younger she would scream and cry, kicking and scratching at the door for all she was worth. This had only served to increase his anger, especially when her 'infernal racket' brought well-meaning neighbours to their door, daring to question his disciplinary measures.

They had moved at least twice as a direct result of such visits and although those people had only been trying to help, their interference had caused the punishments to be longer and her father's tone more threatening. Silent penance, her father explained repeatedly from the other side of the bolted door, proved to him she was thinking carefully about her actions and trying to hear the guiding words of God. Screaming and even audible crying showed him she still did not understand what it was to be a dutiful daughter. Bringing criticism and meddling to his door undermined him and incurred not only his wrath, but the wrath of the Lord as well, because she was a sinner. Like her mother before her.

Unfortunately, as the years passed, her father became frustrated by her inability to learn her lesson so the penance needed to take longer. And longer. The only thing Cassie could do to mitigate those interminable days in petrifying isolation was to be, at least on the surface, the dutiful daughter her father wanted her to be. Back down. Agree. Keep quiet. Suppress all aspects of her wild character traits in his presence. Deflect, fib—outright lie if the need arose. Do whatever it took to spare herself the agony of being imprisoned again.

'I believe I must have been trapped somewhere once, although I do not remember it.' Lying to Jamie, although necessary, did not come quite so naturally. Cassie stared at her hands rather than let him see the truth.

'It must have been a bad experience indeed to still affect you all these years on.' His hand was still stroking her hair so gently. 'However, the human mind is a powerful thing. It can twist or warp reality cruelly.'

'And we both know I have a mind prone to ridiculous flights of fancy. No doubt I have concocted this silly fear like I do my stories. Weaving fiction into reality and believing my imagination over fact.' Laugh it off, Cassie. Make him see it doesn't matter.

However, he stared at her quietly, worry and some other odd emotion clouding his handsome face. When he finally did speak, it was just above a whisper, almost as if what he was saying was some great secret he was sharing.

'When I was a boy I had a morbid fear of the dark. My mind would play all manner of cruel tricks on me when night time came.'

'You did?' Picturing Jamie scared of anything was difficult. 'Did you have a bad experience, too?'

'I had a father who liked to wake me up with a sound beating in the dead of night. I suppose, after a while, I came to associate the two things as one. The dark and the violence. I think, because I was so confused at being awoken so horrifically, I grew to dread closing my eyes if it was dark. Sleeping became difficult, just in case he came in and I did not hear him.'

'Did he leave you alone if you were awake?'

'No. He still came—with his belt and his anger—but I was prepared for it then, steeled in preparation for whatever onslaught he had planned, so it did not seem as bad.'

'I know what you mean. The door slammed so quickly, I was unprepared. I feel such a fool.'

He must have seen her eyes flick nervously towards the partially open door before they dropped to her hands in shame at being so obviously vulnerable. 'Come. Let us get you out of here so you can compose yourself properly without the fear of the door slamming again.'

He used the wall to lever himself from the ground, then took both of her hands in his to help her up. Once she was upright, one of his arms came reassuringly about her shoulders as he led her from the room and well away from any doors, and still he did not let go of her. His solid warmth comforted her and restored her at the same time. When they were stood in the dim passageway he surprised her. Instead of leading her up the stairs or offering her platitudes, he simply tugged her head to rest on the hard wall of his chest and held her tight. Bizarrely, it was exactly what she had needed him to do.

Cassie lost all sense of time as they stood there, because time did not matter when being close to him mattered so much more. Needing to be closer still, Cassie burrowed her hands beneath his coat to rest on those broad, reliable, loyal shoulders. He might not be shimmying up an apple tree this time, but he was still rescuing her. Saving her from herself and the peculiar workings of her odd mind. Gradually, her erratic pulse began to slow, the vice-like band of terror around her organs loosened as she matched her breathing to his. Slow and steady. In and out. Feeling warm, protected and, rather peculiarly because she had never experienced it before, loved.

Cassie tilted her face up towards his and their eyes locked. She wanted to kiss him, partly as a thank you, but mostly because she needed to. Kissing him would certainly banish the last remnants of any lingering fear. Cassie doubted she would be capable of thinking about anything other than the wonderful sensations his mouth had the power to elicit from her body. She licked her lips and saw his eyes drop to them. Beneath her palm his steady heartbeat was definitely faster, his breathing no longer as slow and steady as it had been only a few moments ago. When he began to lower his face to hers Cassie hoped he might kiss her.

When he hesitated, looking anxious and perhaps a little nervous, she wondered if he was waiting for some signal from her that he should proceed. Tremulously, she reached up and laid her hand on his cheek, watched his eyelids flutter closed, heard the slow exhalation of breath. 'Jamie... I...' His lips were now inches from hers, his intense blue eyes almost black. Hypnotic. She pressed her upper body brazenly against his, marvelling in the power and strength there, before inching closer still so her hips were almost pressed intimately against his. 'I was wondering if...'

'Tea is the solution, I think, and cake of course. Let us go and fetch some and sit outside to drink it. Tea and fresh air!' He stepped back, severing the full body contact and taking her determinedly by the arm. 'You have had a fright and need to settle your nerves.' He took the stairs quickly, too quickly, she thought, because she saw him wince once or twice in his haste to escape the intimate confines of the dusky cellar and her unwelcome amorous overtures. He abandoned her swiftly at the top, calling for the butler and Letty and his brother in quick succession. Because he certainly did not want to kiss her. Not when he could have tea in the garden instead.

Chapter Thirteen

T he incident spoiled the rest of the afternoon. Jamie appeared on edge, smiling far too frequently and determinedly keeping them both busy, ostensibly to take her mind off her ordeal, but more likely to cover his embarrassment at openly rejecting her feeble advances. It was also obvious he was not prepared to discuss it either.

Cassie had tried to broach the subject twice and both times he had changed the subject with as much subtlety as it took to smash a hazelnut with a hammer. It was clear he wanted to maintain the status quo, remind her to adhere to the defined parameters of their unsatisfactory platonic relationship and pretend the sensually charged moment in the cellar had never happened. Just as he had after he had kissed her to prove a point. Then he had tried to divert her using one of his illustrations, now he was trying to divert her again by plotting out the next part of the new adventure for Orange Blossom and Stanley.

But for once, no words or ideas came from her odd brain. His overly friendly, overtly courteous behaviour was so out of character as to become irritating, especially as she was still smarting and humiliated in equal measure at his clumsy withdrawal and the even clumsier aftermath. If she hadn't been so grateful he had rescued her from the locked room so quickly, she would have grabbed him by those splendid broad shoulders of his and shook him in sheer temper.

Even so, Cassie found herself reluctant to leave him until the evening after Letty insisted she stay and have dinner with them. Being with Jamie, even this awkward façade of Jamie, was infinitely more appealing than going home to the unwelcoming, sparse vicarage which had the audacity to be her home. The fact it felt only marginally better without her father in it did nothing to hasten her return. Since meeting Jamie, and spending a brief amount of time with some of his boisterous family, she had come to realise what a true home really was and it certainly wasn't anything like hers.

A true home was a place of laughter and camaraderie. The Warriners were a noisy, nosey sparring riot of a family who passed insults across the dining table alongside the potatoes. However, the unbreakable bond and loyalty they had for one another was as plain as the freckles on Cassie's face. Their conversations were so natural. Nobody watched what they said or feared incurring the wrath of another, because despite all of the banter, they clearly loved one another unconditionally.

Cassie's relationship with her father was so diametrically opposed to theirs as to be laughable, except laughter was not tolerated in her house. Not that there was a great deal to laugh at. Nor was industry, imagination or freedom and it all seemed more stifling now than it had a few short weeks ago. Too stifling if she experienced the overwhelming urge to turn somersaults every time her father was called away. Even with him gone, her home lacked heart. Was it any wonder she sought to escape it either by riding outdoors or inventing a better place to live in her mind?

She stared at it mournfully after settling Orange Blossom in the tiny stable. At least she would be spared the ordeal of her father tonight. The Bishop of Norwich had insisted the Reverend Reeves would also have to attend a meeting of the diocese tomorrow after their necessary conversation today, so the earliest she would encounter his miserable face was late afternoon at the earliest. With any luck, a freak torrential rainstorm would flood the roads and prevent him from returning for a month. By then, a publisher might have bought her book, giving her enough money to pay for lodgings somewhere, to finally escape from her father's sermons, rages and punishments. And Cassie did not care if thinking such errant thoughts made her a bad daughter either, she was in far too much ill humour to worry about eternal damnation as well.

She spied the Bible lying on the kitchen table the second she stepped into the house. Unless he had forgotten it, its presence could only signal one thing. He was home and, seeing as the clock on the side stated quite clearly it was nine o'clock, there was every possibility she was already in a whole heap of trouble.

'Cassandra. You are home.'

The words came from above, but she could not see him on the landing. His voice was calm. Cold.

'Yes, Papa. As I was not expecting you, I took the opportunity to visit some of your parishioners. You remember Mrs Sansam, don't you? I promised to watch her children for her.'

Already the fear was seeping into her limbs, making them seem leaden and stiff as she hoped he might believe the lie if she got it in quick enough.

'Come upstairs, Cassandra.'

Cassie was sorely tempted to run, where she had no idea, but knew fleeing would confirm her guilt and only briefly put off the inevitable. Deflection might work better. 'Of course. In a minute. I am going to put the kettle to boil first. You must be wanting a cup of tea after your long journey tonight.' If he had only recently come home, then maybe he would be open to explanations. If he had been home for hours...

'Come upstairs now, Cassandra. I have something I should like to show you.'

He did not sound angry, she reasoned. Cold was normal, so was terse. Perhaps there was nothing to fear this time. And perhaps hell had frozen over. Resisting was futile, especially as she had no idea what she was resisting against. Better to find out, then temper her response accordingly.

'What is it, Papa?'

Cassie made a show of slowing removing her bonnet in case he was watching, putting it away neatly and swinging the kettle over the hearth as if she had absolutely no qualms about his request whatsoever.

'I have an issue with the laundry. Hurry up, girl, I have not got all day.'

There was something about the way he delivered this, with its impatience and frustration, which put her at her ease. As it was the way he always spoke to her and because it was about a domestic task she relaxed. He was always highly critical of her efforts, no matter how hard she scrubbed and cleaned. No doubt his preaching tabs were not starched enough or one of his black coats had not been sufficiently brushed, showing a laxness in her duties which was reminiscent of her mother.

Cassie climbed the stairs and entered his bedchamber, only to find it woefully missing an irritated vicar. Dread settled heavily in her gut as she realised he was in her bedchamber—a place he usually avoided unless he was camped outside her locked door reading the scriptures and praying for her infected soul.

With the certainty which came from years of his abuse, she realised she had walked into a trap. This was a new and terrifying development. It smacked of another level of distrust. In that moment, Cassie understood he had not just arrived home. He had arrived home hours ago. His suspicions would have been raised by her initial absence, but as the afternoon wore on and she had not made an appearance, his temper would have bubbled. Creating more force behind it. Waiting to erupt with potentially explosive consequences. If ever there was a time to run, Cassie knew it was now.

Behind her, she sensed him and slowly turned. He was blocking the top of the staircase, almost as if he had known she would bolt, his eyes narrowed with hate and malice. One snowy white cravat dangling damningly from his clutched fist.

'What is this?'

It had to belong to Jamie, although why it was there or where he had found it she had no clue. He must have lost it on the night he had hidden in her bedchamber. Cassie could already feel the guilty blush creeping up her neck and the icy terror in the pit of her stomach. If he ever found out she had had a man in her bedchamber, then it would confirm all of his worst fears about the state of her tainted soul.

'It must be one of yours, Father. I have no need of a cravat.'

'I would not be seen dead in something as fine as that one—this linen is of the best quality. An unnecessary frippery bought out of vanity. Which begs an interesting question, Cassandra, doesn't it? If it is not yours, and it is very definitely not mine, whose is it? And, more importantly, what was it doing under your bed?'

He did not give her the chance to answer. The back of his hand hit her soundly across her cheek, causing her head to reel back. Cassie clutched her face, stunned. He had never struck her before; it was another terrifying new deviation in his behaviour.

'I swear to you, I do not know!'

'Liar! His initials are on it! You are a disgrace, Cassandra! Like your mother before you!' The hand lunged out again, this time violently grabbing her hair above her ear and yanking for all he was worth, pulling her head down and dragging her like a yoked animal. The heels of her boots scraped along the floor as she resisted, because this time Cassie knew she had to resist and she had to leave for good. There could be no coming back from this. She could feel the fury emanating from him. Violent, boiling fury—much worse than any she had encountered before. But he was too strong. Too angry. His nails dug into her scalp so fiercely he had to be drawing blood. Even with Cassie exerting all of her strength, he still managed to easily drag her the few feet to her bedchamber.

'Do not fight me!' He practically threw her to the floor.

A floor covered in every belonging she possessed. Automatically, she used her legs to push herself away from him, still reeling from the unexpected and horrendously violent assault.

'Did you bring your lover here? Did you let him raise your skirts and spread your legs in my house?'

'No, Papa, there is no lover! I swear it! I would never—'

'Liar!' The arm still gripping the cravat swung and hit her hard on the cheekbone. The blow was so severe it blurred her vision for a second. 'You have dishonoured me under my own roof just like my treacherous wife. She denied it, too, then left me! But like her you prostitute yourself in harlots' clothes!' He snatched up a pair of her silk stockings which he had placed on the bed and then rummaged in his pocket to produce her pretty floral garters. He flung the garters at her. 'Do you deny those are yours, girl?'

Tears of desperation had begun to silently trickle down her face. 'I just wanted something pretty...'

'Something pretty to lure men to your bed! How many have there been? And do not lie to me—I have found your stash of coins. The money they left on your nightstand after they had paid to fornicate with you.'

His fist plunged into her hair again and he used it to force her eyes to look at his. The maniacal gleam in them was beyond anything she had witnessed there before. The raw hatred glowering down at her. 'I have never lain with a man, Papa! I promise you. I am still a virgin!'

He yanked her to her knees and wrapped one hand

tightly over her windpipe, not forcefully enough to choke her, but enough to convince her he still might do so. The other anchored her in place with her hair.

He began to chant to the sky. 'Lord, what shall I do with this filthy girl? Leviticus tells me *"The daughter of any priest, if she profanes herself by harlotry, she profanes her father; she shall be burned with fire."* Do you want her dead, Lord?'

Cassie began to feel light-headed as his grip around her throat tightened. She clawed at his hands ineffectually, fighting for her life. 'Please, Papa.' The words came out in a barely audible whisper. 'Papa...'

'Never call me that again! I have no daughter.'

Both hands came about her neck and squeezed. As her bedchamber began to fade away, Cassie thought about the only two things she cared about. Her pretty little pony and her handsome pirate. When she closed her eyes there was a sunset and she was riding towards it.

Free at last.

'Cassie is lovely.'

Jamie's elder brother said this a little too casually over the breakfast table as he popped a crisp bit of bacon into his mouth. The fact Letty was missing this morning was also a little too convenient. She had taken her breakfast on a tray in bed when she never took her meals alone. It all smacked of an imminent elder-brother chat. Jack had even dismissed the footmen. No doubt some great, earth-shattering wisdom was about to be imparted unless Jamie could sidestep it with indifference.

'I suppose she is.'

'You suppose? What an odd turn of phrase. Especially as you continually look at the girl exactly like a man besotted looks at a girl.'

'I am not besotted.'

I'm in love. Hopelessly, desperately, miserably in love and I have no idea what to do about it.

'I wish everyone would stop trying to pair us off.'

Usually, this belligerence would garner a witty riposte, but Jack simply stared at him for several moments, then sighed. 'I know you believe no woman will want you now that you are lame, but...' He paused at Jamie's warning glare and sighed again. 'I doubt she cares.'

'I care.'

'It's just a few scars and a limp, Jamie.'

'No, it's not and we both know it. You all know I am not...' What? Safe? Sane? Jamie threw up his hands in exasperation. 'You all know I'm not *right*, Jack. I thought it might have gone away by now, but it hasn't. It's as bad as ever. I am dangerous, Jack.'

'That was months ago and Jacob was unhurt.'

'Only because you and Joe were there to pull me off him. I almost killed him. My own brother.'

'In your defence...'

'There is no defence!' Jamie slammed his palm on the table so hard the crockery rattled. The savage had possessed him and he had not been able to distinguish the face of his youngest brother from either his father or DuFour. In his mind, at that time, all he could see was both of them and both of them had to die.

'In your defence,' his brother continued, undaunted by the quick display of temper, 'you had only just arrived home. You were still so sick. You were in constant pain, confused with the laudanum, and it was obvious to anyone with eyes in their head you were exhausted. And not just physically exhausted. For a long time, you were almost dead inside. Monosyllabic. Isolated. You have come a long way in the last six months. You *will* get better.'

For almost a year Jamie had hoped he would—but the irrational fears showed no signs of abating. If anything, they were now so ingrained he could not remember a time when they weren't present. His peculiar nocturnal madness had become normal. 'Until it is gone, I cannot consider any sort of relationship with a woman as anything more than platonic.'

'Perhaps if you talked to someone about it? You're so stubbornly tight-lipped about it all. Maybe if you opened up and told one of us what happened in that gaol in France…?'

'No, Jack! Not now, not ever. I want to forget about it!'

'Clearly you are doing a magnificent job then. How many pistols do you sleep with? One? Two?'

Jamie scraped his chair noisily as he shot up from the table. 'Stay out of my room, Jack.'

There were three pistols. One under his pillow, one in the drawer of his nightstand and another hidden down the side of the mattress with his dagger. The French cutlass he had taken from Dufour's corpse was stashed under the bed. Despite his outburst, his brother appeared nonplussed as he blotted his mouth with a napkin and then dropped the linen square on to the table before rising as well.

'For what it's worth, your Cassie looks at you in exactly the same way as you look at her.'

'She's not *my* Cassie.'

His brother chuckled and shook his head. 'I recall a similar conversation between us a few months ago, Jamie, during which you rightly pointed out that Letty was *my* Letty and I was just too stubborn to see it. And guess what? You were right and I shall be eternally grateful to you for it. Once I stopped being a stubborn fool, Letty turned out to be exactly what I needed.' He walked to the door, then turned. 'Has it occurred to you that Cassie might be exactly what you need, too?' The words *stubborn fool* did not need to be said. 'Tell her, Jamie. All of it. I suspect she will surprise you.'

Chapter Fourteen

Jamie spent the rest of the morning and a great deal of the afternoon thinking about Jack's advice and his tangled feelings to no avail. He waited for hours on the riverbank for her to trot along on her pretty pony and felt even more wretched when she didn't materialise.

He still did not know what to do. He wanted to her to be *his* Cassie more than anything, but he couldn't trust himself—or more importantly the savage inside him—not to harm her in a fit of blind panic and really did not have any desire to saddle the poor girl with an invalid for the rest of her life. That was no life for a vibrant, generous and whimsical creature like Cassie. Once the bloom was off the rose, something was doomed to happen sooner rather than later when she understood how truly broken he was inside and out, he would see the quirky sparkle in her eyes turn into the flat gaze of patience as he inevitably slowed her down and disappointed her. Seeing that would destroy him.

However, a tiny part of him refused to give up hope. The more he thought about it, the more he became certain that Cassie had wanted him to kiss her yester-

day afternoon. And he almost had. His damned conscience had reminded him of the fact she had only
minutes before been a terrified bundle in his arms—
which had made him hesitate and ignore the desire he
thought he had seen swirling in her eyes. Kissing her
then had felt like taking advantage. Then all the usual
doubts clogged his mind and suffocated the impulse.
He had practically run out of the cellar and no matter how much he had tried to behave as if nothing had
happened he suspected he had made a royal hash of
things. Again. She had left with her button nose in the
air and a look of irritation in those lovely gold-flecked,
big, brown eyes, leaving him stood at the end of the
lane without a backward glance.

Really, there was nothing else for it. Much as he
would rather squirt lemon juice into his eyeballs and
insert red-hot needles under his fingernails, there was
no escaping the fact his brother was right and they
had to talk. It was the mature thing to do. The decent
thing. They would have an honest and frank conversation about exactly what was going on between them in
order to obtain some clarity. Jamie needed to know if
she considered him more than a friend and he would
have to find a sensible, matter-of-fact way of telling
her that he was well on the way to being hopelessly
in love with her and so consumed with lust he could
barely look at her without drooling. Or toned-down
words to that effect.

Just thinking about it made his toes curl. He was
going to have to lay himself bare before her, tell her
about the ugly scars on his body, admit to his physical limitations and his private feelings. Tell her about
his irrational fear of the dark and his propensity for

extreme violence in the grip of a blind panic. In all probability, she would ask uncomfortable questions, so he would have to confess that, yes, he had killed a man with his bare hands—which would dredge up all of the horrors of that dank French hellhole he had been incarcerated in. Kick the blasted hornets' nest he had been doing his level best to forget about and then wait to see if she decided he was worth all of the bother or if he had misread everything and she was perfectly content with simply being his friend.

As he lay listlessly on the bank, staring half-heartedly at the wispy clouds in the early summer sky, Jamie did not hold out a great deal of hope his woeful charms and buzzing hornets' nest were going to be enough to woo the fair maiden by the end of his sorry tale. His only hope was she dismissed the pathetic belief that she was open to being more than platonic friends at the start of the conversation and thus rendering the rest of the mortifying conversation unnecessary.

He heard his horse snort and sighed. 'You're back then, are you? I hope you had a better afternoon than I did.' Disgruntled and bored with his master's long swim in the ocean of self-pity, Satan had flown across the fields as soon as Jamie had removed his reins. The bad-tempered beast had been gone for over an hour. But when he turned his head, Satan was not alone. Next to him stood Orange Blossom.

Instantly his heart soared at the prospect of seeing Cassie and Jamie sat up, but as his eyes hungrily scanned the area for his first sight of her it came to dawn on him that she wasn't there. Like Satan, Orange Blossom was devoid of both reins and a saddle, suggesting she had escaped from her stable or—

the more likely scenario—Satan had broken in to the pretty pony's stall to fetch his lady-love. That he had chosen to bring the minx back here with him, because Satan certainly did not have any issues with going after what he wanted, made Jamie feel inadequate.

'Have you brought her here to rub my nose in it? I suppose you are feeling very smug, aren't you? You have a wife.' Satan snorted and looked down his nose at him. 'Please tell me you didn't kick down the Reverend Reeves's stable door in order to free her, Satan. That man loathes me enough already. I could well do without further ecclesiastical censure caused by your charming talent for demolition.'

Jamie executed an ungainly manoeuvre to get himself upright and stretched, only to find the soft muzzle of Cassie's pony nudge him in the ribs.

'I suppose you are annoyed at me, too, aren't you, Orange Blossom? Is she still angry at me?' He stroked her mane idly. 'I made a hash of things again yesterday. The truth is, I really have no idea what to do for the best. Cassie deserves a man who isn't broken, don't you think? Someone she doesn't have to pity. A real Captain Galahad. Brave, strong, dashing. Not a curmudgeonly, limping former soldier who sleeps with a light on and cannot find the words to say what he feels.' The pony nudged him again, slightly harder this time. 'Do you want me to take you home?'

Because taking the pony home would give him an excuse to see her. Aside from Satan, most horses did not wander the land freely so it stood to reason that Orange Blossom might be a little anxious at being without her rider. And if Cassie's father was home from Nottingham already, then he could hardly assume anything untoward when Jamie was merely being neighbourly.

Good afternoon, Reverend Reeves, I came across this pony whilst I was out riding and thought I had best return it home. It belongs to your daughter, I am told.

Perfectly plausible. She would have to come out eventually to settle her pony back in the stable and Jamie would be hiding there, waiting for her. If the vicar was still away, which he hoped was the case, then Jamie would be able to converse to Cassie openly. Either way, he would see Cassie.

They could talk.

Good grief—his toes were curling inside his boots again at the prospect, but it had to be done. The thought of walking around for all eternity wondering what to do was going to send him madder than he already was. Before he could talk himself out of it, Jamie saddled Satan again, but put the reins on Orange Blossom. He hauled himself on top of his mount, then led both horses across the fields decisively.

To begin with, he thought nobody was home. The vicarage was silent. Every door and window locked and the curtains tightly pulled closed. Something about that bothered him, but he could not quite put his finger on why until he remembered he had never seen them closed before. On his two previous visits, Cassie's bedchamber window was always wide open. Of course, he now knew why. She hated being locked in. A fear he could empathise with wholeheartedly, although to her credit Cassie did not lunge at him with a cutlass between her teeth and try to strangle him. Hers was a quiet, gentle type of blind panic. Civilised. Devoid of a lurking, murderous savage. Unlike his.

Jamie took a deep breath and tried to focus on the task in hand. The hornets' nest could wait until he saw her. To see her window closed must mean she was not there. It made sense she would be out searching for her pony and, having lived in some of the unsavoury places she had lived in during her lifetime, it also made perfect sense she would lock up the house before she left it.

Jamie considered his options. He could return the pony to the stable and leave. An unsatisfactory solution which denied him the chance to see her. Or he could go off and search for her—and perhaps waste hours doing so. The only reasonable alternative was to sit close by and loiter until she came home, and in case her father caught him there he would keep Orange Blossom with him. A readymade excuse for his distasteful presence, and one he could also use on Cassie if she made it plain she did not wish to see him.

In view of the fact he was not supposed to be skulking around, Jamie walked both horses to the front of the house and left them munching on the lawn while he eased his backside on to the low wall closest to the building. Really, he reasoned, what happened next was down to her. He intended to ask her outright about it straight away.

Did you want me to kiss you yesterday?

Too blunt.

I was wondering, should I have kissed you yesterday?

Pathetic.

Cassie, yesterday there was a moment when I was convinced you wanted to be kissed. Like a fool I let it pass. Was I right to do so?

Jamie groaned aloud. His toes would cramp up before this awkward debacle was concluded, in fact...

He heard a chair scrape on wood close by and realised the only place the noise could have come from was the vicarage. Somebody was home, which meant he could hardly remain sat in their front garden rehearsing all of the cringingly bad sentences he intended to say. Jamie stood up, straightened his coat, smoothed down his wayward hair, then smartly rapped his knuckles on the front door.

More wood scraped against wood and footsteps made their way to the door, but did not open it. 'Who is it?' The Reverend Reeves's tone was wary and unwelcoming, something which did not bode well when he could have no idea who his visitor was.

'Captain James Warriner. I should like to speak to you, Reverend.'

'Go away. You are not welcome here.' Well, it had started well. Things would undoubtedly get much worse before this conversation finished.

'I appreciate that, Reverend Reeves, however I come here with a purpose. A neighbourly purpose.' When this was met with stony silence Jamie knocked again. 'I have something for you.' He bit back from telling the man he had Cassie's pony in case the man told him to take it to the stable without opening the door. He could hardly argue with such an obviously sensible request. 'It is important.'

The bolt slid noisily open behind the door and it finally opened a crack. Half of the vicar's face came into view. He appeared quite dishevelled. His hair was sticking up on one side of his head, the shoulder seam of his cassock torn, but it was his eyes which began to bother Jamie. They were quite manic.

'Go away, Warriner. Whatever you have I do not want.'

'I found this pony wandering riderless—I believe it is your daughter's.'

'I have no daughter!' This was spat with venom—a worrying amount of venom—then the vicar tried to close the door.

Jamie wedged his foot inside.

'This is your daughter's pony, sir! Your daughter Cassandra...'

'Do not speak her name in my presence!'

Foaming spittle was gathering in the corners of the man's mouth again, not that Jamie needed to see it to know something was amiss. Jamie was instantly, loyally furious.

'Where is she?' He angrily pushed at the door with his shoulder, ignoring the resistance from the other side. The Reverend altered position to brace his full weight against it to close it, allowing Jamie to see the whole of the man's face for the first time.

Four deep scratches marred his left cheek. More were visible on his neck and on the backs of his hands. Not scratches, perhaps. Claw marks. Human claw marks. And was that blood on his shirt?

His neck prickled with fear. 'Where's Cassie?'

The vicar refused to budge, still denying him entry. 'Did she open her legs for you, Warriner? Did you use her for your pleasure or to get petty revenge on me for daring to speak the truth about your sins?'

Every instinct Jamie had was positively screaming. Something was very, very wrong.

He stepped back, then lunged at the door with a primal grunt of exertion. As he had intended, the odious vicar fell backwards as the full force of the impact knocked him off his feet.

Wasting no time, Jamie strode into the stuffy kitchen. 'Cassie! Cassie where are you?'

There was no reply, and her father was already scrambling to his feet. He threw himself in front of Jamie as he stalked towards the narrow staircase. *'Get thee behind me, Satan!'*

The bitter taste in Jamie's mouth, his palpitating heart and the way every hair on his body had suddenly stood to attention were warning signs he had grown to trust. They had kept him alive in the Peninsula and he was damned if he would doubt them now. He grabbed her father sharply by the lapels. 'Get behind me!' Unceremoniously he shoved him back to the floor and took the stairs two at a time.

'If you have so much as harmed one single hair on her head, I will kill you!'

When her bedchamber door refused to open Jamie felt the bile rise in his throat.

'You locked her in, you bastard! The thing she fears most in the world! Give me the key!'

Below him, the Reverend Reeves walked towards one of the plain wooden crosses nailed to the wall and closed his eyes, his body rocking back and forth as he began to chant in a monotone. 'The Lord is my rock, and my fortress, and my deliverer; in him I will trust. He is my shield, and the horn of my salvation and my refuge. Thou savest me from violence…'

'The *key*!' Jamie no longer existed, he could tell. Wherever the Reverend's mind had gone, it was no longer in this building.

Chapter Fifteen

'I will call on the Lord, who is worthy to be praised, so I shall be saved from mine enemies...'

The man was quite mad. Clearly lost in his own fevered recitation of the scriptures, trying to reason with him was only wasting time. Wondering about the sort of life Cassie endured with him did not bear thinking about. Not yet at any rate, because he still had to find her.

Jamie threw his shoulder repeatedly at the door with a strength he had not known he possessed. As he did, he called to her and each time she failed to answer he rammed the barrier between them harder. For the first time since his injuries, Jamie was thankful those bullets had torn through his leg. Because his weakened leg had forced him to rely more on his arms, and those arms, these shoulders, were now stronger than ever. The door really did not stand a chance. Once the ancient wooden frame began to splinter he was able to break through in a matter of seconds as it all gave at once under his relentless onslaught.

'Cassie!'

Although daylight outside, the room was dark. The
heavy curtains were pulled tight and it took his eyes a
moment to focus properly. The tiny bedchamber had
been ransacked. The blankets and sheets from the
bed hideously tangled and strewn over the floor. Her
clothes were scattered around, ripped and torn as if
some ferocious beast had rampaged through the room
and gone at them with its bared teeth. All around him
was carnage, yet he could still not see her.

Jamie clambered over the mess to search on the
other side of the bed and there she was. On the floor.
Slumped against the solid leg of the headboard. Most
of her hair covered her face, but he saw enough to feel
sick. Gagged. Hands bound tightly behind her back,
whatever held them together had also been lashed securely around the bedpost. One sleeve of her dress
hanging limply where it had been torn from the bodice.

Whatever rage he felt for her father was temporarily
forgotten in his rush to help her. Jamie ignored the protest in his thigh as he dropped to his knees beside her.

'Cassie?'

He smoothed the bulk of her hair from her cheek
and saw the bruising. Her cheekbone was covered in
an angry raised mark. Her lovely eye swollen from another blow to her face and she wasn't moving.

'Oh, my darling, what has he done to you?'

Instinctively his fingers went to her neck and located
her pulse. It vibrated strong and steady beneath his
touch, easing some of the tension clouding his mind.
He wrenched the knife out of his boot and carefully cut
through the bond which held her to the bed. It wasn't
rope or cord. Whatever it was, it had the distinct texture of silk. Those binding her hands were harder to

remove. The ribbon, and he was certain it was ribbon, was covered in some raised decoration which made slicing through without harming her skin problematic. Jamie had to lean her heavy head against his upper body in order to do it. When they finally came free, he glanced down at the tangled mess in his hands and recognised part of it instantly. Her floral garters, and if he was not mistaken the other restraint was made out of a single silk stocking.

Jamie gathered Cassie close and began the arduous task of trying to stand with her in his arms. Unconscious, she was a dead weight, but his arms were strong and he was damned if he would fail her.

Something hard and angular caught him unawares on the back of the head.

'She needs to repent!'

Jamie almost dropped her. Almost. Instead he managed to lower her carefully to the ground just as another blow caught him across the shoulders. He twisted around in time to see the crazed vicar coming at him again, brandishing one of the austere wooden crosses from the kitchen. He allowed his assailant to attempt to strike him again, lunging for the makeshift weapon and using its downward momentum to destabilise the man. Jamie wrenched the crucifix from his hand and tossed it out of harm's way, before heaving himself awkwardly to his feet to go on the offensive.

As he topped the man by over six inches, he did not bother crouching to take him down. Instead he stalked towards him menacingly, grateful for the burning fury and hatred which coursed through his veins and rid him of any guilt at what he was about to do. This time he welcomed the savage inside, happily opened the cage and let it out to wreak chaos. This man deserved nothing less.

His palm shot out, gripping Cassie's father firmly about the throat, then marched him back against the wall to loom over him.

'You hit her.' And he wanted to kill him.

'She is just like her disgraceful mother!'

Jamie felt his palm squeeze tighter of its own accord and didn't care.

'You tied her up. Gagged her. Locked her in!' Dear God, he hoped she had not been imprisoned for long.

'She prostituted herself for money!'

'You're a monster!' He could feel the vicar struggling to breathe and still he didn't care. 'A raving madman!'

'*She's* the monster. She is possessed by the devil himself. I saw the evidence of it with my own eyes! Pages of blasphemy where animals talk! Harlots' clothing. Wanton lust. In my house! With *you*!'

Behind him, Jamie heard the magnificent sound of Cassie moaning. She was coming to. It distracted him and her father used it as an opportunity to wrench his neck free.

'I know it was you who fornicated with her. JW! *JW!* It was on your cravat. I did not put it together till now. James Warriner. Debaucher. Fornicator!'

The need to smash the man's head against the wall was instinctual, because this man had hurt Cassie and therefore he needed to die.

'And don't forget, Reverend, I am the devil's own henchman. This face will be the last thing you ever see and it will be laughing as it chokes the life out of you.'

Both of Jamie's hands wrapped around his neck. One violent twist and he would have the satisfaction of hearing and feeling it break.

An execution.

Justice. And Jamie would be the executioner.

She moaned again and without thinking he turned to her. Saw her eyes. The pain and fear in them and knew he couldn't allow her to see him as the monster he truly was. With a growl of sheer frustration, he smashed her father's head against the wall. The older man's eyes rolled back in his head and his knees gave way. But the man was still breathing as Jamie left him on the floor.

'It's all right, Freckles. You're safe now, darling.'

Feeling choked with emotion, shaking like a leaf in a gale and still desperately fighting to control the anger, Jamie went to her, helped her up and supported the bulk of her weight as he led her from the bedchamber. She swooned slightly at the top of the stairs, clutching at his waistcoat and collapsing against him. He didn't trust his leg to carry her like a lady. If it gave way on the staircase, then the fall would add to her injuries. Thinking about her in more pain because of him made his stomach lurch. All he could do was bend down and fling her over his right shoulder like a sack of flour, and let his undamaged right leg bear the brunt of the lifting as he carefully picked his way down.

She hung limply behind him, but he did not stop. He took her to where he had tied Satan and deposited her gently across the saddle, then he hauled himself up behind her, positioning her damaged body to sit safely in the cage of his arms. His temperamental horse appeared to understand the gravity of the situation and set off a fair lick in the direction of home. Next to him, Orange Blossom galloped alongside. Even though it was not possible, Jamie could almost see the worried expression on the pretty pony's equine face.

Only when he was certain he had put enough distance between Cassie and her crazed father did he stop to remove the tight gag in her mouth. The task made Jamie's heart ache with regret, because he recognised what her father had cruelly used to silence her. It was his cravat. Letty's tiny embroidered initials—JW, in the distinctive pattern which was reserved only for him—a damning reminder of his part in her fate.

Cassie had a vague recollection of the events which had ultimately brought her to this soft, comfortable bed in Markham Manor. Obviously, she wished she did not recall exactly the dreadful things her father had subjected her to. The beating, the choking and being practically shackled to her bed were memories which would always haunt her. It was her dramatic rescue which was a little hazy. Flashes really. Jamie's voice calling out to her. His look of complete disgust as he threw her father to the ground. His arms around her as they galloped away, when ironically, the sun was setting. It might not be the happily ever after she had often imagined, but it was a definitive ending of sorts. After what her father had done this time, Cassie was determined never to go back.

It really did not matter that the only possessions she had escaped with were the torn clothes on her back. Everything else had been violated by her father. Her writing had been shredded before her eyes, the pretty fripperies she had hidden for so long were used to tie her up. The few plain dour dresses she had owned meant nothing to her and almost seemed like the uniform of her father's oppression. The only thing she cared about was her pony and Orange Blossom had had the great good sense to accompany Jamie back to Markham Manor. As soon as they were all safely ensconced inside, those enormous imposing gates were ceremonially closed, meaning she was safe from harm in a virtual fortress. Never had a bolted door given her such palpable relief.

Of course, everyone had made a huge fuss over her. The physician had been fetched by the Earl himself. Her injuries were declared to be temporary. Nothing which a good night of bedrest and several hearty meals could not fix, and now that the awful after-effects of her latest incarceration were waning, Cassie felt like a fraud lying here, in one of Letty's fine night rails, being waited on by a family who had shown her nothing but kindness and for whom she had caused nothing but trouble.

There was a light tap on the door before his dark head popped in. 'I just wanted to check you were comfortable.'

Cassie beckoned him in, feeling an overwhelming surge of love and gratitude for this man who had come to her rescue yet again. He took a few steps towards the bed and stood awkwardly. 'Come. Sit.' She shuffled her bottom across the mattress and patted the space she had created. With trepidation he did as she asked, his posture stiff and barely meeting her eyes. 'What is wrong?'

'I feel dreadful. What you were subjected to—that ordeal—it was all my fault. He found my cravat, didn't he?'

Technically, yes, but Jamie did not deserve to absorb the blame. He deserved the truth. 'This time it was your cravat. Last time it was because I spoke out of turn. The time before it was because the points of his shirts were not properly starched. Once I was locked up for three days because he caught me humming when I was scrubbing the kitchen floor. The slightest thing will send him into a rage, Jamie, and they now occur with such alarming frequency I doubt it matters what is the cause. I have come to believe his moods send him half-mad and then he finds everything about me offensive.'

'Half-mad?' His hand had found her hand and he was lacing his fingers through hers. 'I hate to say this, Cassie, as he is your father, but he is a lunatic. I wish you had told me about all this before today. I could have helped you.'

'I have learned through bitter experience to keep my father's behaviour a secret. He could be relentless if others interfered, and in my defence I was trying to help myself. I had a plan to escape. I knew that now I am of the age of majority he could not drag me back once I left, but I did not want to be at the mercy of the streets either. In many ways, the life some of those poor wretches endure is a life more brutal than mine. At least I had a roof over my head and food in my belly. Most of the time my father is oblivious of my existence, so I was able to carry on until I had made all of the preparations to escape properly. Once and for all. To that end I had been saving a little money each week. A pitiful amount really, but I hoped eventually

I would have enough to afford to rent lodgings before seeking gainful employment somewhere.'

'You still should have told me.'

'When you move around as frequently as I do, you assume all friendships to be transient and I did not want to burden you with my problems.'

'You are not a burden, Cassie.' The hand holding hers squeezed tighter and he stared down at their intertwined fingers. 'I asked you if he was violent towards you and you denied it.'

'Until yesterday he had never struck me. My father believes silent penance in solitary confinement is a far better punishment.'

'Which is why you are afraid of locked doors.'

Cassie sighed and rested her head against his strong shoulder. 'Something, I am sure, which made the punishment more fitting in his eyes.'

'You cannot go back there.' His arm came about her shoulders and gathered her close. His chin rested comfortably on the top of her head.

'I know.'

Her father had almost killed her. If there was a next time she might not be so lucky. For several minutes they simply sat there, Cassie burrowed against his chest, his free hand idly stroking her hair. For the first time in the hours she had been here, she felt totally relaxed. Content. Sleepy. He felt her stifled yawn.

'You are exhausted. I shall leave you to rest.' He began to remove his arm to rise and she lazily wrapped her arms around his middle. Now that he was here she couldn't bear him to leave.

'Don't go yet. I know this is silly and irrational, but I would feel safer knowing you are here. Just for tonight.'

* * *

There was nothing safe about him in the night. But a lamp was burning low on the nightstand and Cassie was clinging to him as if her life depended on it. Added to that was the desire to comfort her after everything she had been through and to know for himself she was all right. Being here would ease his own mind on that score. The red marks around her delicate neck troubled him. To know her father had attempted to strangle her, that she would have had to watch his crazed face as she was robbed of breath was too close to home and unsettling. He suspected what she had told him already about her father was merely the tip of the iceberg.

The Reverend Reeves had effectively tortured his daughter for years. It was testament to her strength of character that she was not a meek and terrified creature all of the time. Jamie did not need to be told this episode had been the second one in as many weeks. The pinched, strained expression she had worn in church that day matched the one he had seen on her face when she had accidently been trapped in the store cupboard. The remnants of it still stained her lovely face now, hours since he had carried her from that dungeon, and it was obvious it had taken its toll. Angry bruises stained her skin. Bruises he wanted to avenge because he could not undo them. If she needed his comfort, right at this minute he did not have the heart to deny it.

'I am not going anywhere, Freckles.' He would sneak out once she was sound asleep and lock himself in his own bedchamber. A bedchamber, which by his own insistence, was as far away from Cassie's as it was possible to be within the constraints of the house.

Without dislodging her from her comfortable position against his shoulder, Jamie swung his legs up on to the mattress and reclined on the fluffy pillows behind his head. Instantly, she burrowed against him, the lower half of her delectable body fortunately covered in blankets. She snuggled closer still, her silken hair falling over her face and his waistcoat, touching all the way down his side from that shoulder to the middle of his booted calf, yet the tough leather nor the covers formed a satisfactory barrier. Every nerve ending was alive.

Bizarrely, it was not lust which pulsated through him, it was something quite different. A sense of wonder, of rightness and the primordial need to hold her close. Protect her as if she were his woman.

So he did. Muttering reassuring platitudes against the crown of her head, allowing the golden tendrils of her hair to run through his fingers. Enjoying, just this once, the heady feeling of being with the woman he loved, cuddled up together.

Like lovers.

The bright slice of daylight shining through the gap in the curtains was a revelation. As was the feel of a delightfully rounded womanly bottom under the palm of his hand. He must have nodded off. A foolhardy and dangerous thing to have done considering his propensity for violence, but also a miraculous one. Cassie was still in his arms, the majority of her body sprawled atop his. One leg hooked proprietorially across his and her face was buried under a sea of hair. One errant strand tickled his nose and he blew it away rather than wake her by moving. Her breathing was the heavy, rhythmic sort of a person not inclined to rise any time soon and if anyone deserved the rest, it was Cassie. Besides, his hand was perfectly happy resting on the curve of her hip as if that particular curve had been carved by a master craftsman to be the perfect fit for his meaty paw.

A quick glance towards the nightstand confirmed the lamp still burned, although its glow was pointless now. It was definitely morning. What time in the morning he was blissfully ignorant of, but as he could not hear any sounds of servants mulling about, if was fairly safe to assume it was early. With nothing better to do, Jamie tried to piece together the events of the night to ascertain at what point of it he had been taken by Morpheus.

He remembered clearly holding her for at least an hour because it had been a perfectly splendid way to spend an hour. He had stroked her hair, then he had a vague recollection of burying his nose in it. After that was a huge gaping blank. Which meant he had inadvertently spent many hours snoozing contentedly with this woman in his arms. And she truly was a glorious armful. Clearly she had long ago fidgeted out of the bedcovers. The only thing separating her bare skin from his touch was the soft, gauzy nightgown. He had touched Cassie's waist before, but without the layer of stays and petticoats, it was deliciously soft. Jamie suddenly became aware of the feel of her breasts flattened against his chest. The flash of lust was instantaneous and made him suck in a breath, causing the sleeping woman to stir. She burrowed and wiggled against him and he bit down on his bottom lip to avoid groaning out loud.

Lust and wiggling was a heady combination indeed.

Hot blood rushed to his groin, adding to his sudden discomfort.

She wiggled again and sighed into his neck.

Good grief! She was going to kill him. There were worse ways to go, he reasoned, than burning up with the flames of unspent passion. Under his palms he felt her body stiffen, then her freckled face emerged out of the sea of hair and she blinked down at him, startled.

'Hello.' The smile she bestowed upon him made his heart melt.

'Hello, yourself.' Thank goodness his aroused state had not affected his ability to talk normally, but by God she was beautiful. All mussed from sleep, hair all over the place and that face so close to his he could count every freckle. Jamie had never seen anything quite so lovely in his life.

'I slept well.' She had braced her head on one hand, the elbow of which was propped happily on his chest and showed no signs of moving. It should have felt awkward, but didn't.

'Glad to hear it. Sleep cures all ills, or so I am told.' She shifted slightly, reminding him of those breasts pressed intimately against his chest and making his body throb with need.

'You stayed.'

'You asked me to'

'Thank you.'

It was the sleepy eyes that did it, he would recall later, she was looking at him dopily through those long lashes and he was seduced by her beauty and completely burning with desire. For her. Of their own volition, his arms wound possessively around her ribs and tugged her until her mouth fell within kissing distance of his. Then it was completely natural to close the small distance and press his lips to hers.

Later, he would also recall the way she melted against him, which encouraged him to roll her over on to the warm, rumpled sheets and kiss her some more. And Cassie kissed him back, coiling her arms tightly about his neck and plunging her fingers into his hair. She felt the evidence of his desire and it did not repulse her. In fact, it apparently did quite the opposite. She arched against him, sighing into his mouth. Jamie could not have asked for a better response. Cassie in the throes of passion took his breath away.

At some point his hand found the hem of her nightgown and his hands dived underneath, running his greedy palms over the creamy, soft skin of the thighs which had haunted his dreams since he had spied them in the apple tree. They ventured further, lingered for a while on the ripe cheeks of her bottom before they were filled with her full breasts and he went to heaven. Of course, by then he was lost. All that mattered was the woman in his arms and the way she was making him feel.

Having never woken up with a man before, Cassie did not know what to expect. But as soon as she had begun to wake, she had been aware of his big body beneath hers. Initially, she felt safe, such an unusual emotion when she was used to living with her father, under constant threat of another of his cruel punishments that a constant sense of unease felt normal. Only when she was out in the open, riding Orange Blossom, did that state wane. It had never completely gone before, yet it was gone now and it was wonderfully liber-

ating. So liberating she was giddy with it and wanted
to giggle. Maybe that was because she knew she could
never return, even though she had absolutely no idea
how she was going to support herself in the short term,
but it probably had a great deal more to do with who
she had woken up with. Jamie looked positively delicious all rumpled. Cassie had immediately wanted to
run her fingers through his hair and bury her nose in
his neck. As it turned out, they were doing something
infinitely better.

Yes, she should have rolled off him the moment
she realised she was shamelessly sprawled across him,
however, he had seemed perfectly content with their
intimate position. He had instigated the kiss, tugging
her close and then brushing his mouth over hers, and
that kiss had been so achingly perfect, so charged with
emotion, it had brought tears to her eyes. It was very
different from the first kiss they had shared, the one
tinged with anger and done to prove a point—this time
Jamie made her feel precious and special. The fact he
was taking his time over it was also interesting. Each
time his lips touched hers, her body reacted. Tingles,
shivers, an unfamiliar awareness of her womb and her
breasts, an awareness which grew when he began to use
his teeth and tongue as well as those intoxicating lips.

When it heated and became more, she welcomed
it, loving the nearness and the intimacy of his weight
above her. She could feel the evidence of his desire
pressed against her belly, yet it was not close enough
for her needy body. When his hands touched her bare
skin it had come alive, the secret parts of her crying
out to be explored and caressed. Cassie heard herself

moan when he found her breasts and grazed the pad of his thumb over her aching nipples.

That guttural noise had an interesting effect. He shifted position and tugged her nightgown up her body to see her nakedness with his own eyes. Those bright blue windows to his soul had darkened with passion as they lazily took in every part of her from the pointed tips of her breasts to the triangle of hair at the apex of her thighs, before coming back to lock with hers. 'You are beautiful, Cassie. I hoped there would be more freckles and now I know for sure. His finger trailed slowly down one breast to rest on one of the blemishes before it traced the outline of her nipple. The grin he gave her was totally wicked, possessive and wholly male, and instead of feeling ashamed that she was bared before him her arms and legs became heavy and her body craved more of his touch. When he bent his head to kiss her, it was not her lips he sought, he kissed that freckle and, heaven help her, she wanted more. So much more.

Shamelessly, she wriggled closer until his tongue began to trace the edge of her nipple and still it was not enough. Shockingly, she wanted to ask him to kiss all of it, thoroughly, and to touch her between her legs. Too shy and too frightened, Cassie kept angling her hungry nipples towards his mouth, yet each time his tongue came close to where she wanted it, he would change course and kiss another part of her breast. When she felt him smile against her heated skin she relaxed and accepted the sweet torture he was subjecting her to, waiting for his tongue to find the throbbing tip. He sucked it into his mouth and did wicked things to it, and like the true wanton she was, Cassie moaned and grasped his head in her hands, clamping him to her body so that the sensations would not end.

But they did, thank goodness, because he worshipped the other breast with equal devotion. Needing to feel his skin on hers, Cassie clawed at the hem of his shirt, yanking it up towards his head while he went in search of more freckles. It got caught. Twisted. And he laughed and tugged it over his head for her. It gave her the very first look at the shoulders which she longed to touch properly. Broad and beautifully muscled, strong arms and a chest which made her mouth water. Her hands immediately went to it, explored the dips and planes, marvelled at the solid feel of it. The smoothness of his skin. The tantalising roughness of the dark hair which dusted it before narrowing and disappearing beneath the waist of his breeches. And this time, when he lowered himself on top of her to kiss her deeply, there was the joy of feeling him. Jamie. Her hero and knight in shining armour. His naked skin on hers. Almost no other barriers between them.

Almost. Because he was still wearing his breeches. Emboldened by everything they were doing, Cassie set her fingers to work on the buttons of his falls, giving up to feel the long, thick length of him beneath the fabric and rejoicing when she heard the guttural sounds coming from his throat this time. One of his hands came down to assist her with the buttons, until between the pair of them they had managed to get a few undone before she pressed the flat of her hand against him again through the fabric. An open invitation that she was determined to be thoroughly ruined. In case he missed it, Cassie finally found the courage to tell him what she desired. 'I want you, Jamie. Right now.'

Beneath her palm, his arousal twitched, so she slowly traced the outline through the taut fabric with the tip of her index finger to torture him as he had spectacularly tortured her. 'I want to see you naked and kiss every inch of you.' Shocking words, yet the truth nevertheless. She had never wanted anything more. His hand came on top of hers and he closed his eyes, pressing her palm firmly against that part of him. The part which would join their bodies. The part her body craved so much she could not hide the urgency in her voice. 'Let me see you, Jamie. I need to see you!'

He sat back on his heels sharply and stared down at her, his dark brows now drawn together in a frown, his chest rising and falling as rapidly as hers. Whatever trance of passion had bewitched him no longer held him now. She could sense his withdrawal and didn't understand it.

'I'm sorry.' Before she could stop him, he was off the bed and hastily buttoning his breeches back up. 'I can't do this.'

'Why not?'

'I can't.'

'But I want you to.' Surely he could see that she wanted him to?

'No. It's not right. I can't explain.'

He was shaking his head in agitation, unaware his rejection was like a knife to her heart. All at once, she no longer felt beautiful and tempting, but ashamed and exposed. She dragged a blanket to cover her nakedness and watched, devastated, as he snatched up his shirt and hurried to put that on, too. All the while, he resolutely refused to look at her. He was halfway to the door when he stopped and turned around, looking every bit as wretched as one would have expected a disgusted man to be. 'For what it's worth, I am sorry. I never should have let things go this far. Forgive me.'

Then he was gone and Cassie was left staring at the closed door, wishing she had not allowed her true nature to surface and shock him. The evidence of her wantonness was everywhere. The limp and crushed nightgown was in a puddle on the floor. The sheet knotted from her shameless writhing, her hair a riot of tangles to match. And even now, even after he had spurned her so vehemently, beneath the blanket her breasts still ached and her secret area yearned for his body to join with hers.

She did not need her father's words to confirm the truth. She was her mother's daughter after all.

Chapter Sixteen

He avoided her for the rest of the day, riding the grounds aimlessly rather than face up to what he had done and tell her what was wrong. To say he was ashamed of himself was an understatement. Every muscle and sinew had been clenched in mortification since he had abandoned her naked on the bed. But he had panicked.

Let me see you, she had said, and in one fell swoop he had remembered it was daylight. Broad daylight. And he was broken—something which around Cassie he had a tendency to forget.

The early summer sun was already streaming through the gap in the curtains to highlight his deformity. Every hideous gnarled scar would be illuminated and he would have had to watch the wondrous sight of her passion-filled dark eyes cloud with distaste at the unpleasant spectacle. In daylight there could be no hiding it—which in turn meant he would undoubtedly have to talk about it. Then he would have to explain why half of the French garrison had been shooting at him and that he had murdered a man in cold blood when not completely in control of his faculties. Because he had been asleep when DuFour had come, and just as he had when his father had woken him with violence, the terrible uncontrollable savage which lay waiting inside him, the beast Jamie tightly controlled, had sprung forth and taken over.

Even if the sight of him did not horrify her, if they had continued what had so naturally started, Cassie would be ruined. They would have to marry. Whilst he would happily marry her right this minute, he had to consider the hornets' nest which she would have to contend with as his wife. There were so many things she did not know about him, things a wife would need to know before she said her vows. It hardly promised to be a casual chat.

Before this goes any further, you might find the following information useful, my darling. I cannot abide the taste of cheese and I have a tendency to break people's necks in my sleep.

Separate bedrooms, obviously, but he would have to explain why. Not just what he had done, but what he was capable of. The danger he would pose to his future wife and future children. His irrational and pathetic fear of the dark. That ridiculous arsenal of weapons he slept with. Any one of which could kill her in an instant. He never wanted to put her in harm's way again, let alone directly from his murderous hands. All of that had to be properly discussed, rationally, and understood before he could act on his desires.

Properly discussed rather than the ham-fisted hash he had made of it this morning. God only knew what she had to be thinking. She had looked positively wretched and on the cusp of tears when he had left her so abruptly. He could not make her his, and potentially create a child in the process, without being honest. Although in bringing her home with him, he had ruined her anyway, so the poor girl was very likely stuck with him whether she wanted to be or not. Yet how did one begin such a dreadful conversation?

With heavier feet than usual, Jamie limped back into the house. It couldn't be put off any longer. He found Cassie in the drawing room with Letty and Jack, looking withdrawn and more than a little alarmed at his arrival.

'There you are!' His brother was annoyed and rightly so. He had brought Cassie home here last night and then disappeared as if she wasn't his responsibility, when she so clearly was. 'I was about to send out a search party. Where have you been?'

'Riding.' He did not need Jack to make him feel any worse when his mood was already trawling the depths of despondency. 'Cassie, might I have a word?'

'Can it wait?' Her voice was shaky and her eyes were darting every which way except at him.

'Not really.'

'Oh, for pity's sake, Jamie, leave the poor girl alone!' Even Letty sounded irritated with him and who could blame her? 'Cassie has been through a dreadful ordeal, not helped by your silly disappearance this morning, and besides I have ordered tea, which the three of us are going to enjoy. You can join us, if you can bear to grace us with your presence, or you can scurry off again and hide. I dare say it will make no difference to any of us regardless.' Her attention went back to her sewing, but by the way she was jabbing the needle in the fabric, Jamie could tell his sister-in-law was imagining it was his thick head. He was tempted to offer her his actual head in the hope it might make both of them feel better. 'What were you saying, Jack? Before your idiot brother came in and interrupted us.'

Just like that they closed ranks around Cassie and Jamie was forced to sit ignored, in painful isolation, feeling like the worst sort of cad. The object of his misery said little, although once or twice he caught her looking at him before she blushed furiously and resolutely stared at her hands. All Jamie could do to pass the time was stare angrily at her bruises and castigate himself for his part in her misery.

Chivers appeared silently out of nowhere and addressed his brother. 'My lord, the Reverend Reeves is at the gates, demanding to be let in. He is accusing Mr James of kidnapping his daughter and holding her hostage. How would you like me to proceed?'

Jamie surged to his feet. 'I will deal with him!' And deal with him he would. Once and for all. Without Cassie there to see, he was going to beat her father into a pulp, one which would need to be scraped off the driveway with a shovel by the time he was finished. His fists were clenched in preparation as he started towards the door.

'Wait!' Jack grabbed him forcibly by the arm. 'Whilst I completely appreciate your anger and whilst I would like nothing better than to see that man get his comeuppance, this is not your decision to make or mine. It's Cassie's.'

Yes, it was. Damn it. 'Marriage has made you soft, Brother. A few months ago and you would have been the first one out of the door.' Jamie's irritation at being thwarted disappeared when he saw Cassie's reaction to the situation. All colour drained from her face, eyes wide and clearly terrified. Without thinking he went to her and pulled her close. 'I won't let him harm you. You're safe here. I promise.'

'Jamie is right.' Jack came to stand loyally beside him. 'You are under our protection now and out of your father's jurisdiction. Do you want me to have him sent away or should I send for the constable? Or would you prefer Jamie to deal with him?' The brothers exchanged a look of understanding. Jack knew that it was not his place to step in and Jamie was grateful his brother acknowledged it.

'I would like to speak to him.' Her voice came out so small. She stepped stiffly out of his unwelcomed embrace and stood proudly. 'I want to tell him I am never coming back. I want him to see that he hasn't beaten me.'

They let him in. Cassie could tell Jamie wasn't happy with the decision, but he abided by it and stood next to her like a ferocious tiger ready to pounce as her father was led into the drawing room, flanked by the Earl on one side and a particularly burly footman on the other. Their presence reassured her, but did nothing to stop the nervousness and sense of vulnerability at seeing him again less than twenty-four hours after he had almost killed her. Despite that, her father showed not an ounce of remorse, although she had not really expected him to.

'These thugs of yours do not frighten me, Cassandra. We are leaving.'

'No.' In all her twenty-one years she had never said that tiny word to him. Even with the Warriners and their servants at her side, saying it still took every ounce of courage she possessed.

'I said we are leaving. I have had my fill of Retford and the patronising bishop. When we get home we shall pack.'

'And I said no. I am staying, Father.' The word Papa was too familiar and affectionate to use ever again. 'I granted you this audience because I wanted you to know I am never coming back to live with you again.'

'Under God's holy law, you must obey me.'

Cassie shook her head. 'I am of age. In the eyes of the law I can do as I please.'

'No law supersedes the word of our Lord! Honour thy father, Cassandra!'

She was done with being bullied. Done with all the punishments she did not deserve. Done with being a disappointment because of wayward character traits she could not suppress. 'Yesterday, by your own admission, you had no daughter. Only a harlot.' Her voice wavered on those terrible names because she suspected they were close to the truth. If only Jamie had not seen her completely naked and consumed with wanton lust. Though it made no difference to her decision concerning her father. 'You beat me.' Her fingers lightly touched the raised bruise on her cheek, yet her father's eyes did not appear horrified to see the evidence of his brutality. 'You tied me up. You put your hands around my neck and choked me until I passed out. I might have died. I will not live with the threat of such violence again.'

'You have duties to attend to.'

'Nor will I skivvy for you. I will find a job and earn money for my labours instead. That money you found, the money you accused me of prostituting myself for, it was my running-away fund. As soon as I had saved enough I was going to leave anyway. Your actions only served to expedite the process.'

His temper began to fray; she could see it in his eyes because she had never openly disobeyed him before. All her rebellions had been secret, but there were no secrets now. Her father had found everything and cruelly destroyed it. The only piece of her writing not torn to pieces was *The Great Apple Debacle*, and that was with a publisher and safe from his petty controls. And they *were* petty, she realised, because the paper he had ripped up so cruelly before her eyes was only that. Paper. The stories were still there in her head and they could easily be written down again.

'I am going to live my own life, exactly as I want to.'

"Favour is deceitful, and beauty is vain: but a woman that feareth the Lord, she shall be praised!"'

His hand lurched out and grabbed her roughly by the arm, only to have it yanked away by Jamie with twice as much force. He glared down at her father, still holding the offending arm in a vice-like grip, and practically snarled as he spoke.

'How convenient, Reverend, that you should be sparing with that particular verse of Proverbs. I suppose the rest of the verse doesn't suit your particular needs. Do you remember it? Because I do. Word for word. *"Give her of the fruit of her hands; and let her own works praise her in the gates."* In other words— and do correct me if I am wrong—God demands you treat your women well, *Reverend*. Respect them. It says nothing about beating them, restraining them, imprisoning them like criminals, and it certainly does not tell you to try to strangle the life out of them!'

'You have turned my daughter against me and dragged her to this den of iniquity!'

'If you speak another vile word about Cassie, you will have me to answer to!'

Her father's lip curled scornfully. 'And who are you to usurp the word of her father?'

'I will be her husband and you can rot in hell, or a lunatic asylum where you belong! And make no bones about it, Reverend, I shall drag you there with my bare hands and make sure they throw away the key!'

Cassie stood frozen for several seconds, reeling.

Husband.

Where had that come from?

This morning he had left her naked because her wantonness was so abhorrent. She had seen the disgust and horror written plainly on his face. Almost the same sort of disappointment she received daily from her hateful father. A marriage on those terms did not bode well. All she would be doing was swapping one miserable existence for another, lesser one, doomed to disappoint another man with her wayward tendencies and break her own heart in the process. Because a bad marriage to Jamie, when he meant the world to her, would be a living hell.

'Over my dead body!' Her father managed to wriggle out of Jamie's hold to lunge at her again. Quick as a flash, Jamie caught him and twisted an arm painfully behind her father's back, effectively anchoring him in place.

'That can be arranged. Touch her again and I *will* kill you this time!'

'Oh, stop it!' Cassie felt bitter tears sting her eyes. This was all so awful. 'You need to leave, Father. I have made my decision and I am never coming back.' She turned, not to Jamie but to his brother. 'Can you show him out, please?'

Jack and the burly footman took an arm each and dragged her father from the room, all the while he spouted the scriptures and glared at her menacingly. Perhaps Jamie was right and he was a lunatic. Suddenly she felt chilled to the bone and more miserable than she had a scant few minutes ago. And so hopelessly lonely. She had believed Jamie was coming to understand her, like her even, but her exuberant personality had repulsed him, too, because she had let her guard down and allowed him a glimpse of the real her.

As if this morning had not happened, Jamie stepped towards her with his arms open, clearly intent on offering her more comfort, yet the thought of his hands on her again was too painful even though she desperately wanted to rush into them and absorb his strength. She backed up and held her palms up in warning. A warning he ignored. His fingers reached out and lightly brushed her cheek. 'Cassie...'

The tears fell then, noisily and filled with anger. 'Just leave me alone!'

'We need to talk.'

'No, we don't. I have nothing to say to you, Captain Warriner. I never want to talk to you again and I am certainly not marrying you!' Cassie picked up her borrowed skirts and fled from the room.

Chapter Seventeen

❦

'Can I come in?'

The sound of her sobbing behind the door was breaking his heart.

'No! Go away!'

He heard something hard bounce off the wood, some missile she had found to hurl at his head no doubt. Ignoring her, he turned the handle. He had a hard head after all and he had procrastinated long enough, and in doing so had upset her further when she had so much to be distraught about already. Cassie had thrown herself on the bed, but raised herself quickly to her knees at his unwelcome intrusion. The murderous look she shot him could have curdled milk. 'I need to talk to you.'

'And I have already stated I have nothing to say to you!' She pouted sulkily and searched the vicinity for something else to throw. Finding nothing of any substance, she turned her back on him.

'Well, that is fine. I will talk to you and you can listen.' Stony silence. Jamie approached the bed gingerly and perched his bottom on the edge of the mattress, twisting slightly to address her back. 'Firstly, as

has been loudly, most vociferously and completely unnecessarily pointed out to me by Letty, I should like to
apologise for my horrendous proposal—if one could
call it that. I did have every intention of asking you
properly. I still have every intention of asking you properly. But I need to tell you some things first. Things I
have been putting off because I couldn't find the right
words to tell you.' Words Jamie was still struggling to
find. 'The thing is…this morning I…'

'I definitely do not want to talk about this morning!'
She practically jumped off the bed and stalked towards
the window with her hands fisted against her sides. 'I
would prefer to pretend *that* debacle never happened.'

'But I want to explain…'

'No explanations are necessary. I know perfectly
well what I did wrong!'

Obviously he had made a spectacular hash of things
if she thought she was to blame for any of this. 'You
did nothing wrong.' He saw pain wash over her face
and felt wretched. 'Why would you think you did anything wrong? I was the one who panicked.'

'You panicked? I didn't… I didn't disgust you?'

'Disgust me?' Where had that come from? 'Quite
the opposite, Cassie. You were perfect.' Which actually gave him the perfect opening. 'And I am not. In so
many dreadful ways. So I panicked because I did not
know how to tell you and fled. I wish with all of my
heart I hadn't if I made you doubt yourself in the process. You are the most beautiful thing I have ever seen
and the simple, awful truth is I do not deserve you.'

This time when he reached out to touch her she did
not recoil. She allowed him to take her hand and tug
her to sit on the mattress beside him.

'I don't understand.'

Jamie took a deep breath. 'It's hard to explain. It might be easier if I showed you.'

The scars.

The guns.

He stood stiffly and tried to steel himself for her reaction to it all. 'Come. I need to take you to my bed-chamber.'

She followed him warily without question, still allowing him to hold her hand. Jamie tried not to hope this was a good sign. Once she knew the truth she might not be so keen to hold it. No matter, she deserved the whole truth. 'You should probably sit down.'

She did, cautiously, her pretty face awash with questions while Jamie paced nervously to the window and then back again, wondering where the hell to start. 'When I escaped from that goal, I barely escaped with my life. The alarm had been raised and the whole garrison were searching for me.' He would tell her why that was later, if this part did not send her screaming down the landing. 'I was shot. Four times. The damage was substantial.' At a loss at how to explain the full extent of his injuries, He shrugged out of his jacket and began to undo his waistcoat.

Cassie sat watching him, alarmed. 'What are you doing?'

'I thought it might be prudent to show you what those musket balls did. It's more than just a limp, Cassie.'

Briskly he tugged his shirt over his head and tugged the waistband of his breeches down enough to see the raised pair of scars which sat like bookends on either side of his left hip. They were the least offensive marks and if she balked at them then there would be no point showing her the others. 'One bullet entered here and came out the other side.'

To her credit, she did not balk. Instead she bent her head to get a closer look and then surprised him by running the tip of her index finger over the mark at the front. 'That must have been agony.'

'Compared to the others, it was insignificant. It hurt like the devil at the time, but it was a reasonably clean shot and hit nothing important.'

'What did the others do?'

'They have left me deformed.' Jamie felt sick. 'Hideously deformed. This morning I was embarrassed. I didn't want to disappoint or disgust you and I blame myself for letting things between us go as far as they did…especially when you were probably expecting a whole man rather than what is left of me.' Her eyes widened and he fought the urge to flee again. Damn and blast, he had never been so humiliated or felt so useless.

Come on, Jamie. Be matter-of-fact about it. Show her. She deserves to know why you left her unsatisfied this morning. 'It's not pretty. Are you sure you want to see it?' Because if she did not, he would probably be relieved. And then truly miserable, because this was his only chance of any sort of future with Cassie. He wouldn't marry her without brutal honesty.

She nodded, but he could see her trepidation. He briskly undid the buttons on his falls and watched her eyes stare intently at the area of his hips as he began to inch the fabric down. 'There's nothing to be done about it and I can only apologise for inflicting this on you…' Revealing it inch by inch was pathetic and only served to prolong his agony and her horror. Better simply to do it quickly, let her see, then cover up the mess and promise never to sully her eyes with it again. He would suffer the dark to make love to her if she would have him. Which she probably wouldn't when she saw the state of him. Utterly degraded and mortified, he yanked the breeches down far enough to expose all of the vile damage and squeezed his eyes closed so he did not have to witness her initial reaction. As the silence dragged, he couldn't bring himself to open them.

After an eternity she huffed out a breath. 'But it is still there. Does it no longer work?'

'You know it works—you've seen it work—but it will always limp.'

'It limps?'

'When I walk, I limp. You know that. Did you think I had a wooden leg?' He had not thought his limp was that bad! Jamie risked cracking open one eye and found her staring not at his ruined left thigh, but at his manhood. It also brought him up short and had him hastily gathering up the sagging breeches and holding them in place. He had been so fixated on showing her the dreaded scars he had quite forgotten she might never have seen a man's privates before.

'And your...your...' She waved her hand in the direction of his jewels and blushed as red as a beetroot. '*That* part of you still works?'

'Perfectly well.' She still wasn't looking at his leg. Apparently her eyes were resolutely locked on his groin, something both strangely disconcerting and erotic at the same time when one considered the situation.

'Oh, thank goodness!' She started to giggle, her eyes never leaving that particular area between his legs, her lovely face as red as a face could be without the aid of paint. 'I assumed…when you said you weren't a *whole* man…well, I assumed that it had been shot off or damaged in some way as to render it…useless…but then I felt it this morning and it seemed to be functioning… as I am led to believe that part of a man's anatomy should function.'

Thank goodness?

Not at all what he had expected her first words to be when at best he had hoped for a cursory *it doesn't matter, just kindly keep it covered up.* A tiny part of him began to hope in earnest. A bigger part needed to hear her verdict on his deformity. 'The scars are repulsive, aren't they?'

Her eyes flicked to the covered damaged area, lingered, then slowly swept up his body to look incredulously into his. 'You were ashamed to show me them?'

'You're so lovely and so perfect and I am—'

'Brave and strong.' Her interruption brought him up short. 'Did you really think me so shallow that I would think less of you because of a few scars, Jamie? If I am completely honest, they humble me. To think that you have suffered all of the pain of those wounds and not only survived, but fully recovered leaves me in awe.' Her eyes travelled back down his body again, reminding him of the fact aside from bunched fabric in his hand he was stood practically stark naked in front of her. Her fingers reached up to trace the shape of the scar on the front of his hip. 'Does it still hurt?'

Jamie shook his head, transfixed on the peculiar sensation of being touched. There. And with affection. 'Parts of it are numb. Other parts over-sensitive.' The involuntary twinge as she found one of those places made her hesitate. 'Is my touching it uncomfortable?'

Uncomfortable. An understatement. Despite himself, Jamie laughed. 'My breeches were just around my knees, I am allowing you to scrutinise all of my imperfections and I inadvertently flashed you my...' He flapped his hand in the vicinity of his crotch and felt himself blush like a virgin. 'Why on earth would any of those things make me uncomfortable?'

'I suppose it is a little awkward, but...'

'But?'

'As you have already seen me naked, I think it is only fair that I get to see you in all of your glory.'

There were no words. Jamie opened his mouth twice to speak and twice he closed it while he digested what he thought he had just heard. 'Hardly glorious. My leg is a mess.' He must have misheard or misinterpreted her words out of desperation. He wanted her approval so very much, clearly his poor, besotted heart was attributing false meaning to the tiniest things. Yet she appeared totally sincere. Not even the slightest bit repulsed.

He watched in frozen wonder as the flat of her hand pressed against his abdomen, smoothed up his chest and then one finger traced the line of hair all the way down to his navel. 'To you perhaps it is a mess. My eyes find plenty of other bits of you to feast on which are much more interesting than a few insignificant scars.'

Cassie sucked in a breath of surprise and dropped her wandering hands firmly back into her lap. Gracious! Where had those words come from? She could hardly believe she had thought them, let alone said them out loud. But really, seeing him stood in all of his natural splendour in such intimately close proximity was making her giddy. Her palms itched to touch him again. All of him. Especially *that* part of him she had oh-so-briefly glimpsed and wished she were still able to see because it had not at all been what she had expecting and had held her momentarily transfixed.

Shocking thoughts which a proper young lady would never dream of thinking, but Cassie could not help because her passions were just too exuberant and always too close to the surface. With Jamie, it was impossible to control them—and with this morning's enlightening interlude still so fresh in her mind, knowing what those clever hands and mouth could do to her body— those passions had never been so close to the surface. She was practically vibrating from the force of them.

He caught her staring longingly at the arrow of dark hair on his abdomen which pointed down to *that* part— she supposed she was being rather blatant about it— and for a moment his dark brows drew together in a frown. Instantly, guilt and shame at her uncontrollable wantonness had her staring at her hands. She did not want to disgust him. 'I am so very sorry. I do try to control my passions—I really do—it's just that...' Her voice trailed off miserably and she buried her flaming face in her hands. She was hardly controlling her wanton tendencies if she was about to confess that the sight of him stood before her was making her think the most impure of thoughts.

Cassie felt the mattress depress beside her as he sat. Then she heard his breathing. Slightly erratic. More than a little heavy. Much like her own. 'Am I to understand the sight of me…naked…pleases you in some way?' His voice was gruff.

Hesitant.

Cassie risked glancing at him through her fingers and was surprised to see blatant longing in his deep blue eyes as if the idea of it was so preposterous, yet not unwelcome by any stretch. He was staring at her so intently. Waiting for her answer. It compelled her to be honest.

'Naked you are quite…splendid.'

He stood jerkily, still clutching the waistband of his breeches, and appeared bemused for a second. Relieved. Then in an instant he was all seriousness again. 'There is more, Cassie.'

'More scars?'

'Sort of—but not scars you can see… I am broken on the inside, too. Horribly broken and I cannot seem to fix it no matter what I do. The truth is, I have a morbid fear of the dark.' Not quite what she had expected his next words to be and unsure of how to react to them, Cassie merely blinked. 'I tell you this because if you marry me we can never sleep in the same room.' Not what she wanted to hear, but as he was speaking in such a rush now there was no time to interrupt. She had the feeling that whatever it was which was troubling him needed to come out; she suddenly understood he had held it all inside for so long, festering, because he could never say the words. Interrupting him in mid-flow now that he had finally found them was probably not the best idea. Especially when the poor man appeared completely mortified to be confessing it all to her in the first place.

'I am unsafe, Cassie. Dangerous. I have a tendency

to lash out at anyone who comes near me. I killed a man once. Snapped his neck. His name was Capitaine Du-Four and he was my gaoler in France. He used to come in the night and beat and torture his prisoners. That night I was exhausted—he had been interrogating me all day. He woke me from a deep sleep and I lost control. The savage inside me took over and I lost all reason. I was crazed, Cassie. It was as if I had the strength of ten men yet the sense of none. I wish I could say it was an isolated incident, one created by an extreme set of circumstances but it wasn't. I almost strangled my father for doing the same when I was barely fifteen. I wrapped his belt around his neck and watched him turn purple as he fought for life. When he fell to the floor I thought he was dead. I didn't feel any remorse, merely relief that I had killed him. I hadn't, as it turned out, but at the time I wanted him to be dead so very much. I tried to attack the surgeons who wanted to amputate my leg. They had to resort to tying me to the bed to stop me from lashing out. I even tried to kill my own brother when he woke me up to give me some laudanum. It took the other two of them to restrain me else he would be dead, too. So you see, you can never spend the night with me. I need you to understand that—really understand that and the dangerous implications before I dare take this further. I care too much about you…' His anguished voiced caught and he seemed to sag with exhaustion at the confession.

'But I have spent the night with you.'

It was almost too much information to take in and her brain was whirring, trying to make sense of what he was telling her and link it to what she already knew about him. Loved about him. 'I came to no harm.'

'A fluke. I could have killed you. This thing within me...' he clenched his fist and pressed it to his abdomen '...it feeds off the dark and kills all of my reason. When it possesses me it is as if I am outside of my body, watching myself. All that I feel is the urge to destroy. To kill. You have seen it for yourself. I wanted to kill your father when I discovered what he had done to you. I am a menace. I cannot control what I do.'

'Yes. You can. I watched you do it.' He had not been outside of himself when he had gone at her father. Jamie had been totally in control. And he had stopped because of her. Their eyes had locked and he had tossed her father to the floor. Stepped back. Centred himself. He had not been a crazed beast, merely her rescuer. Her knight in shining armour. A man who painted every detail of the delicate wings of a bee on a beautiful flower was not a man who would willingly harm anything—unless he had great cause to.

She remembered what he had said about his own father, of how the man had sought to beat the urge to paint out of him and pictured the little boy he had been, terrified and vulnerable at the hands of someone so much bigger, suffering for years and years at the hands of a sadist, and understood why he had eventually fought back so ferociously. If this Frenchman who haunted him had tortured Jamie repeatedly, then she hated the man with a vengeance just as much as she hated his dead father and certainly without needing to know any more. 'Your father and this DuFour were evil men who had come to harm you. Repeatedly. It is hardly surprising that you snapped eventually and fought back.' Cassie could find no sympathy for those vile men. 'Although extreme, they are wholly natural reactions. When your life is in danger you fight back. And you do the same for those you care about.' She had witnessed his loyalty to his family and now to her.

He cared about her.

How wonderful was that?

'I have spent my life cowering before my father in the hope it might make things better, yet it only made it worse. The more subservient I became, the more irrational and cruel his punishments. I fought my father when he tried to harm me and I will not feel bad for doing so. I am glad his face is covered with the scratches I gave him. His arms are covered in my teeth marks, too. If I had had a weapon to hand, I would have gratefully used it against him yesterday even if that action would have resulted in his death.' Cassie touched his arm gently. 'Tell me about the surgeons.'

He swallowed hard and tried to calm his breathing. Clearly that memory was also a painful one to recall. 'They wanted to cut off my leg when I first arrived. They said it couldn't be saved, but I wouldn't let them. When the infection set in they were adamant it needed to go, when I refused they restrained me. Tied me to the bed. It was too dark to perform the operation so they decided to leave it till morning. They left me strapped to the bed all night, but I managed to escape. Found a pistol. After that if any of them came near me I threatened to shoot them. They washed their hands of me. Said I was mad. Sent me home to die.'

'But you didn't die.'

'No. My brother Joe has been studying medical books since he was a boy. He made medicines and ointments to treat the infection. Even then it took months.'

'You were still ill then, when you attacked your brother, and drugged with laudanum.'

'I won't excuse it, Cassie. I cannot be trusted. I am not rational. I still sleep with a pistol because the darkness terrifies me.'

Aching with pity for him, Cassie went to him and wrapped her arms around him. No matter what he said, no matter what he had done, she knew he had a gentle soul and would never hurt her. 'Oh, my poor darling! After months of incarceration and torture, to then have to fight for your own life as well—it is hardly surprising you came home fragile and a little confused. Does your brother blame you for your outburst?' She had yet to meet Jacob Warriner, but if he was anything like the other three she suspected he was cut from the same cloth and would remain loyal to the end.

'No. He felt dreadful for creeping up on me and trying to drip the laudanum in while I slept. But Jake is my brother, Cassie!' His eyes were pleading now, desperate to convince her of his unworthiness. 'I attacked my own brother!'

'Almost a year ago, when on the cusp of death and still traumatised from your ordeal, and you are still flagellating yourself for it. Tell me, does Jake fear you now?'

This appeared to flummox him for a moment. 'He should—but, no, he doesn't. He's just the same as he always was around me and still does not knock before he enters my bedchamber when I have warned him a thousand times.'

'Perhaps because he trusts you and loves you.' Jamie clearly hated himself and did not think he was worthy of those things. 'Just as I trust you. And I love you, Jamie. With all of my heart.'

He stopped breathing and blinked. Swallowed hard, those fathomless bright blue eyes disbelieving. So she leaned close and kissed him, a soft brush of her lips over his, and took his hand. 'I don't think you are afraid of the dark, Jamie. I think you are afraid of yourself. Did you leave me this morning because you feared I wouldn't understand?'

She felt his head nod next to hers, felt his fingers lace with hers tightly. 'You love me?'

'Hopelessly. I have done pretty much since the moment you rescued me out of that stupid tree.'

'That's funny,' he said, not laughing at all, 'I think I fell in love with you at exactly the same time. Just after you flattened me. I remember opening my eyes and there was this beautiful creature staring down at me. Big brown eyes. Freckles. The most amazing hair filled with twigs and leaves. I never wanted a woman as much as I wanted you then. I painted you.'

The image of that lovely picture sprang into her head and Cassie realised that was exactly how he saw her. 'The orchard picture. And you want me?' He nodded again, perhaps a little uncertainly, and her heart soared. As he clung to her, Cassie choked out a laugh of relief. 'I thought you were disgusted by my wantonness.'

He held her out at arm's length and stared at her in shock. 'Are you mad? What would give you such a preposterous idea?'

'My father has always told me that desire and passion were a sign of wickedness. My mother left him for another man, you see. He was worried I had inherited her tendencies. Such things, he was adamant, were unwelcome in a marriage.'

To begin with he merely blinked at her, then he shook his head incredulously. 'As I said before, your father is a lunatic to have filled your head with such nonsense. I bet he had a number of convenient biblical quotes to prove his point. Sins of the flesh and all that. However, as I understand it, marriage was created to allow two people to enjoy one another without sin.'

'Enjoy? My father taught me that the only purpose of fornication is procreation.'

'But the marriage vows state *"with my body I thee honour"*—why would they say that unless they were acknowledging the physical manifestation of love between two people? If the act is solely for the procreation, then why did he design our bodies to find the experience pleasurable? In fact, the creator made a very specific part of the female body for no other purpose than to feel pleasure.'

'He did?' How shocking and wonderful was it to have a conversation like this with a man, although his claim baffled her. Every part she could think of had another, more important purpose. Giving birth. Feeding children. He saw her confusion and grinned. His hands let go of her arms and slid around her waist.

'It's very small. Very hard to find. Would you like to know where it is?'

The air became charged with an odd sort of tension. Of expectation. Cassie's own clothes suddenly felt tight and constricting. She became very aware of her breasts, her womb and all of the tingling flesh in between. 'Yes.' It came out in a whisper because he was pulling her to stand flush against him and she could feel his desire through her clothes. Felt it grow. Harden.

'I am afraid you are going to have to be quite naked again.'

'Will you be, too?'

She saw the trepidation, but he nodded. 'If you would like me to be.'

She licked her lips, she couldn't help it, and let her gaze drop to his magnificent chest.

'Yes, please.'

Was that really her voice? Urgent, breathy, laced with need, but she was hypnotised by the intense way he was gazing at her and the way all logic appeared to vanish when he was so near. When he bent his head and kissed her, she could taste his passion and happily gave herself over to it and to him. This man she loved and who loved her in return, despite all of her many faults and peculiarities.

He stood and walked to the door. Turned the key in the lock. Cassie's heart began to beat in panic, but when he came back towards her he pressed the key into her hand and she loved him for that thoughtful gesture which only he would understand. Cassie smiled and lifted the pillow, placed the key next to his pistol and carefully replaced the bedding to hide them. They both had their irrational fears and foibles. Perhaps together they would find the courage to overcome them. And perhaps they wouldn't. It didn't matter.

Jamie wrapped his arms around her, gently edged her back towards his bed and eased her to sit down on to it with a kiss. Then stood back. She watched the muscles in his arms bunch as he bent to tug off his boots. Only when they were gone did he allow t~~ breeches to drop.

Except this time, her eyes got to feast on the sight of him aroused, a far more impressive state than before and that had been impressive enough. Wordlessly, he took her hand and pulled her back upright, staring deeply into her eyes as he began to undo the back of her dress. When it fell off her shoulders, he slowly peeled the muslin down her body, then did the same with her corset and petticoat. As each layer came off, Cassie's body came alive. Now, stood in only her chemise, he trailed his fingers over the aching tips of her breasts lovingly before he cast that garment to the growing puddle around her feet.

Both completely laid bare in every sense of the word, he opened his arms and she stepped into them, feeling for the first time the blissful sensation of his warm skin completely against hers. He kissed her again, deeply, and within seconds she was moaning into his mouth, her arms wrapped as tightly about his neck as she could to increase the contact of her breasts against his chest. Her belly against his hardness.

He picked her up like she was something precious and lay her reverently on his bed. 'I have to kiss your freckles first. All of them.' His mouth wandered over her body, licking and nipping every tiny blemish until she was writhing beneath him.

Unashamedly wanton, because he was not at all disgusted by it, she moaned her appreciation and those moans seemed to fire his passion further. Yet he still tortured her body mercilessly, kissing each of her breasts before sucking the puckered nipples into his mouth and making her cry out from the exquisite

⌐ny. By the time he came to lay alongside her, Cassie ⌐was desperate. 'You still haven't shown me the part of my body designed solely for pleasure.' Wherever it was she needed his hands and mouth on it. Immediately.

His fingers trailed lazily up her thigh, causing her hips to buck. 'I think you have an idea where it is, don't you?' And he was obviously enjoying her discomfort, a state wholly of his making. His hands were rubbing lazy circles on her abdomen. So close to where she wanted them and yet too far away. Her most secret area was screaming for his touch, but she was not brave enough to tell him. She hoped it was there so he would put her out of her misery.

'Please, Jamie…show me!'

His fingers toyed with the soft curls at the apex of her thighs and Cassie unashamedly opened her legs to allow him to explore her. This was no sin if they were husband and wife, and in her heart they were already married. Jamie was propped up on one elbow, watching her face intently and clearly enjoying the sensual spell he held her under. 'Let me see…' One finger probed her sensitive flesh gently and then—

'Oh, my!' He caressed something wonderful and Cassie's hips came off the mattress. With the tiniest amount of pressure and the smallest of movements he managed to create sheer ecstasy. With every stroke he watched her. With every stroke she lost herself.

It was bliss.

Heaven.

Yet it kept building and building and she kept wanting more and more until the need became almost painful. Her muscles tensed, her breathing became laboured and Jamie kissed her lips softly and nuzzled her neck.

'Don't fight it, Freckles. Relax. Let it happe.

And it did. Something gave way inside her, h muscles pulsed and lights exploded behind her ey For an eternity all Cassie was capable of doing wa feeling until she collapsed boneless on to the mattress, stunned. Too stunned to care that he was grinning at her so smugly, clearly feeling extremely pleased with himself for being the cause of her current state.

Yet as strange and wonderful as that state was, it still wasn't enough. Her hand reached out to touch him, closed around his hardened flesh. 'I want you, Jamie. Every bit of you.'

Those intense blue eyes instantly became almost black and he seemed to grow larger in her hand. 'If we do this, we have to marry. Will you marry me, Cassie? Even though I'm broken?'

'Yes. In a heartbeat.' There was no point arguing with him. He believed he was broken and unworthy and she would make it her life's work to prove to him that he wasn't. He was perfect. 'Although I think we might have to find another vicar to do the deed for us.'

He was laughing as he rolled on top of her, his lips nuzzling her neck, ears and then her mouth, and settled his body in the cradle of her thighs. 'I suspect the Bishop of Nottingham might be sympathetic. Will you marry me as soon as possible? Because I cannot wait.'

Cassie couldn't answer. He was doing wicked things to her with his lips and his tongue and her wonderfully wanton body was desperate for his. Everything about him was glorious, so she shamelessly ran her hands over the hard planes of his back, those broad shoulders she had always desired, his bottom, his face. Emotion clogged her throat when he began to inch inside her.

was so gentle, moving with such aching slow-
so as not to hurt her, despite the fact she lustily
comed the intrusion. The discomfort was insignifi-
ant and fleeting. Then he filled her, his lovely blue
eyes locked intently with hers, and she saw the love
shining out of them and knew she was home. When
he moved inside her, further pondering was impossible. Nothing else mattered or existed aside from the
place where their bodies joined. She did not fight the
passion as it built this time. There was no point. She
gave herself to it completely, let it consume her, glo-
ried in it until they both cried out together, clinging
to each other for dear life. Exactly as they had been
created to do.

If his brother or Letty had any inkling of what he
and Cassie had spent the entire afternoon and most of
the night doing, thankfully they said nothing. Even
though Cassie's cheeks was reddened from the rasp
of his morning whiskers and her lips were plumper
and pinker than usual from his kisses. Nor did they
make mention of the soppy way he and Cassie kept
smiling at each other over the breakfast table. In fact,
it was a positively civilised meal. Far too civilised,
filled with a great many pointed and knowing looks,
and that amused him. Jamie knew the pair of them had
to be burning with curiosity and Letty at least would
have a million questions. Purposefully, he held back
from telling them that he and Cassie were engaged
for no other reason than that he knew it would irritate
them. Letty was gripping her teacup with such force,
he feared for the porcelain.

Chivers appeared out of nowhere and addressed his brother. 'A messenger has arrived with a letter for a Mrs Cassandra James.' Letty grabbed it and tore it open before anyone else had a chance. To vex everyone no doubt because her thirst for gossip was so far unquenched, she read it silently to herself, then smiled before folding it again. Both Jamie and her husband knew how the game was played and ignored her. Poor Cassie was beside herself.

'Is it from the publisher? Does he like the book? Does he hate the book? What does he say?'

Jamie hoped she would always babble when she was nervous, he enjoyed it immensely. It was one of the many things he loved about her.

'Please, Letty! What does it say?'

Letty sipped her tea, then blotted her mouth daintily with a napkin before finally caving and taking pity on her. 'It says he absolutely loves *Orange Blossom and the Great Apple Debacle*, as I always knew he would, and that he is keen to purchase any new stories by this wonderfully talented new author. He's going to publish it, Cassie. Do you have a new story?'

'We have been working on a story about a dragon.'

'Called Brimstone,' added Jamie as it had just occurred to him, 'He kidnaps the silly but intrepid Miss Freckles and locks her in a tower.'

Cassie was smiling. 'And Captain Galahad, Orange Blossom and Stanley come to rescue her.'

'Does it end with another wedding?' his meddling sister-in-law asked pointedly, 'With a guard of honour complete with an arch of crossed carrots?'

'Of course not.' Cassie's hand came to rest affectionately on the back of his. 'It will end perfectly. The silly but intrepid Miss Freckles and the brave and long-suffering Captain Galahad will ride off into the sunset together. Until the next adventure.'

Letty sighed and patted her protruding stomach. 'The perfect happily ever after. Cassandra James will soon be a household name.'

It occurred to Jamie then that things had changed. 'What your father thinks no longer matters. You are free from his rules. You do not have to hide behind a pen name now, Cassie. Perhaps it is time for Cassandra Reeves to step out of the shadows and shine.'

'The book was a joint effort and I rather like Cassandra James. As Letty pointed out, it is a marriage of sorts.' She blushed at her unsubtle hint for him to tell his family the good news because he had toyed with them for long enough.

Jack appeared perplexed. 'I fail to see why both of your names shouldn't be on the cover. Miss Cassandra Reeves and Captain James Warriner has a ring to it.'

'I'm no longer a captain.' It was time he was honest with everyone, including himself. 'My soldiering days are over, thank goodness, and I am resigning my commission. Even if a miracle occurs and this blasted leg heals, I am an artist now. An illustrator. And I like Cassandra James, too. The names merge perfectly together...almost as if they were meant to be.' Which of course they were. For always. 'I was wondering, if you two have nothing better to do, then perhaps you would like to accompany us to Nottingham?'

This invitation earned a scowl from his brother. 'Nottingham! No, thank you. I loathe the place and I am certainly not dragging Letty all that way when she is so heavy with child!'

'That's a shame,' Jamie said, sipping his own tea nonchalantly. 'You will miss our wedding and I was going to ask you to be the best man.'

Epilogue

'Jamie!'

The voice was loud and he was being shaken. Quite violently.

'Jamie!'

'What the blazes?' His eyes flew open and it was dark. Very dark. He was in a strange bed. In a strange room. His chest constricted with panic.

Then he realised there was some moonlight. A lamp was burning low nearby. He was in the inn. In Nottingham. Simultaneously, he realised there was a very lovely, very dishevelled-looking naked woman knelt on the mattress beside him.

Cassie.

Her new silk stockings were hanging limply on the bedpost where he had tossed them after peeling them reverently from her legs last night. Heaven only knew where the saucy pink garters he had also bought her had gone, although he suspected they were somewhere in the tangled mess of his and her clothing scattering the floor. The moonlight glinted off her wedding ring and the lamplight picked out the copper fire in her hair.

As she continued to shake him with some force, her lovely breasts bounced and drew his eyes straight to them before he remembered she was distressed. 'Cassie?' This was not time for lust. He sat bolt upright, wrapped his arms around her, wishing he could recall where the devil he had put his pistols. 'What's wrong?'

'Nothing.' She was grinning and nudged him playfully.

'Then why the devil did you wake me up like that!' He was instantly furious. Didn't she realise the danger she had just put herself in? Hadn't he explained to her what he was capable of at night? Repeatedly. 'And what the hell are you still doing in my bedchamber?' He had taken two rooms at the Red Lion specifically to keep her safe. Two rooms at either end of the corridor just in case.

One for him and one for her.

'You promised me faithfully you were leaving to go to your own bedchamber.' At the time, he recalled hazily, his eyes had been drooping and his voice was thick with fatigue after they had made spectacular love for hours. Cassie had left him exhausted. 'Damn it, woman, I could have killed you!'

'But you didn't. Just as I suspected. You are far too fond of me to hurt so much as a hair on my irritating, odd little head. Admit it. The thought never even crossed your mind.'

She had a point. He had experienced a flash of brief panic before he had been distracted by the sound of her voice. Seduced by the sight of her nakedness. His wife.

Just thinking the word made him smile before he remembered he was livid.

'Next time you might not be so lucky. What would you have done if I had tried to strangle you?'

'I would have grabbed your pistol which is conveniently located under my pillow and clocked you over the head with it.'

Now she was giggling and Jamie wanted to remain angry, really he did, except the giggling made her fabulous breasts jiggle more and he couldn't seem to hold on to the anger for long enough to make it sound convincing.

'You woke me up just to prove a point?'

'Not entirely. Doing something simply to prove a point would be churlish and childish, wouldn't it? I did have another reason, seeing that you've asked.'

'Then spit it out, woman.' A difficult sentence to say with venom when her fingers were tracing the outside of his lips and she was so close he could smell her perfume.

'I want you again, Jamie. Do you mind?'

'Mind?' His lusty wife wanted him. Again. How splendid was that? 'For pity's sake, woman, have a care. You must be gentle with me—I am an invalid, you know.' Although he never felt like one with her, especially when she was already looking at his chest as if it was smothered in the finest roast beef and she was starving.

'You did promise to honour me with your body.'

'I did. And you promised to sleep in your own room.'

She sat back on her heels and pouted prettily. 'So you do mind?'

His arm shot out, grabbing her, and she tumbled giggling on to his chest. The blasted woman would be the death of him. 'For future reference, you never need to ask me that question again, Wife.'

Because she was the woman he had always dreamed of. That elusive soulmate who enjoyed nature's beauty as much as he did and who would want to sit with him while he happily painted, every day for the rest of his life. The woman his sensitive artist's heart beat for. His future. His bright and brilliant and purposeful future.

'You have made me the happiest man on earth, Miss Freckles, and if you want me, rest assured, I will *never* mind.'

And he never did.

* * * * *

If you enjoyed this story you won't want to miss the first great read in Virginia Heath's
THE WILD WARRINERS *quartet*

A WARRINER TO PROTECT HER

And look out for the next two stories, coming soon!

YES! Please send me **The Hometown Hearts Collection** in Larger Print. This collection begins with 3 FREE books and 2 FREE gifts in the first shipment. Along with my 3 free books, I'll also get the next 4 books from the Hometown Hearts Collection, in LARGER PRINT, which I may either return and owe nothing, or keep for the low price of $4.99 U.S./ $5.89 CDN each plus $2.99 for shipping and handling per shipment*. If I decide to continue, about once a month for 8 months I will get 6 or 7 more books, but will only need to pay for 4. That means 2 or 3 books in every shipment will be FREE! If I decide to keep the entire collection, I'll have paid for only 32 books because 19 books are FREE! I understand that accepting the 3 free books and gifts places me under no obligation to buy anything. I can always return a shipment and cancel at any time. My free books and gifts are mine to keep no matter what I decide.

262 HCN 3432 462 HCN 3432

Name	(PLEASE PRINT)

Address	Apt. #

City	State/Prov.	Zip/Postal Code

Signature (if under 18, a parent or guardian must sign)

Mail to the **Reader Service:**

IN U.S.A.: P.O. Box 1867, Buffalo, NY. 14240-1867
IN CANADA: P.O. Box 609, Fort Erie, Ontario L2A 5X3

* Terms and prices subject to change without notice. Prices do not include applicable taxes. Sales tax applicable in NY. Canadian residents will be charged applicable taxes. This offer is limited to one order per household. All orders subject to approval. Credit or debit balances in a customer's account(s) may be offset by any other outstanding balance owed by or to the customer. Please allow 4 to 6 weeks for delivery. Offer available while quantities last. Offer not available to Quebec residents.

Your Privacy--The Reader Service is committed to protecting your privacy. Our Privacy Policy is available online at www.ReaderService.com or upon request from the Reader Service.

We make a portion of our mailing list available to reputable third parties that offer products we believe may interest you. If you prefer that we not exchange your name with third parties, or if you wish to clarify or modify your communication preferences, please visit us at www.ReaderService.com/consumerschoice or write to us at Reader Service Preference Service, P.O. Box 9062, Buffalo, NY. 14240-9062. Include your complete name and address.

2 Free Books,

HARLEQUIN®

Western Romance

Plus 2 Free Gifts—
just for trying the
Reader Service!

Get 2 Free Books,
Plus 2 Free Gifts—
just for trying the Reader Service!